MR. REAL RICH

A MANHATTAN MEN NOVEL

JACOB PARKER

BRIXBAXTER PUBLISHING

Mr. Real Rich
A Manhattan Men Novel

Copyright © 2022 by Jacob Parker

First Edition.

Editor: Eric Martinez
Cover Designer: Ryn Katryn Digital Art

FIND JACOB PARKER

Jacob Parker

https://jacobparkerbooks.com/

DEDICATION

To my beautiful wife, Ali Parker.
None of his would have been possible without you. You are the love of my
life and the inspiration for all the romance in my books. I love and cherish
our relationship more than anything in the world and I am so glad I get to
spend my days with you.

Jacob Parker

1

CASE

I nodded while jotting down notes as the client sitting across the table from me spoke. The note-taking wasn't really necessary, but I did it to make my clients feel like I was really paying attention. I was. It was all being filed away in my memory bank. I prided myself on my ability to remember details.

"Miller's?" I questioned. Yes, I heard him the first time, but it was part of the game.

"Yes." He nodded. "I want it. I know I can kick Hershey's ass if I can get my hands on that company. They have what I need to elevate my brand."

"Miller's Chocolates?" I repeated. "I've never heard of them."

The client, James Lyons, was one of our biggest. He was used to getting his way in every aspect of his life. He was one of my father's old friends, which put just a little more pressure on me to give him what he wanted.

"They sell high-end liquor chocolates," he said. "I need that company in my portfolio. I can take it to the next level. I want to get the chocolates in hotels, upscale venues, and around the world. The current owner thinks small. I can take it international."

"Have you approached the owner?" I asked.

He smirked. "I have. My offer wasn't accepted. I want it."

"Have you done a financial evaluation?" I asked.

He shrugged as if it didn't matter he could be buying a money pit. "I figure that's your job. The company seems to be in good shape. It doesn't matter. I'm going to completely restructure and expand. I just need the recipes."

"I'll get my people to do some investigating," I said.

"I want it," he said again. "I'm prepared to offer a very fair amount. I just need you to get the owner to agree to sell it."

I smiled and put down my pen. "That won't be an issue. I can be very convincing. I'd like to dig into it a bit. I need to find out what kind of financial shape the company is in. I'll do what I can to pull the financials. It will give me an edge. I'll know where to push."

James smiled, flashing a set of veneers that didn't quite match his face. The man was pushing sixty but was convinced he was thirty. The hair plugs and obvious plastic surgery on his face weren't helping. But I didn't criticize. When I hit sixty, I might be longing for my thirties. "Your dad said you would take care of me," he said.

"We always do," I said. "I'll get right on this. Give me a few days to do my research. It'll probably be best if I meet with the owner in person. I tend to be a hard man to say no to."

James chuckled and shook his head. "The Manhattan men have never had a problem with people telling them no. You boys get that from your father. He's a smooth one."

I flashed my megawatt smile. "He taught us everything he knows."

"I look forward to hearing from you," he said. "I'm counting on you to get this done."

"It's already done." I smiled and walked him to the elevator. "I'll have a deal done soon."

We shook hands as we walked out of my office and he stepped into the elevator. I waited until the doors slid closed before turning and heading back to my office. I checked the time and decided to head to the gym early. There were no more meetings on my schedule, and as one of the top guys at the firm, I could sneak out the door a little early.

"I'll see you tomorrow," I said to my assistant, who was just coming down the hall.

"Have a good night," he said.

I stepped into the elevator and got a glimpse of the bustling office. Being an accountant wasn't exactly a dream people had when they were little. I didn't wake up one day when I was five and declare I was going to be a CPA. But I realized early on I had a knack for numbers. I loved numbers. I loved looking at a math problem and solving it.

I nodded at the security officer that manned the front door of the building our offices occupied on the prestigious Fifth Avenue in midtown Manhattan. The moment I stepped outside, a gust of icy-cold wind blew across me. I shuddered once before stepping to the curb to get a cab. It took all of thirty seconds for one to pull up. I hopped in and gave the driver the address of the private gym a few blocks away.

I walked in, scanned my card, and headed for the locker room where I kept several workout outfits. I changed and headed out to the gym doing the typical nod and wave to those I recognized. It was early, before the six o'clock rush when all the corporate workers hit the gym.

I stepped on the treadmill and began a slow, steady pace. A woman climbed onto the treadmill beside mine. She was vaguely familiar. "Hi." She smiled.

"Hello." I nodded back.

"Aren't you usually here with another guy?" she asked. "The tall, dark, and almost as handsome as you are guy?"

"Yes." I nodded. "My brother. He'll be here soon."

"Who's the oldest?" she asked with a sexy smile.

"I am," I answered.

"I'm Taya," she said.

"Case," I replied and picked up the speed a bit.

She kept her pace slow. I remembered why she was familiar. She was somewhat notorious. Usually, she traveled with a pack. The ladies treated the gym like their personal man market. I wasn't interested in being one of the many names under her belt. I was halfway through my usual workout when I caught a glimpse of Edwin.

"Have a good workout," I said to Taya and hopped off the treadmill.

Edwin was walking toward me, likely to get on his own treadmill. I shook my head. "Skip it," I said.

He looked over my shoulder and grinned. "Taya." He laughed.

"You know her?"

"I know her friend Penny," he said. "And your warning is warranted. Chest day, right?"

"Yes," I said and followed him across the gym to the state-of-the-art machines the gym boasted.

"Did she get you to take her out?" he teased.

"No," I said with a shake of my head. I gestured for him to take the first turn on the machine. "She didn't get that far. She wanted to know who was older out of the two of us."

"Ah, she wants to get with the heir." He laughed. "She wants to make sure she marries the one who will inherit the family fortune."

"I didn't tell her shit about who we were," I replied.

"You don't have to. She knows who you are. You don't think she did her research? I bet her and the pack have files on every one of us here."

"Great," I muttered.

"How'd it go with the big fish?" he asked.

That was something I loved to talk about. "He wants me to buy a company for him."

"He wants *you* to buy the company?" He grunted as he pushed the bar up.

"Yep," I said with my fingers under the bar and ready to take the weight should he lose strength. "He's got his eyes on it, but the owner isn't willing to sell. When you want something done, you call in the big guns."

He groaned, seated the bar, and sat up. "You're the big guns?" He laughed.

I pointed to my mouth. "All I have to do is flash a smile and turn on the charm. I don't care who it is. No one can resist this package."

"Yeah." He scoffed as I took my turn on the bench. "One of these days, that ego is going to blow up in your face."

"It's not an ego," I replied. "It's confidence. My confidence is what makes people want to give me what I ask for. I've been told I'm very charming. I think that's the word."

"Charisma," he said. "You have charisma. Some people are born with it, and some are not."

"Guess I'm glad I was," I said on a breath as I pushed up the two hundred pounds on the bar.

"Where is this business?" he asked.

"Pennsylvania," I grunted. "Harrisburg."

"Is it another hotel?" he asked.

I took a few seconds to catch my breath before pushing up the weight again. "Chocolate."

"A chocolate hotel?" he teased.

"Chocolate factory," I managed to say before returning the bar and sitting up. I wiped my face on a towel. "Booze-filled chocolates."

Edwin laughed. "That sounds like it's right up Lyons's alley," he said. "Of course, he wants it."

"He plans on taking it international," I explained. "According to him, the current owner is small potatoes and not thinking big enough. You know how he is. He looks for moneymakers. This place is on his wish list, and whatever James wants, James gets."

"Do you think you'll get the job done?" he asked.

I gave him a dry look. "I'm not paid the big bucks for nothing."

He rolled his eyes. "One of these days your ego is going to get walloped. Don't come crying to me when it does."

"My ego is just fine," I told him. "It's not in any danger."

We finished our workout and I headed for home. My home in the city. I kept an apartment near the office for days when I worked late or didn't have the energy to go home to my house in Great Neck. I walked through the door and dropped my keys in the dish on the table by the door.

I went straight for the shower. Once dressed in my sweats, I picked up my phone to order dinner from my favorite Italian restaurant. I opened a bottle of wine and poured a glass before going into the den to do a little research on my target.

A quick internet search led me to the Miller's Chocolates website. I clicked on the about page and found myself pleasantly surprised. "Well, well, well," I said as I stared at the head shot of the founder and current owner of the company. "Miss Emma Miller, so nice to meet you."

She was not what I expected. I assumed it was going to be some crotchety old guy unwilling to give up his family's company. I was not expecting Emma Miller. I quickly opened another window to do a personal search of the business owner.

"Twenty-six and never been married." I nodded as I read through the information that was frighteningly easy to find out about a total stranger.

This could work to my advantage. I wasn't necessarily arrogant, but I knew the ladies liked me. My looks were not my fault or even something I could control. That was all my parents, and I wasn't complaining. They gave me the black hair, blue eyes, and my height, but I took full credit for keeping my body in tiptop shape. I was a gym rat and not ashamed of it. It was how I stayed sane. When I had a problem, I hit the gym. When I was mad, I hit the gym. It was my outlet.

I went back to the company page and stared at the picture of the woman who was about to be the recipient of my charm. Gorgeous green eyes stared at me from the screen. Her hair was a honey brown with streaks of lighter shades through it. Her hair fell around her shoulders, perfectly framing her pretty face. She was wearing minimal makeup in the picture. She was a natural beauty.

"Miss Emma, we are about to meet," I whispered as I pulled up the contact page. I quickly typed out a message asking for a meeting.

I made sure she knew I was willing to meet in her hometown. It was all about making her feel relaxed.

I sent the email and couldn't help but take one last look at the woman I was about to make very rich and very jobless. She was pretty, and if this were any other situation, I could see myself asking her to dinner. Unfortunately, this was business, and a dinner date was not part of the job.

2

EMMA

I put on my safety glasses and pushed open the door to the kitchen. This was where the magic happened. The kitchen was where I spent the majority of my time crafting our new products. I considered myself a chocolate connoisseur.

"Good morning," my head developer said as I walked into the kitchen.

"Good morning," I replied. "It smells amazing. What am I smelling?"

"Strawberries." She grinned. "Are you ready?"

My eyes widened and I clapped. This was going to be our Valentine's surprise for our anxious customers. We had been working on this particular product for two years. I was certain this recipe was the one. "I'm so ready!"

We walked to her perfectly clean station. A tray of chocolates was awaiting me. "Okay, now, I had to tweak a few things to get the sugar content just right. I switched to that other strawberry rum, and I think it works."

I reached for one of the chocolates and took a bite. Some of the liquid center oozed down my chin. I quickly wiped it away and focused on the flavors bursting in my mouth. I inspected the other half of the chocolate in my fingers and was very satisfied with the product.

"Nailed it," I told her. "It's delicious. It's perfect. This is what I have been imagining for years. I can't believe you finally perfected it!"

"It wasn't me." She laughed. "This was all you. I have to admit I wasn't sure it would work or taste good, but these work. These really, really work."

"Send the recipe to production," I told her. "I'm going to get back to the marketing. I want to get these on the market ASAP. We're a little behind the eight ball for Valentine's but we'll make do. I've got social media ideas. I think that will be our most effective option for now."

"I'll get it into the factory," she said with a nod. "Everyone is ready to go. We've got the machines cleaned and have the red boxes. We're still going with the red, right?"

"Yes," I answered. "We have the stickers that will be added at the end of the assembly line."

"Okay, we'll get started," she said.

"Thank you, Wendy," I said. "I couldn't do any of this without you. You are a hero."

"Thank you, but I'm your sidekick. You're the hero. I suspect you have a cape or some sexy little bodysuit under that outfit."

"Shh, it's our secret," I said and walked out of the kitchen.

I walked down the hall lined with framed pictures of our products. I took the stairs up to the second floor where our offices were held. I was greeted almost immediately with a hot cup of coffee from my assistant, Robyn.

"Did it work?" she asked excitedly.

I grinned. "It did."

"Yes!" She fist pumped the air. "I knew it. Is it in production?"

"Heading in there now," I said. "So, I'm going to work on some quick, simple ads for social media and local radio. Can you please call our local vendors and let them know what we have in the pipeline?"

"On it."

"And submit that design to the box supplier," I said as I started walking away. "Please."

"I got it," she said. "It's a go. This is not a drill. Go, people, go!"

I was laughing as I made my way to my office. My business was small, and I knew the names of everyone I employed. We were a family. Because I insisted we keep things small, it often meant my staff had to work a little extra hard. I paid them well and their loyalty was worth every penny.

I shrugged out of my blazer and adjusted the blouse I was wearing before sitting down at my desk and pulling up the file I had been working on. I didn't have a marketing team. When I needed to, I consulted with a firm, but it didn't make sense to pay someone six figures to work three months out of the year. I handled the bulk of the marketing. I loved to draw and create and liked to come up with my own ads.

I reviewed what I had come up with and loved it. It took another hour to get the ads scheduled for the various social media platforms we used. Next year, I would probably hire a marketing firm to push the strawberry-rum-infused chocolates nationwide. First, we needed to get some reviews under our belt.

With the most important stuff out of the way, I turned to my email. It was the usual stuff until I came across one from a CPA in New York. I frowned as I read the short and sweet email. He wanted to meet with me about the business. I had a CPA. This guy clearly wanted something and was even offering to fly here to meet with me. I quickly replied I was willing to set a meeting. I wasn't going to switch firms, but it couldn't hurt to hear him out.

I spent the rest of my day busting ass to get the new product rolled out along with the rush of Valentine's orders around the corner. This was the busiest time of the year for the business, but I made a commitment not to spend sixteen hours a day at work. I shut everything down, put on my blazer and then my coat, and prepared to brave the cold January air in Harrisburg, Pennsylvania.

I walked to my SUV in the employee parking lot. Once inside, I blew on my hands to warm them before pulling out of the lot and heading to pick up Lucy. I walked into the school and signed the sheet to pick her up from the after-school program.

"Aunt Emma!" she squealed when she saw me.

I bent at the knees to accept the hug I knew was coming my way. "Hi, baby girl," I said and wrapped her up in a warm hug. "How was your day?" I asked before dropping a kiss on top of her head and standing.

"We drew pictures of trees and elephants!" she declared.

One of the women that helped in the program approached us. "Lucy had so much fun with the paints today," she said.

I smiled down at my five-year-old niece. "She loves painting."

"She's a very talented little artist." The woman smiled. "Show your Aunt Emma the picture you made when you get home."

"I will," Lucy said with a bright smile. "She's going to hang it on the fridge. She always hangs my pictures on the fridge."

"She's not wrong." I laughed. "I'm just so proud of you."

"We'll see you tomorrow," the teacher said as I took Lucy's backpack in one hand and her little hand in the other.

She was jumping and skipping as we walked to the car. I buckled her into the booster seat before climbing behind the wheel. "What should we have for dinner?" I asked.

"Pizza!" she declared.

I did a mental check of the pantry at home. "Okay, we'll make pizzas." I smiled in the rearview mirror.

I drove down the quiet street of the new subdivision where I had purchased my first house almost two years ago. When I got Lucy three years ago, I had been a babe in the woods. I lived in a small apartment in town and never thought twice about the need for more space or a backyard. Lucy had only been two when she came to live with me, but it quickly became obvious my apartment wasn't a home. She needed room to run and space for all her things.

Buying my first home had both been exciting and devastating at the same time. I bought the home on my own because I had to raise my sister's baby girl.

I pulled into the driveway and pushed the button to open the garage. Every time I came home, I thought about Marie. My older sister had died way too soon. She should have been the one coming home after a long day to make her daughter dinner. Instead, it was me.

"Alright, Miss Thang," I said and helped her out of the seat. "Let's get this party started!"

After washing up, we got started on the homemade pizzas we usually made once a week. I was a fulltime working mom who owned and operated a successful business but making pizza with Lucy was a top priority. It always came first.

"Cheese me," I said and slid the prepackaged crust down the counter. She was on her little stool, the one she always used when she helped me with dinner.

She giggled and sprinkled the cheese mixture over the mini pizza crust. "Pepperoni!" She laughed as she pushed it back toward me.

I carefully arranged the slices in a happy face just like she liked. "Alright, I'll put these in the oven, and we'll work on your words, okay?"

"I know my words," she said.

"Okay, then show me," I replied and rubbed her head.

She hopped off the stool and pulled the sight-words flashcards from the drawer. I was determined to make sure she kicked ass at school. I promised my sister I would give Lucy the best education possible. I got her into a great preschool, and she was already way ahead in her kindergarten class. I didn't want to lose the momentum.

After dinner, I put her in the bath, read with her a bit, and then it was off to bed. After getting her tucked in, I went downstairs to go through my normal nightly chores. I poured myself a glass of wine and started the cleanup of the kitchen. The pizza-making tended to get a little crazy. With the laundry going, the dishwasher running, and the snacks packed for tomorrow, I finally sat down on the couch for a little quiet time.

My eyes went to the coffee table where I kept several photo albums and scrapbooks. I wanted Lucy to be able to look at her mama whenever she wanted. Lucy sometimes called me mom and sometimes Aunt Emma. I never tried to pressure her to do either. She knew who I was and who her mommy was, even if she didn't really remember her.

I reached for the album that held pictures from Marie's adult life. I felt that familiar sting as I looked at the pictures of Marie and her boyfriend, Lucy's dad. They were so happy. So in love. When they found out they were pregnant, they were thrilled. Lucy's father never got to meet her. He died in a tragic car accident a few months into the pregnancy. As if fate wasn't done showing our family just how cruel it could be, Marie was diagnosed with breast cancer a month after Lucy was born.

I flipped through the pages and came upon the pictures of Lucy's second birthday. Tears rolled down my face. Marie had been so sick and so weak, but she was determined to make sure Lucy had the best birthday party ever. She died the following week.

My fingers touched the picture of Marie and Lucy smiling at each other. "So not fair," I whispered. "She's beautiful, Marie. So beautiful. She looks so much like you. Every time I look her in the eyes, I see you. You can be proud of her. She's smart, funny, and so kind."

I flipped the page. The pictures of Marie stopped. It was just like her life. It just stopped. She was gone and it was just me and Lucy. I blew out a breath and put the album back on the table. I had plans of getting married and having my own children one day, but I wasn't planning on becoming the mother of a toddler at twenty-three.

The best laid plans.

It was all good. Lucy enriched my life. All the stress and exhaustion that came with being a single mom was worth it. Lucy was worth it, and I would never change a thing.

I finished the wine and carried my glass to the sink. Then it was lights out. Tomorrow morning would come too soon, and it would all start over.

3

CASE

I stepped out of my office and nearly ran into Edwin. "Woah, what are you doing here?"

"I was bored." He shrugged.

"You're not bored," I said dryly and stepped back into my office. If he was stopping by in the middle of the day, it was because he had a problem. "What'd you do?"

"It's not what I did," he said and flopped down in a chair. I sat down on the small couch in the area I often used to talk with clients.

"Who?"

"Just office drama." He shrugged. "I don't want to be there at the moment. Where are you off to so early?"

"I'm heading to Pennsylvania to get that chocolate factory," I said.

He smirked and sipped the coffee he was holding. "You just assume you're going to get it."

"I know I'm going to get it," I said confidently.

"And if you don't?" he asked.

"I'm sorry, have you met me?" I teased. "I did my research. She's going to be an easy mark. I'll turn on the charm and she'll be signing it over in a flash. She'll get a fat check and I'll come home to a very happy client."

"And you'll get to brag to daddy that you impressed his friend," he said with a nod.

"And maybe win a few points with Aunt Anne."

"As if you need to do that," he said. "You know they're going to tap you to run this place if Victor ever retires."

"I don't think Victor is going anywhere soon," I said. "I don't want him to. I like my setup. I don't have to be the big boss and work all the time. I don't have to deal with the boss nonsense. I get to come in, do my thing, and go home."

"I suppose there are perks to being number two or three on the company ladder," he said.

"So, is that what's got you rattled?" I asked.

"I'm not rattled," he said.

I stared at my little brother. He had chosen to go the real estate path. We both had the benefit of having the family name, money, and clout to get our foot in the door of whatever we wanted to do. I went with the accounting firm owned by the family. He went with the real estate firm, starting in the mailroom just like I did.

"You didn't close a deal," I said. I knew him well and this was the face of a bummed-out man.

"I didn't close it, but it's not totally lost," he muttered.

"You're worried Uncle Henrick is going to fire your ass." I laughed.

He scowled at me. "He isn't going to fire me, but I'm not interested in going back to the office."

"You'll get it done," I told him. "You always do. You just need to take a step back and rethink your approach. Are you buying or selling?"

"Buying," he said. "My client is locked into a price, and he won't budge. The seller isn't budging."

"Sweeten the pot," I suggested. "You know how to make it happen. Fall back on that old Manhattan charm. No one can resist the Manhattan name. We built this city. Tap into the ancestral power."

He rolled his eyes. "Like that actually works."

"It will," I said. "Now, I've got a flight to catch. I'll be back tomorrow hopefully."

He got to his feet and together we walked to the elevator. We said goodbye, and I hopped into the hired car and was off to the airport. I hoped his bad juju didn't rub off on me. I had to close this deal. If we both fucked up, our father would not be happy.

After arriving at the airport, I made it through security.

"Thank you," I said to the TSA agent and carried my briefcase and shoes to a bench to put them back on.

My flight left in thirty minutes. On my way to my gate, I stopped when I saw a small display in one of the gift shops for Miller's Chocolates. I walked into the shop and checked out the offerings. Strangely enough, I had never noticed the chocolates before. I was certain I had seen them, but I never actually noticed. They weren't exactly advertised all that well. The only reason I saw them was because I knew the name.

I grabbed one of each offering and carried them to the counter. "ID," the cashier said.

I raised an eyebrow. "You don't believe I'm over twenty-one?" I smirked.

"I'm sorry, sir, anyone under forty has to be carded," she replied.

I pulled out my license and proved I was more than old enough. "Thirty-two," I said.

"Thank you," she said and quickly rang up the liquor-filled chocolates.

"Have you had these?" I asked conversationally.

She wrinkled her nose. "I don't think tequila and chocolate go together."

"Do you sell a lot?"

She shrugged. "I suppose. People like to buy them for gifts or pop a few before they get on the plane."

She handed me a bag with my chocolates. I paused at the display once again. I noticed the pink ribbon in the corner. Five percent of all sales went to cancer research. That was very noble, but if I wouldn't have looked closely, I wouldn't have noticed. I didn't want to help the woman be any more successful, but the marketing could use a little kick in the ass.

I popped one of the chocolates in my mouth as I walked to my gate. "Damn," I said aloud when the liquor erupted in my mouth. I wasn't a big brandy drinker, but when combined with the chocolate, it was delicious.

I opened another package and gave it a test. It was really good. I was thoroughly impressed. I hadn't expected them to be good. I'd had the same opinion as the girl that sold them to me. It just never clicked to combine the two. I boarded the flight and a quick hour later I was landing in Harrisburg, Pennsylvania.

I checked into my hotel and found a basket of mini Hershey chocolates. That wasn't a surprise given where I was. I sat down and checked in with work before going out to check out the city for a bit. Pennsylvania wasn't exactly one of the places at the top of my list to visit.

It wasn't long before I found myself standing in front of the Miller's Chocolate factory and storefront. There was a sign on the door reminding people they would be carded. I pulled open the door and stepped inside. Glass cases with a variety of chocolates on silver trays were on display. I meandered around the space and noted the many flavors.

The place was doing a lot of business. People were taking advantage of the free samples while others were placing special orders with one of the helpful sales associates. The store was cramped with the number of people in the rather small space. If it were my business, I would want to expand just a bit. The more people that could comfortably crowd into the store without feeling like they were being pushed into a sardine can, the better.

"Would you like to try our newest creation?" a pretty blonde girl asked.

"Sure," I said and accepted the offering. "What is it?"

"Strawberry rum." She grinned.

"Strawberry rum?" I asked skeptically. I found myself sniffing the chocolate. I could smell strawberries and chocolate. My nose was telling me it was going to taste like chocolate-covered strawberries.

"Our competitors infuse the chocolate with strawberry paste, but we have switched things up," she said with a bright smile. She was giving me the pitch, which I didn't mind.

"Does it matter if the strawberry is in the liquor or the chocolate?" I asked. It was a test. I wanted to hear what she would say.

Her smile grew bigger. "It matters. See for yourself."

I popped it in my mouth, and I couldn't say if it was mind over matter, but it did taste like a chocolate strawberry. "Good." I nodded. "Very good."

"We have a limited supply in store," she said. "They're going fast."

"I'm sure they are." I smiled.

"We also have champagne truffles," she offered. "Those are really hot right now."

"I'll give them a try," I said. "Thanks."

I continued to make my way around and helped myself to the variety of offerings. I was probably going to make myself sick, but I wanted to know exactly what I was dealing with. I had seen all I needed to see. I understood why James wanted the business. The potential was huge. It wouldn't take much to bring the company into the Fortune Five Hundred stratosphere. The owner was on to something.

I turned to walk away and slammed right into a body. Chocolates went flying. "Oh shit," I gushed and reached out to steady the woman I had run into.

She looked up at me with her green eyes cutting right through me. It was her. The owner. The woman I'd secretly been fantasizing about since I first laid eyes on her picture a few days ago. "Sorry," I said.

She pursed her lips together. She was not happy. Her eyes dropped to the floor where the chocolates were scattered around our feet. "It's fine," she said in a tight voice.

"I'm so sorry," I said and rushed out of the store.

I was so embarrassed. So, so fucking embarrassed. I was such an idiot. Normally, I could be just a little more graceful. That was not exactly the first impression I wanted to make. I just hoped she didn't recognize me when we met for dinner that night.

I walked back to the hotel and caught a glimpse of myself in the mirror. "Are you kidding me?" I groaned. There was chocolate smeared on my leather jacket.

I had made a total ass of myself. That was not my usual style. I tended to have a little more finesse. "Dammit."

I unzipped the garment bag with my suit and hung it on the back of the door. My only hope was to disguise myself in a five-thousand-dollar designer suit. I'd been told I looked like a different man when I was at work versus the gym. For my jaunt to the chocolate factory, I'd worn jeans and a hoodie. Would it be enough?

Nothing I could do about it short of hiding my face behind sunglasses. For now, I was going to take advantage of the hotel gym. A workout would get me through the humiliation. I changed and headed down to the ground floor to work up a sweat.

4

EMMA

I stared at the door where the man had fled. He was a real piece of work. "Let me help you," one of my staff said and dropped to her knees.

"Thanks, Cara." I sighed as I looked at about a hundred-dollars' worth of product scattered on the floor.

"Thankfully it wasn't the strawberry ones," she said.

"Very true," I agreed.

I looked toward the door once again. Sometimes I was surprised by the rudeness of people. I knew it was an accident, but he could have at least offered to help clean up. We tossed all the chocolates in the trash, and I added them to the waste list to be tracked in inventory.

Feeling irritated and not in the right frame of mind to deal with customers, I retreated to the processing area and jumped on the line. I never forgot my roots. Not to mention, it was good to rub elbows with the crew that stood in front of conveyor belts eight hours a day. I liked to think of it as quality control and team building.

After picking Lucy up from school, I went home to get ready for the dinner meeting. My best friend, Jennifer Brown, showed up a few minutes later with a treat for Lucy. "You didn't have to do that," I said when she handed Lucy the Happy Meal.

"I'm living vicariously through her." She laughed.

"Uh oh, have a job coming up?"

She sighed and nodded. "Swimsuit ads," she said. "A piece of bread and I'll look three months pregnant."

"You know you're gorgeous," I said.

"Thank you, but I want to look good on paper. That means I have to be a good girl. No fries and burgers for me. Once the shoot is over, you better believe I'm digging into a juicy burger."

Jennifer was a model. She wasn't on Cosmo or other fashion magazines, but she stayed busy enough with catalogs and local ads. "Help me pick something out," I said as we went upstairs to my room.

"What are we going for?" she asked. "Hot and sultry or prim and proper?"

"It's a business meeting," I said. "With an accountant. I don't think it's going to matter what I wear."

"He could be hot," she suggested.

I stepped into the walk-in closet. "He's a CPA. I'm guessing bald, round, and nerdy."

"Woah, way to stereotype." She laughed.

"I'm not going to dinner with him to flirt," I reminded her. "This is strictly business."

"You haven't been out in forever," she said. "You need to pretend this is a date just so you don't forget how to do it."

I laughed and pulled out a little black dress. "I remember how to eat and speak. That's all I have to do."

"What if he turns out to be hot?" She grinned. "You could pretend it's a date."

"No, thanks," I said. "Speaking of hot."

"You met someone!" she asked excitedly.

"No, I got steamrolled by some dude today," I told her. "Slammed into me and knocked the chocolates out of my hand. He barely said he was sorry as he rushed out the door. He didn't see if he hurt me and didn't bother to offer to help pick up the mess he made. Total jerk."

She waved a hand. "Those guys are out there, but there are good ones as well."

"I haven't found one yet."

"You haven't looked," she reminded me. "Not since—"

"What about this one?" I cut her off. "Simple, but not total schoolmarm."

She inspected the black dress that fell just above the knee with short sleeves and a pretty sparkly belt around the waist. I had only worn it once before to get a bank loan. It was business casual, which was perfect for dinner.

"Strappy heels," she said.

"I can do that."

Once I was dressed and ready, I gave Lucy a goodbye kiss and asked her to be good for Jennifer. The last bit was really not necessary. Lucy was a good girl and loved Jennifer. I put the name of the restaurant into the GPS. It was a very fancy, expensive steakhouse. I hoped he was paying.

When I walked in, I gave my name to the hostess and was quickly shown to a table. She gestured to the empty chair, but I shook my head. *No way.* This could not be who I was meeting. It was the jerk from earlier. The one who steamrolled me. Seeing him now when he wasn't running out the door, I understood why he was able to knock me down. He was a wall. A redwood tree trunk. The man was solid and big. Maybe he was a linebacker.

"You?" I said.

He offered me a sheepish smile. "Me," he said and got to his feet. "Case Manhattan."

I debated turning around and walking out. I didn't. I wasn't someone who ran away. "Emma Miller," I said and shook his hand before taking my seat.

"Let me start by saying I'm sorry," he said. "I'm not usually so clumsy."

His apology felt half-assed. "Thanks," I said and thought about my options here. I could sneak my hand into my purse and send Jennifer a text. We had a code. All I had to do was send her the number three. She would call and claim there was an emergency at home.

"I hope I didn't hurt you," he said.

I took a moment to really look at him now that we were eye level. I hated this kind of guy. He was too hot to handle. Too sexy for my own good. I could get lost in those blue eyes, which I was sure he knew and used. He had a square jaw with a tiny hint of darkness along the jawline. His black hair was short on the sides and just a little longer on top. It was clear there was some serious hair product keeping it perfectly styled. His shoulders were slightly narrower than a refrigerator. It was clear he was buff, judging by the thick neck.

"You didn't hurt me," I said. "You hurt my chocolates."

He smiled and it felt like I had touched the thermostat after running my socked feet across the carpet. "Sorry about that."

"You're from New York?" I asked.

"Yes." He nodded.

"Manhattan," I said. "Is that really your last name?"

He flashed another one of those smiles that probably dropped panties from half a mile away. "It is."

I couldn't do it. I could not sit down and eat a meal with this man. I didn't like him. He was too smooth. At least, that was what he presented. I had the misfortune of finding out how rude he could be when he wasn't trying to impress me. My first impression of him was forever burned into my brain.

"Will you excuse me for a minute?" I asked politely.

He got up like a gentleman when I stood. Manners like that weren't all that common. Someone raised him right. Except for the part where he plowed into me and ran away without saying a word. I walked into the ladies' room and pulled out my phone. It was a swanky place with a small sofa in what I guessed was considered the lobby of the restroom.

"I'm sending up the bat signal," I whispered into the phone when Jennifer picked up.

"The bat signal?" she questioned. "You just got there. Is he a troll?"

"No," I hissed. "He's the douchebag that smacked into me this afternoon."

"The guy that knocked the chocolates out of your hand?"

"That's the one," I said. "I need you to call me in five minutes and say there is an emergency."

"How long have you been there?" she asked.

"About two minutes," I said dryly.

"Okay, you need to give him ten minutes," she said. "Hear him out. If some fancy bigwig in New York has noticed your company, that's a good thing. This could be very good for you. It won't kill you to hear him out. You'll come home and get to tell me all about how awful he is, and then tomorrow, you go on with your life."

"You're supposed to be on my side," I complained.

"I am," she said. "Go back to the table. Is he paying for dinner?"

"He better be," I muttered. "If I have to sit here and listen to him, he damn well better buy me a T-bone."

She laughed. "Go. If you can't stand him, get up and walk away."

"I will. Thanks for nothing."

I hung up and stepped up to the mirror. I really hated that I wasted my expensive makeup on him. I reserved it for special occasions. I could have gotten away with the cheap stuff I wore to work. "Here goes nothing," I muttered and walked out of the bathroom.

When I returned to the table, he was looking at a menu. He quickly stood again. "I wasn't sure what you liked to drink," he said. "I ordered you a glass of red."

"Thanks," I said and picked up the menu.

"So, did you inherit the business, or did you start it?" he asked casually.

"I started it about five years ago," I answered.

"Really?" He looked surprised.

"You think I'm too young," I said with a nod. I had heard and seen the look a million times before. When I applied for the first business loan, I had nearly been laughed out of the bank.

"No." He shook his head. "It's impressive. You built it by yourself?"

"Yes."

"Can I ask what got you into the chocolate industry?" he asked.

The waiter brought our two glasses of wine and took our orders before walking away. "I have always loved baking. I took a culinary class when I was still in high school, and because I love chocolate, it felt like a natural next step."

"And the booze?" he asked with that sexy smile that I suspected disarmed most people.

"I turned twenty-one and my sister gave me a box of boozy chocolates," I told him. The memory stung a bit, but it was that memory that had sent me down the path I was on. "They were good, really good. It got me thinking about my own recipes. Pennsylvania had some rules about the boozy chocolates, but when they went away, I went to market."

"Do you actually make the chocolate?" he questioned.

"Not me personally," I said. "At first, yes, but now we have machines. Not anything like Hershey's or the huge factories, but some stuff is commercial. We take pride in making everything by hand for the most part. We're small but big, if that makes sense."

"It does." He nodded. "I was impressed with what I saw today. Again, I'm so sorry I slammed into you."

"It happens," I said. "What about you? You're a CPA?"

"I am." He nodded. "I work at a firm that's owned by my aunt. It's kind of the family business."

"I see," I said and was about to ask him about why he was there, but he cut me off.

"This is going to sound really dumb to someone who's obviously a chocolate expert, but what's the difference between your chocolate and the guy in the next town over?"

It was a question I loved and had answered more than a hundred times. "My chocolate is different because it's my recipe. My *secret* recipe. Did you get a chance to try some?"

"I did." He nodded. "I actually bought a few boxes in the airport. Why booze?"

"Because as adults, we get to splurge," I said with a laugh. "Who doesn't love champagne and strawberries or a little chocolate with their brandy? It's sinful and that's what sells. People want to be naughty. I let them be naughty while enjoying a treat."

"I see." He grinned. "I have to say, I had never heard of booze-filled chocolates. I was intrigued. I like it. The possibilities are endless."

"I know," I said excitedly. "That's the excitement of what I do. We have a test kitchen that I like spending the bulk of my time in. I get to mix things up."

"How hard is it to come up with a new recipe?"

I thought about it. "I probably try about a hundred different recipes before I get one winner. After I get a winner, my lead developer and I spend days and weeks to fine tune it. Sometimes it works, sometimes it doesn't. Then it's back to the drawing board."

Our meals were delivered, and we continued to talk about all things chocolate. "Can I give you a ride home?" he asked after our dinner.

"I drove, thank you," I said.

"I'll be in touch," he said as he walked me to my car.

I got in and headed for home. It was then I realized we never talked about business. He asked me all about the world of chocolate, but he never mentioned any kind of deals. That was strange. Was it all a ploy? Did he somehow know who I was and thought this was his way of getting a date with me? I got the distinct impression he was the kind of man that flashed that smile alongside his platinum card and got what he wanted.

Not with me. That didn't impress me in the slightest.

5

CASE

"Slow," I whispered. "Wait, wait, wait."

She groaned and writhed under me. Her back arched with her nipples hard and begging to be touched. I lowered my mouth and suckled gently at first and then much harder. She groaned and pulled at my hair.

"Don't stop," she murmured. "Faster."

"No way, baby," I said. "I'm going to savor every second of this."

"I need you," she moaned with her nails scraping down my back.

"I want to make this last," I said. "Think of it as eating one of those amazing chocolates you make. They're meant to be savored. One bite at a time. Feel me inside you. Concentrate on my dick filling you. Close your eyes."

She did as I asked with her lips parting. I could feel her pussy tightening. It was working. I loved that I could do that to her. I rolled my hips, pushing deep and scraping against her tight pussy walls. Her nails dug deeper, encouraging me to keep going. Her pussy grew wetter with every stroke.

"Don't stop," she cried. Her sweet little whimpers fueled my passion.

I didn't stop. I rode her hard and fast all the way to the finish line.

"Fuck," I shouted loud enough to wake myself up. I looked

around my bedroom and realized it was nothing more than a wet dream. A very, very wet dream. That was just a little embarrassing. I threw the blankets off and headed into the bathroom to clean up.

The chocolate lady was under my skin. She had impressed me. She was gorgeous, smart, and funny. We never even got to the business part of our dinner. I had been so enthralled listening to her talk about the chocolate business, I didn't get a chance to offer to buy the business. I guessed that meant we were going to have another meeting. I had a feeling she was going to be a challenge.

I loved a good challenge.

I dressed and headed out to find some decent coffee. I was a bit of a coffee snob. Hotel coffee wasn't going to do it for me. After asking the front desk lady where the best coffee was, I decided to enjoy the unseasonably warm weather and walk to the shop three blocks down.

My phone rang halfway there. I hoped like hell it wasn't James Lyons. Not yet. Thankfully, it was Edwin. "What's up?" I answered. "Are you still hiding?"

"Very funny," he said. "I made the deal. A little here and a little there and we sign today at four."

"I knew you would pull it together," I said with a laugh. "Nothing keeps a Manhattan man down."

"Hell no." He laughed. "What about you? Did you get your deal done?"

"Not yet," I said. "I will."

"I thought you were having dinner with her last night?"

"I did, but it didn't come up," I answered.

"Uh, wasn't that the whole point of you going up there?" he asked.

"Yes, but I couldn't offer to buy the business she so obviously loves," I said. "I will, but last night I wanted to get to know more about the business. She's young and beautiful and very not what I expected."

"Oh no," he said. "Don't you do it."

"Do what?"

"You've got that tone," he warned.

"What tone?"

"You like her," he said. "You want to take her to bed."

"No, I don't," I lied. "She was a little standoffish. I got the impression she didn't like me. I asked her a few questions to disarm her. Before I knew it, I was paying the check and she was going home."

"Did you take her home?" he asked.

"No."

"But you wanted to," he joked. "Don't deny it. I know you. You tried to hit that."

"I offered to take her home, but that doesn't mean I was going to try and sleep with her," I defended.

"Bullshit. Just remember, you're there to make a sale happen. You're not supposed to be there trying to hook up."

"I know, I know," I said. "I just got caught up in the moment."

"This deal is a big one," he warned. "Dad is not going to be happy if you screw it up. You know how close him and Lyons are."

"I know," I said again. "I'll handle it. She wouldn't have been receptive to my offer last night. She's very standoffish. I need to ease into this or she's going to shut me down as fast as she shut down Lyons."

"Oh, so this wine and dine approach is all about easing your way into her good graces. Whatever you say, big brother."

"I'll be home tomorrow. Maybe."

"Maybe?" he asked.

"Probably."

"I hope you know what you're doing," he warned.

"Trust me, I've been doing this for a while. It's all good."

I walked into the coffee shop and ordered the strongest, darkest blend I could get. I sat down at one of the tables and debated my next move. I liked Emma, but this was not a dating opportunity. I had to follow through with my plans. I was supposed to be sealing the deal for my client. That was my priority.

Because I had a feeling I might need her phone number at some point, I had put it in my cell phone. Her digital signature included her cell, which was lucky for me.

Can we go to dinner tonight? I'd like to get to the business we didn't get to last night.

I waited for a response. I wasn't expecting an immediate answer. After all, she had shut me down when I offered to take her home.

Who's this? was her response.

The handsome, charming guy that bought you a steak dinner last night. You distracted me. We didn't get to the business I came here to talk to you about. Can we meet tonight?

I waited for her to reply. *Five o'clock.*

She picked the restaurant and I agreed to meet her there. After killing some time with work at the hotel, I got in another quick workout before I had to meet her. This time, I had to remember why I was there. It wasn't for pleasure. This wasn't a woman I was going to be dating. This was business. I would make the pitch, buy the business, and then leave. Period.

When I arrived at the restaurant she chose, she was already there. Tonight was different. She was wearing slacks and a sweater, which made me feel better about the jeans and dress shirt I was wearing. I liked the idea of scaling things back a little. Last night had felt stuffy. I wanted things to be relaxed and easy.

"Hi." She smiled.

"Thanks for meeting me again," I said. "I'm sure you're busy."

"I am," she agreed.

"I got caught up in your story last night and totally spaced out about the business I needed to discuss with you."

Her green eyes bored into mine. She was very serious. "I'm very interested to hear about this business."

"I have a client that has become very interested in your chocolate factory," I said. "Very, very interested."

"That could mean many things," she said with a coy smile. "Why don't we skip all the pleasantries and stuff? Let's just talk business. I don't want to be rude, but I have something I need to do. Soon."

I wasn't sure what I was thinking this dinner was going to be, but in the back of my mind, I had hoped there would be a perk to our business. I looked at her hand to make sure I hadn't missed a ring.

There was nothing there, but that wasn't saying much. She could have a boyfriend or live with a guy. I was letting my dick do the thinking.

"Okay, fair enough," I said. "My client wants to buy Miller's Chocolates."

Her eyes widened and I saw the shock on her face. "What?"

"I have a client that has taken an interest in your company," I said. "He's willing to offer you five million dollars. He would want all the recipes as well. He would own all of it. You wouldn't be able to pick up and start over with your recipes."

She was staring at me with total disbelief. "He wants to buy my business?" she repeated.

"Yes." I nodded. "Five million. I've done a little homework. I know that is far more than what you make in a year. It's a very, very generous offer."

She reached for the glass of water. "I don't understand."

"From what I understand, he floated the offer to you some time ago," I explained. "He doesn't think it hit home, so he's asked me to talk with you."

"Five million," she murmured. "There was some guy that came in and said he would pay me a few million if I turned over everything right then. I thought he was joking. I dismissed him."

"He wasn't joking." I smiled. "He doesn't always have the best delivery, which is why I'm here."

"You're supposed to smooth things over," she muttered. "You're going to flash your million-dollar smile and buy me a steak dinner and that's supposed to make me hand over the keys."

"That and a cool five million," I added.

"I don't understand. Why? Why does he want my business? Why is he willing to pay that much?"

"Because he is a man with big aspirations and a bigger checking account." I grinned. "When he sees something he wants, he tends to go for it. He's very used to getting what he wants."

"My business isn't for sale," she said. "I thought this meeting was about an investment opportunity. I thought you were some hotshot working for Mr. Money in New York. I thought you wanted to invest in my company. Or your boss. I just—I—this is not what I expected."

"I'm sorry to catch you off guard," I said.

"He doesn't want to invest? My company isn't turning a million-dollar profit, but with an investor, it could. I really thought this was about someone seeing potential and wanting to maximize it."

I felt terrible for dropping this on her. This wasn't the typical business deal. This woman was emotionally invested in her company. I had a sneaking suspicion she might just turn the deal down. I didn't get the impression money motivated her. I was supposed to be the closer. I needed to act fast to save this thing.

I cleared my throat. "No, I'm sorry," I said again. "He only wants to buy the company. He is being very generous because he's serious about the purchase."

"And do what with it?" she asked.

"I'm not entirely sure," I answered honestly. "I would imagine he plans to keep it in business, but with his vision."

She shook her head. "I don't know. This isn't something I ever considered."

"I understand." I nodded. "Why don't we order dinner, and I can try to answer any questions you have?"

"You know, I think I better go home," she said.

"Emma, I hope I didn't upset you."

"I'm not upset," she said. "I told you I've got something to do."

"Can I call you tomorrow?" I asked.

"I don't know," she answered. "I need some time to think about this. This was not the way I envisioned my day going."

"I get it," I said. "I didn't mean to spring it on you."

"Yes, you did," she snapped before smiling. "Sorry, I don't mean to be rude. I am not used to the New York way of things. You guys are notorious for your bold, brazen ways. I'm small potatoes. I'm not used to being steamrolled."

She got to her feet, and I had a sneaking suspicion I had just lost the deal. I followed her out of the restaurant. I was watching my reputation walk away with her. "Call me," I said as she walked down the sidewalk.

She put up a hand but said nothing. I watched her get in her SUV and drive away. It wasn't over. This was just the first shot. She would come back with a higher number, and I would counter. It wasn't usually the dance I did, but I knew how to play. It could be fun.

Anything to get me one more dinner with the beautiful chocolatier.

6

EMMA

I kept it together when I got home. I wasn't ready to talk about the offer with Jennifer just yet. I needed some time to sit with it and get my head around the whole thing. After she left, I spent some time with Lucy before it was time to go to bed. I went to bed early just so I could stay up half the night thinking.

I had to hand it to the man—he had shocked me. I was not expecting an offer to buy my business. Five million dollars was a lot of money. A ton of money. I could pay off the mortgage, set up a college fund for Lucy, and still never worry about money. I could be home for Lucy. I would never have to send her to daycare or an after-school program. I would never have to worry about a slow month or two at the factory and making payroll.

Being debt free and financially stable was tempting. It was a wonderful thought. It would be so freeing to go to the store and buy what I needed without thinking about the costs. Ever since Marie passed away and I was left to care for her daughter on my own, things had been a little strained. The company was doing well, but there was always the fear of failure. If I failed, Lucy suffered. It wasn't just me that would pay the price of my failure. An innocent little girl who had already lost everything would lose again.

But my factory was my other child. I had started it in my kitchen. My tiny little apartment had been the home of my business for almost two years. Way back in the beginning, it was me and Marie helping me out on occasion. Then I hired a single person to help me make the chocolates. I nurtured it from a little bit of nothing to what it was today. I imagined it growing and maybe one day it would be as big as Hershey's. My little chocolate factory was my baby. It was the dream. It was my only dream. Some people dreamed about becoming a doctor or having a big house and six kids. My dream was to make chocolate.

The following morning, it was still weighing heavy on my heart. I dropped Lucy off at school and called Jennifer. "Do you have a job today?" I asked.

"Nope," she answered. "Ready to tell me what happened last night?"

"Yes," I said and couldn't help but smile. She knew me well. Last night, she had simply given me a hug and left with the invitation to call her anytime.

"Let's go for a walk," she said. "I need to get my cardio in. I need fresh air. I'm sick of the gym. It's not too cold and it's not raining. We need to take advantage of the weather."

"Let me clear my schedule," I told her.

We met an hour later at the park we often frequented. "Spill," she said. "What happened last night? Is he a total douchebag? Why'd you go out with him again if you didn't like him?"

"I don't think he's a total douche," I said. "I met with him because, at the first dinner, we never got to the actual business he came here to discuss with me."

"And you did last night?" she asked as we started down the trail.

"Yes."

"Woman, if you don't tell me what happened, I'm going to shake it out of you!"

I laughed and appreciated the lightheartedness. "He wants to buy the factory," I said. "Not him, but his client."

"What? Why?"

"I don't know why, but he offered me a lot of money," I said. "Like a lot."

"How much?"

"Five million," I answered.

She stopped walking and grabbed my arm. "What?!" she shrieked.

"Yep, five million. Five million fucking dollars. Do you know how much that is?"

"Uh, duh," she said. "I don't even know what to say. That's a shit-load of money. You could buy a new house."

"I like my house," I protested.

"Okay, you could pay it off and buy a vacation house," she said. "You could buy a new car, and don't you dare say you like your SUV. That thing is one winter away from breaking down."

"I know," I said as we started walking again. "I could send Lucy to Yale if she wanted to go. I can buy her a car for her sixteenth birthday and put her in that art class next year."

She was quiet for a few seconds. "You could do all those things and yet you're not jumping at the chance to do it. That tells me you're not actually excited about the offer. You haven't accepted the offer because you have misgivings."

"I do," I said.

"Let's hear them," she said. "We'll go through them one by one. We'll figure out what you should do."

"Thank you," I said. "I knew you would see me through this."

"Okay, first reason is because it's your business," she said. "Right?"

"Yes. I started it. I nurtured it. I stayed up for days and gave up so much of my life to make it happen. I missed out on I don't know how many dates. I wore the same clothes for years because I couldn't afford to buy anything new. I scrimped and saved to buy a bag of sugar. It's my blood, sweat, and tears in a very literal sense."

"I agree," she said. "You are absolutely right to feel that way. It's more than just a job. It's *your* job. It's *your* company. Next."

"I worry about the people I employ," I said. "This new owner is probably going to come in and shut down my little operation. All the people that have worked their asses off for me over the years are going to lose their jobs. They depend on me. It isn't fair that I get a windfall of money and they lose their jobs."

"Another good point," she said. "However, let me play devil's advocate. You aren't responsible for anyone except yourself and Lucy. There are other jobs. There is a chance they might land somewhere better. So, while I understand your concern, don't take on that burden. You don't have to take on the weight of the world. You need to think about yourself and Lucy."

I sighed and still didn't feel good about it. "They are like my extended family. When Marie died, they all stepped up and took care of things so I could be home with Lucy. I spend so much time with them they are like my family."

"I understand that," she said. "Does he?"

"Does who?"

"The douchebag."

I burst into laughter. "I don't think he does. But I'm not sure he's a douchebag."

"Oh, you like him!" she exclaimed.

"No, but I don't dislike him," I said. "He's doing his job. He's not buying the company. He's acting on behalf of his client."

"What did you tell him last night?" she asked.

"Nothing," I said. "I told him the business wasn't for sale."

"Then you've already made up your mind," she said.

I groaned and looked up at the sky in the hopes the answer would be in the clouds. "No. I don't know. The money would change our lives."

"But you would be selling a piece of your soul," she said.

"Yes. Exactly. What am I going to do every day if I'm not going to work? Yes, I think the first few weeks and months would be amazing. I would be able to do all those things I've been wanting to do. I would get to take Lucy on a weekend getaway."

"And you would be bored out of your skull," she pointed out. "You love what you do. You have chocolate running through your veins. You could step away, but you won't be able to stay away."

"I have to," I said. "If I take the deal, he wants it all. He would have all my recipes. I'm sure there would be a million strings attached to the money. I wouldn't be able to compete against my own chocolates. Like you said, it would be selling my soul. I would have to come up with new recipes. I've spent years coming up with my chocolate recipe. I don't know that I could change it and be happy with it."

"Before you make a final decision, why don't you invite this guy behind the scenes?" she said. "Show him the love that goes into your chocolate. It isn't just about a business. It isn't about the money."

"I doubt he cares how chocolate is made," I said.

"Does he know that you donate a percentage of your profits to cancer research?" she asked quietly.

"I don't know."

"Does he know about all the charity events you host and contribute to?" she pushed.

"I doubt it."

"Before you give him an answer, why don't you invite him to the tasting event tomorrow?" she suggested. "Take him behind the scenes. Show him why Miller's is different than the typical chocolate factory. Your business is built on love."

"And then what?" I asked. "What will that do?"

"He will get to see how special Miller's is," she said.

"Because I want him to offer more money?" I asked.

"Or maybe just understand why you have to reject the offer," she answered. "When you tell him no, you want him to go back to his client and let him know it isn't going to happen."

I thought about it for a few seconds. "Ah, because I'm dealing with some big city billionaires that play dirty, right?"

"I don't know if they play dirty, but if this guy asked once and you shut him down and now he's sending in his henchmen, you have to wonder what comes next."

I groaned again. "I don't know if I'm flattered or pissed," I said. "It's great they noticed my little factory, but it pisses me off they think they can throw money at me and I'll just take it."

"There you go," she said. "That's my girl. Fight back. If you don't want to sell, don't do it. If you want to sell, take your time making this decision. Bring the douche into your world. Maybe he'll have a heart and walk away and leave you alone."

"And he'll take his money and go." I sighed.

"It's a lot of money." She laughed. "Man, the things you could do."

"Stop! You're supposed to be convincing me not to sell."

"I am?" She laughed.

"I've got dollar signs in my eyes and dread in my heart," I told her. "I know the right thing to do, but I also know what I can live with."

"Call him," she said seriously. "Show him the business. See it through his eyes. Take a step back and try to get a new perspective. If you still feel like the business is your heart and soul, don't sell. You'll make money. If you look at it and you see it is just a business, sign on the line and walk away a wealthy woman."

I knew she couldn't give me all the answers, but she had helped. I was going to step back and reevaluate everything.

7

CASE

I tapped my fingers on the table and stared out the window of my hotel room. I was wasting time here. There was nothing I could do here that I couldn't do from home. Spinning my wheels was not something I did. I made my pitch and now I had to give her the time she was asking for. Pushing her would likely back-fire in my face. I needed to take this one slowly.

I started packing my things when I got a phone call. My immediate thought was it was James Lyons calling to check on the progress of the deal. I didn't quite have the balls to tell him I failed. Techni-cally, I hadn't failed yet, but it felt like it was leaning that way. Unless she saw the benefit to having a few extra million in her bank account.

I glanced at the screen and grinned. "And that's why they send me in to do the hard jobs."

Yes, I was just a little cocky. But I earned it. "Hello, Emma Miller," I answered with all my usual smoothness.

"That's very formal." She laughed.

"How are you?"

"I'm good, thank you," she replied. "I was calling to invite you to a chocolate-tasting event."

I frowned. "A chocolate-tasting event?" I asked.

"Yes. It's the chocolatier way of schmoozing. A number of companies get together and hold tasting booths. Investors and retailers are invited. It's how we check in on our competition while securing more deals to market our goods. Some of us even attract investors that want to help grow our companies."

I didn't miss the not-so-subtle dig at my offer to buy rather than invest. "Tonight?" I questioned.

"Yes," she answered.

I really, really should get my ass back home, but the thought of spending another evening with her was far too tempting. No one had to know I was enjoying the wooing of the owner of the company. It wasn't like anyone was really going to check up on me. "Okay," I said. "What's the dress code?"

"Semi-formal," she answered. "The suit you wore the other night would work."

"Where should I pick you up?" I asked. It was my attempt to make this just a little more date-like instead of all about the business. I had to disarm her enough to let my natural charm work its magic.

"I'll text you the address," she answered, to my surprise.

"Great, what time?"

"Six," she said.

"I'll be there," I said and hung up.

Things were looking up. I wasn't going to have to go home with my tail tucked between my legs. First things first, I needed a new suit. I wasn't about to wear the same one. I also needed a car service. I got to work getting what I needed to impress this woman that had captivated my attention. I would go home and chastise myself for breaking the barrier between professional and personal desire.

The town car pulled up to the address Emma had given me. It was a nice house in a quaint suburb. It was one of those new builds that popped up in a subdivision with all the houses being cookie-cutter versions of their neighbors.

I walked up to the front door and rang the bell. The door opened with a very pretty blonde checking me out. She looked me up and down, and not for the first time in my life, I felt like a horse at an auction. I expected her to ask me to open my mouth so she could inspect my teeth. When she was through checking me out, her blue eyes met mine.

"Is Emma here?" I asked with a smirk. She knew damn well what she had done and the defiant look on her face told me she didn't care. I didn't care either.

"She is," she said. "You're Case?"

"I am."

"Case *Manhattan*," she stressed my last name.

"Yes." I nodded.

"Is that your stage name?" she joked.

"Nope, family name," I answered with a shrug.

"Manhattan?" she questioned skeptically. "That seems rather bold."

"I don't think they got to choose their name," I answered with a smile. "Did you?"

"Yes, actually, I did," she said. "It was part of my career plan. Why Manhattan?"

"I couldn't tell you. Like I said, they didn't choose the name. Maybe back in the fourteenth century they did, but none of the ancestors I know had anything to do with the name."

"What came first, your ancestors or the city?" she teased.

I leaned forward and lowered my voice. "My ancestors. It's very common for cities to be named after the founders."

Her mouth dropped open. I winked and was about to give her one more little jab when I caught a glimpse of Emma coming into the room. She was stunning. I couldn't breathe for several seconds.

"You're a Manhattan!" the woman exclaimed.

Emma looked confused. "What does that mean?" she asked her friend.

The blonde pointed at me. "He's a Manhattan! Like the Manhattans. They built Manhattan! They're like the Kennedy's Camelot but New York!"

Emma looked at me, and for the first time, I was a little embarrassed. I had a feeling she would not be impressed by my name or what it meant. "Oh," she said and shrugged a dainty shoulder in the red shoulderless dress she was wearing. The cutouts at the shoulders exposed her collarbones, something I had a very weird but real fondness for. I could already imagine myself kissing along those sharp points.

"You look stunning," I told her. It wasn't a line. It was a fact. The red dress was hot. It just so happened to be one of my favorite colors, although I leaned more toward lingerie in red. Her hair was done in big, chunky curls that were left to hang around her shoulders.

"Thank you." She blushed a little before turning to her friend. "I'll see you guys later."

I wasn't sure who she was referring to. I waved at the woman who still seemed to be a little shellshocked by me. She was looking at me like I was Elvis come to life.

"Don't mind her," Emma said. "She tends to be a little on the dramatic side."

"Is that your roommate?" I asked and opened the back door for her.

"No, my friend," she answered. "Jennifer."

We got into the car and Emma leaned over me to wave out the window. I found it a little odd she'd be waving to her friend. When I turned to look, I discovered it wasn't her friend she was waving to. It was a little girl with long dark hair waving back.

A kid? Nothing in her bio said anything about a kid. I looked at her waving hand one more time to make sure I hadn't missed a ring. There wasn't one. Maybe she had a live-in boyfriend. That was probably more common than being married with kids.

"Are you ready for this?" she asked as she settled into her seat.

"I think so," I said. "Is there something you're not telling me?"

"I'll give you a few tips," she said with a grin. "There's going to be a lot of chocolate. Like more than a trip to Willy Wonka's factory. There will also be a lot of booze. I'm not the only company that makes liquor chocolates, so you'll be given a double whammy. There will be appetizers served. I recommend you go for the salty, high in carbs choices."

"Why?"

"Because when you're eating chocolate and drinking alcohol, it's easy to forget just how much you're drinking until you've crossed over into drunkenness."

I smiled and nodded. "I think I can hold my own."

"Don't be afraid to drink water," she said. "There will be bottles all around the place. Trust me, you'll want to cleanse your palate now and again after all the sampling. Oh, and take these." She opened her little black purse and pulled out a bottle of Advil. She shook two out and handed them to me.

"Why am I going to need these?" I asked.

"Because I don't know about you, but when I mix a lot of different alcohols and top it off with more sugar than any single person should have in an hour, I get a killer headache."

I reached for one of the bottles of water in the car and quickly took the offered meds. "Thanks. Any more tips?"

"Beware of the pitches," she said. "Just try and enjoy yourself."

I was anxious to step into her world. I didn't want to tell her I had been to a thousand of these boozy parties and could handle my own. If she wanted to be my guide, I was happy to be her willing student. When we arrived at the hotel where the event was being held, I was impressed by the number of people in attendance.

"Damn," I said under my breath. "I smell chocolate. So much chocolate. And liquor."

She flashed me a grin. "I hope you're ready for this."

I followed her lead, stopping at a table arranged with a variety of chocolates in shiny gold wrappers. That seemed to be pretty standard fare and wasn't all that impressive. "Try this one," she said and handed me a small chocolate blob.

I popped it in my mouth and was rewarded with a burst of tequila that, surprisingly, didn't make me choke like it usually did. "Wow," I said. "This isn't yours."

"No, but I can appreciate a good recipe." She smiled.

"I would have never paired tequila with chocolate," I said.

"People will put chocolate with anything." She laughed and pointed to another table. "Ever had chocolate-covered bacon?"

My lip curled. "I don't think I want to."

"Come on," she teased. "You're here to learn and have fun."

I took a bite of the offering and was impressed. "Those could be dangerous," I said with a laugh.

"Ah, here comes the liquor," she said under her breath as a woman wearing a black dress approached us.

"Would you like to try our Cherry Chocolate shots?" she asked us.

"Please," Emma said and took one from the tray.

I looked at the shot glasses that weren't actually glasses. "Is this chocolate?" I asked.

"It sure is." Emma laughed. "You take the shot and eat the glass."

"Creative," I said and took one.

After the woman walked away, Emma looked around. "Their chocolate is shit," she whispered. "But I love the cherry-flavored liquor."

"Oh, is this your competition?" I teased.

"As if." She scoffed. "I don't make these chocolate glasses, but if I did, you would actually want to eat them."

"Good to know," I said with a smile. I liked the feisty, competitive side of her.

"I need bread," Emma said with a groan after we'd been at the event for less than thirty minutes. "There's a table of apps, or what some of my colleagues will call the quitters' table."

"Why the quitters' table?" I asked.

"Because the people over here can't hang," she explained. "I am not too proud to surrender. The ones that don't visit this table are going to be the ones making asses out of themselves by the end of the night. I'll wave the white flag all day."

I was glad she was willing to say uncle. I was already feeling a buzz. I didn't think I had drunk all that much, but it was all going straight to my head on blood thickened with chocolate. I couldn't let myself get drunk and make a mistake I might regret.

Or would I regret it?

8

EMMA

I was feeling a little buzz and knew I better slow down a bit. I was actually having fun, which I never expected. Not with him. He was enjoying himself as well, judging by the laughter I heard coming from him as he hammed it up with a small group of guys that were clearly enjoying the free booze.

"There you are," he said with a big smile when I approached the group. "I was just telling these guys how amazing your new strawberry chocolate is. They are interested in tasting."

"I'm sorry, guys," I said with my own smile. "It's a very new product and it is still in production. I wasn't able to bring any tonight."

There were some exaggerated pouts with the promise to buy it as soon as it hit the market.

"I think I might have a tiny buzz," he said as we made our way around the large room and sipped champagne.

"You think?" I laughed. "We better hit the apps before we both end up sloppy drunk."

"I can't believe this is a thing," he said and gestured to the room as a whole.

"What do you mean?"

"I go to about a million charity events, dinners, and what not," he said. "I'm not bragging, but my family is invited to something every week. We usually try and take turns about who has to go. Fortunately, the family is huge now and we can rotate in and out. These things are always a drag."

"Why?" I asked curiously. He had mentioned his family but never really told me much about them. The little tidbit about him being one of *the* Manhattans was a surprise. I probably wouldn't have put it together without Jennifer's help.

"We go and rub elbows with people who either want something from us or want to be friends with us because of the family name," he explained. "Again, I'm not trying to sound like a dick, but it's just the way it is. We've all been used once or twice. Some a lot more. We hate going to these things because it's like being fed to the vultures."

"Ah, everyone wants a little piece of the Manhattan family," I teased. "I bet it's a lot like the old days where mamas with big aspirations for their single daughters were thrusting them at the eligible noblemen with the hopes of getting a title and a big bank account."

He looked at me a little strangely. "I guess it's kind of like that."

I was suddenly embarrassed. "Sorry. I read a lot of historical romance novels. You're my first real-life prince. Or duke. You know what I mean."

The champagne was getting to me. I was rambling and making a total ass out of myself. He didn't seem to mind all that much. He was staring at me with that cocky grin on his face. "Should we take a walk outside and get some fresh air?" he asked before leaning close. "Would that cause a scandal? Should we have a chaperone?"

"Very funny." I smacked his shoulder. But a little fresh air was exactly what I needed to clear the bubbles from my head. And because we were in the now and the threats were a little more serious than some overzealous man hoping to steal a kiss, it would be nice to have a big burly man to guard my body.

We followed the discreet signs that directed us into the hotel courtyard. It was chilly but several heaters were placed around the area along with soft lighting. The fresh air felt good, but it wasn't clearing the bubbles just yet. I couldn't believe I had let myself get buzzed. I was usually much more careful.

"Are you cold?" he asked.

"No, the cool air feels good," I told him. "It's warm in there."

"Maybe it's the alcohol pumping through your veins," he teased.

"Maybe." I laughed. "So, tell me more about yourself."

We stood in front of a heater with our hands held out like we were in front of a campfire. "I'm really not that exciting," he said.

"I'll admit, I don't really follow the gossip of the New York elite, but I have heard of your family. Are you guys famous?"

"No," he answered right away. "My father and his siblings were famous in their day. There's so many of us kids it's impossible for the press to keep up with all of us. We fly under the radar most of the time. We're not exciting enough. The only time we make the news is on a Sunday when there is nothing else to report."

"I guess a CPA probably doesn't live a super exciting life," I teased.

He chuckled and shook his head. "No, not really."

A small group of young people ventured into the courtyard. Our quiet moment was interrupted. "We should probably get back inside," I said. "I can't afford to get sick."

We walked back to the door only to find it was locked. "Shit," he muttered. "I guess we'll go around."

He shrugged out of his suit jacket and wrapped it around my shoulders.

"Thank you," I said and was actually grateful for the extra layer. Being away from the heaters reminded me just how cold it was outside.

As we walked, we tried every door until we finally found one that someone else just happened to be coming out of. I looked down the long hallway. "Where are we?"

"Not a clue," he answered. "We'll find our way back eventually."

"I think we're in an employee-only wing," I whispered.

There was a loud machine and a few room-service carts parked along one side of the hall. We stopped walking and looked at each other. He grinned and something hit me. My eyes dropped to his mouth. His grin fell away, and a moment later, I was pushed against the wall with his mouth covering mine. The kiss went from zero to oh-my-god in a millisecond.

I opened my mouth and let his tongue inside. Our tongues slashed against each other as my hands gripped his upper arms. Strength radiated from his body. He stepped closer, giving me a full-body press with the wall behind me keeping me from going anywhere. His hands slid up my sides with his thumbs brushing over the sides of my breasts before dropping back down to my hips. I heard myself moan and it was the alert I needed to push him away.

I turned my head, giving him the signal to stop. I couldn't quite say the word. I was breathless. My chest heaved up and down as I struggled to catch my breath. My knees actually felt weak. It was a very good thing I was slumped against the wall. I probably would have dropped to the floor in a shameless puddle had it not been there.

"I should go," I said.

"Should I apologize here?" he asked and ran his hand up the back of his head.

"No," I quickly answered. "No need to apologize. We've had a little too much to drink. I'm going to call an Uber."

My purse was slung over my shoulder, which was when I remembered I was still wearing his jacket. I shrugged it off and handed it to him. "I'll get the car service to pick us up," he offered.

"No!" I said just a little too forcefully. "I mean, no thank you. I think it's best I take my own ride."

His lips quirked. "Worried I might steal another kiss?"

I wasn't going to acknowledge that statement. I was already ordering a ride. "Thanks for coming tonight," I said and was going to walk away, but I had no idea where I was or where the exit was.

"This way," he said and pointed down another hall.

I followed behind him. The whole time, I was lecturing myself for making out with the man that was trying to buy my company. He had ulterior motives. I knew that. He pushed open a door and we were in the lobby of the hotel.

"Thanks for coming tonight," I said and made a beeline for the doors before he could say another word.

I hoped like hell he didn't follow me. The car showed up and I climbed in. The entire way back to my house I kept replaying what had happened. What in the hell was I thinking? When I got home, Jennifer was curled up on the couch and watching *Friends*.

"Hey," she said and sat up. "You're home early."

I walked to the couch and flopped down in a very unladylike fashion. "I'm an idiot!"

"What'd you do?" she asked. "Did you sell the company?"

"No," I groaned. "I kissed him."

"You kissed who?"

"Him!"

Her eyes widened. "Manhattan?" she gasped.

"Yes. Case. I kissed Case Manhattan. The man that's trying to ruin my life by buying the company I've poured my life's blood into."

"I don't know if he's trying to ruin your life," she said. "Technically, he could be changing your life for the better if you decide to accept the offer."

"You're not helping." I scowled.

"Let's agree he's not trying to ruin your life and get back to the part about the kissing," she said with way more enthusiasm than necessary. "How was it? I bet it was amazing. The guy is gorgeous. I'm not into the big rich socialite types, but I could so get into him."

"Stop," I scolded. "This isn't funny. I don't do this kind of thing. If we hadn't been in a public place, I probably would have ended up hiking up my dress and letting him fuck me right in the hallway!"

Once again, pure shock covered her face. "You did what? Where?"

I covered my face with my hands. "I cannot believe I did that," I muttered. "I'm so embarrassed and ashamed of myself."

"Why are you embarrassed?" she asked. "You certainly have nothing to be ashamed of. You were out with a gorgeous man. I probably wouldn't have made it out of the car before dropping my panties."

"Jennifer!" I gasped in shock.

"It's true." She laughed. "You've been out of the game for too long. Making out with a hot guy is pretty normal. You have nothing to be ashamed of. Did anyone see you with him?"

"I don't think so," I said. "We got lost and ended up in some maintenance hallway or something."

"Then let's skip over the embarrassed part and give me the good stuff." She grinned. "Details. Was it good? He looks like he would be a good kisser. He had very good kissable lips."

As much as I wanted to clutch my pearls and pretend it wasn't amazing, I couldn't lie. "Amazing," I breathed. "I've never been kissed like that. Then again, it's been so long since I've been kissed, I couldn't really say if it was as good as I think it was."

"Tongue?"

"Absolutely," I said with a laugh. "He pushed me against the wall and—"

I stopped. I couldn't finish the sentence because it was already making me very squishy inside. She was looking at me with a huge smile. I was about to blush again.

"And then what happened?" she asked. "Did he get to second base? Did you find a room?"

"Nothing happened," I said. "I stopped it before I could totally lose my mind. I called a ride and here I am."

"Are you going to see him again?"

"No!" I said and remembered the little girl asleep upstairs. "I can't. No way."

"Why not?" she asked. "He's single and obviously interested. I saw the way he looked at you. He likes you."

"He lives in New York and is a member of a social class I am not a part of. He's the prince and I'm the lowly peasant girl."

She rolled her eyes. "We're not in the twelfth century anymore."

"Same thing, different times. Besides, I'm not interested. It was a moment of weakness brought on by champagne and way too much sugar. I'm going to reject the offer. He'll go home and that will be that."

"Fine, it doesn't have to be him, but now that you've had a taste of it, don't you want more?"

"More what?" I asked.

"Sex!" she burst out. "Lucy is stable. She's not going to suffer if you go out on a date once a week. I'm here. She knows she is loved. She has a beautiful home and she feels safe. You need to start dating again. Find her a daddy."

"I'm not looking for a daddy," I replied.

"Then look for a man for you, but just make sure he's a good daddy."

I had no interest in looking for a man. I didn't have the energy to date. I was certainly not going to risk bringing the wrong man around Lucy.

We said our goodbyes and I headed to bed with the taste of him still on my lips.

9

CASE

The first thing I thought of when I opened my eyes was her. The kiss had lingered with me all night. It was a tease. I wanted more. I had kissed plenty of women, but this one felt different. Maybe it was the forbidden fruit. Whatever the case, I wanted more, and I planned on getting what I wanted. I knew she wanted it as well. I had felt it in the kiss. She kissed me back. Given another five minutes and I would have made use of one of those maintenance closets.

I got up, used the bathroom, and then checked my phone. "Shit," I sighed when I saw eight missed calls. Some were from my dad, some from Edwin, and the others from James Lyons. This did not bode well.

Going by order of importance, I called my dad first. "Dad, it's me," I said.

"What in the hell are you doing?" he growled.

I looked at the date. I didn't think I had anything scheduled. "I'm in Pennsylvania."

"No shit!" he barked. "We all know where you are. Have you talked to James?"

"Lyons?" I asked with confusion. I felt like I'd been dropped in the middle of a movie with no context. "I haven't talked to him this morning. It's not even eight o'clock."

"He's been trying to reach you," he said in a tone that said I was in trouble. Big trouble.

"Why?"

"You're up there to do a job. You're not supposed to be sleeping with the woman!"

"What are you talking about?" I asked.

"It's all over Twitter and whatever other stupid social media networks people use these days," he growled.

"What's all over social media?"

"Why don't you see for yourself and then you figure out how you're going to fix this with your client?" he snapped. "I'll expect to see you back home by the end of the day."

He ended the call.

"Fuck me."

I pulled open the Twitter account I had but never used. It wasn't long before I saw what had my dad so pissed. There were several pictures of me kissing Emma. One of them looked especially risqué. My hand was on her breast and my body was pushed against hers. To anyone that hadn't been there, it looked like we were about to have sex. If only they had stuck around for another minute. Whoever "they" was.

It wasn't exactly a big deal. We were consenting adults at a party. We stole a few minutes to make out. It wasn't newsworthy, but because I was who I was, it was news. This was one of the serious downsides to being a Manhattan. We couldn't get away with anything. There was always someone with a cell phone.

I was going to have to do a lot of explaining and that was best to be done in person. I booked a flight and quickly packed. Before I left, I needed to talk to Emma. If she saw the pictures, she was not going to be happy with me either. I wasn't done with her just yet, but that was going to have to wait until I settled this with James Lyons.

I had the cab take me to Miller's Chocolates first. I wanted to tell her I was leaving in person. "Excuse me," I said to the young woman behind the counter.

"Can I help you?"

"I'm looking for Emma. Is she in?"

"Let me see if she's available," she said and walked through a door to the back.

I looked around the store once again. There weren't as many customers but it was still pretty busy. People were picking out boxes and selecting chocolates with other service workers. It all seemed to be a very smooth process. Her business seemed to run like a well-oiled machine. That was all credit to her.

Emma appeared from the back with a black apron with the name of her company embroidered on the left side. "Hi," I said and expected a smile or something.

She looked around nervously. "Hi."

"I wanted to let you know I'm flying back to New York for a few days," I said.

"Okay." She shrugged.

It wasn't exactly the response I expected. "I'll be back. We have unfinished business to discuss."

"I don't think we do," she said. "I think email would be fine."

She was acting like we were fifteen and had been caught kissing under the bleachers. "I'll call you," I said.

"Okay, I need to get back to work," she murmured without making eye contact.

While I would have liked to say more, something told me it was better if I left things alone. I had enough holes to dig myself out of. I didn't need to make any more. "I'll see you later."

She was already walking away. I headed back to the cab. It wasn't exactly the goodbye I had been hoping for. Maybe she'd seen the pictures. Hell, I was sure she had seen them. She was probably pissed at me. Again, I chalked that up to a problem to deal with on another day.

I was in New York by the end of the day. I went to my office first and was welcomed by a very angry father. "Dad—"

"Don't," he said and pointed to my office.

Thankfully, there were only a few people left at the office. I didn't appreciate being scolded like I was a three-year-old with my hand caught in the cookie jar. I was a grown-ass man and felt like I deserved to be treated as such. Unfortunately, what I felt and what was happening were very different. I was just grateful he was giving me the courtesy of letting me get my ass handed to me behind closed doors.

"Do you want a drink?" I asked as I walked to the sidebar. I knew I was going to need one. I knew that look on his face. It meant I was in deep shit. I was thirty-two and my father still had the power to make me feel like a little boy.

"No," he said. "Sit down. We need to figure this shit out."

I poured myself a drink and sat down across from him. "Get it out of your system," I told him. "When you've said your piece, then we'll talk. No point in me saying a word because you aren't going to hear it."

"James Lyons is not only one of the oldest family friends, he's one of the best clients in all our firms," he said angrily. "I don't have to tell you just how valuable his account is at the accounting firm, let alone the law firm. I can't have my son embarrassing the family with this kind of behavior. There are a million women around here and you go after the one you can't have. Do you know what this looks like? Do you know what will happen if he decides to pull his business?"

"He's not going to pull his business," I said. "There would be no reason for him to do that."

"When he called me, he made it clear he wasn't happy with what he was seeing," he said. "You haven't returned his calls. He thinks you're up there chasing ass instead of taking care of business."

"I was taking care of business," I insisted. "I wasn't chasing ass."

"The pictures I saw made it pretty clear you were doing a lot more than handling business," he growled.

"The pictures don't tell the whole story," I argued. "We were there on business. I'll close the deal."

"Really? Because from what I saw, you were closing an entirely different deal. One that Mr. Lyons is not impressed with."

"Dad, I have always done my job," I told him. "Always. I have upheld the family name for my entire life. I've been discreet. Whatever those pictures captured was not the full story. Nothing happened between us. It was a kiss. Nothing more."

"Son, I know you think I'm old, but I'm not that old," he said with a sigh. "I remember those times."

"It wasn't that," I insisted. "It's just business. She wanted to go out. I'm closing a deal. You're the one who taught us how to wine and dine our clients. I put on some of that infamous Manhattan charm. It'll get done."

I was lying just a little. It was more than business, but I wasn't going to tell him that. It wasn't going to help anything. All he needed to know was I was doing my job. What I did in my personal time was none of his business. It hadn't been for a long time.

"You need to square this with James," he said. "I will not let you ruin our good name."

He got to his feet and walked out of the office. I had been properly chastised. Now, it was time to call James and work this out. It wasn't that big of a deal. Sometimes, it wasn't always fun being in business with the family. It was like being watched all the time. My dad and his siblings were from a different generation. They didn't get it.

I downed the last of the drink and poured another before moving to sit behind my desk to make the call. "James!" I greeted like there was nothing wrong.

"Case," he said in a tight voice. "I've been trying to call you."

"I understand," I said. "I'm back in New York."

"What the hell is going on?" he snapped. "Why am I seeing pictures of you with your tongue down the throat of the woman who owns the business I want? That doesn't make me think you were very serious about getting what I wanted."

"You've met the woman," I said. "You know she can be very stubborn. Your way didn't work. I'm trying something different."

"You're going to fuck her until she agrees to sell?" he spat.

I flinched at the words. "No, sir. I'm working on getting her to like me enough to consider selling. She isn't going to jump at the chance to sell the business she loves. It's a work in progress. I need to slowly disarm her."

"Just how slowly are we talking?" he asked. "I'm not interested in how you get it done. I just want it done."

"And it will be done," I assured him. "I'll keep you updated, but you don't need to worry about if my goals have changed. Have I ever let you down?"

"I'd hate for you start doing it now," he replied.

"I won't," I insisted. "I know how to close a deal. I told you I would make this happen. It will happen. Let me worry about how it gets done."

"Someone better make it happen," he said and hung up the phone.

I felt like I needed to shower. I felt dirty. I hated lying, but I wasn't going to tell him or my dad what was really going on. I wasn't entirely sure what was going on myself. But I knew I wasn't done with Emma Miller.

Not even close.

10

EMMA

I was struggling to focus on the task at hand. I had about a million things I needed to get done and was running in circles. Valentine's Day was around the corner. There was no time for me to sit in the office and do paperwork or other administrative tasks. It was all hands-on deck. The entire staff was in the factory. Part of my training program included everyone learning the ropes in the factory. I didn't expect my HR girl to mix the chocolate, but she and the rest of the staff knew how to sort and package.

"Incoming," someone up the line called out.

Chocolates filled with a rich brandy started to come down the conveyor. One by one, I plucked them off the belt and carefully wrapped them and put them in a box. I had considered buying equipment to do all this, but we didn't do enough volume to make it worth the cost. I liked to think this was another way for me to do a little more quality control.

"We're busier this year, aren't we?" one of the ladies working beside me asked.

"We are." I smiled. "About ten percent."

"That's awesome!"

"It is and it's all thanks to you guys," I said.

"It's your spectacular chocolate that has made us all very busy," she replied. "I love the strawberry ones. They are really, really good."

"Thank you."

I zoned out while I packaged the candy. My mind kept going to the kiss. The kiss was good. Really, really good, and if I was being honest, I wanted more. I wanted more of those kisses. Maybe even a little more than a kiss.

I would love to take Jennifer's advice and jump at the chance to break my celibacy streak, but it had been so long. I wasn't even sure I remembered how. What if I did it wrong? He was the kind of man that would know. Judging by the way he kissed, he had plenty of experience in the art of lovemaking. I would look like a total fool if I tried to tangle with him.

He had kissed me because I was there. We were both a little buzzed and the moment presented itself. If we had been back in the ballroom with the extensive list of available women that would absolutely love the chance to get in bed with him, things would be different. He would have picked up one of them. I was just in the right place at the right time.

"Emma?" I heard my name.

I blinked and brought myself back to reality. "What?"

"Suzy is here," she said. "She's ready to take over for you."

"Oh, thanks," I said and took a step back.

I left the line and went upstairs. The second shift had arrived, which meant it was time for me to go pick up Lucy. We were running eighteen hours a day to keep up with demand. It was only temporary, and the employees loved the extra hours.

I left the building and headed for the school. Once again, my thoughts went back to Case. The more I thought about it, the more I believed he only made the move on me because he had an ulterior motive. He wanted my company. What better way to get me to sign on the line than to woo me? He was flashing that cocky smile and those sexy blue eyes to get me to do what he wanted.

I was not some naïve little girl. I knew what he was doing. The light turned red. My fingers tapped against the wheel as I considered my options. What if he did call me? Would I answer? Would it be terrible if I enjoyed the fun he offered for just a bit before turning him down? Did I want to turn him down?

So many questions and zero answers. This was a problem I needed to sit and think about. That was assuming he called me again. He might be gone for good and all of this stressing about what to do would be for nothing.

"Don't borrow trouble," I told myself. Worrying about something that had not happened wasn't going to do me any good. I parked my car and headed inside to pick up Lucy. I was in the here and now. This was my priority, not him.

I greeted Lucy and accepted the usual hug. "I missed you."

"Can we go to the park?" she asked as we walked to the car.

"It's dark," I told her.

"Can we go to the playground?" she asked instead.

I probably should have said no, but I didn't. I was going to regret spoiling her one day, but I would deal with that then. I wanted nothing more than to make her happy, and a little cheeseburger was not going to mess up her world too much.

"Okay, but we can't stay for too long," I warned her. "It's a school night."

She grinned and I was certain she knew exactly what she had done. I was wrapped around her little finger and everyone knew it. She was a good girl. She had respect and didn't really do anything to get into trouble.

"Can I go play?" she asked three seconds after we had walked through the door of the restaurant.

"Let's order first," I said. "I need to keep an eye on you."

She looked like she was going to protest but quickly zipped it up. We ordered and found a table near the play area. The girl was running up the ladder before I even sat down. I watched her play and found myself smiling. After all she'd been through, she was relatively normal. She was having fun and playing like a normal kid.

I often thought of her as my own. She was my baby. I loved her like she was mine. When I watched her play like this, I wished like hell I could take pictures and send them to my sister. Unfortunately, I had no one to send them too. Jennifer had stepped up and treated her like family, but poor Lucy was seriously lacking in that department.

I wished she had grandparents and cousins to spend the holidays with. I wanted her to know the love of a big family. She was such a special girl. I felt like more people should know her the way I did. Everyone should get to love her.

"Lucy!" I called out once our tray of food was delivered. "Come eat!"

A few minutes later she returned to the table and sat down. "Is your boyfriend coming over again tonight?"

I almost choked on my fry. "What boyfriend?"

"That man that came to pick you up last night?" she asked. "Is he coming over again?"

"No," I said.

"I like him."

"You didn't even meet him," I said with a laugh. "How do you know you like him?"

"He seemed nice and you were smiling," she reasoned. "That means you like him."

She was way too smart for her own good. "I don't know him either."

"But you got in the car with him," she pointed out. "You said we can't get in the car with strangers."

One day I was going to learn to watch what I said. "He is someone I know a little bit," I explained. "I was safe, but you're right, we never get into cars with strangers."

"Aunt Jennifer said he was very nice," she said.

I hoped that was all Jennifer said. "He's a nice man and now he's back home."

She seemed satisfied with the answers and went back to her dinner. I let her play another twenty minutes before I called it a night. After we got home, she took her bath while I tidied up.

"Can we watch Willy Wonka?" she asked.

Once again, I was torn between telling her we had to read and giving in to something we both wanted to do. I loved the movie and so did she. It was our thing.

"We can watch half of it," I said. "And then we'll watch the other half tomorrow night. If you put up a fuss when it's time for bed, then we don't get to watch the other half, deal?"

She grinned. "Deal."

I was probably breaking all the parenting rules. I pulled up the movie on our purchased movie titles and settled in on the couch with her and our favorite blankets. We had watched the new version and had been unimpressed. We kept with the classic.

As I listened to the grandparents singing, my mind drifted back fifteen years. I remembered sitting on our couch at home. Marie and I would watch Willy Wonka at least once a week. It was our thing. The movie was so special to me on so many different levels. It reminded me of simpler times. It reminded me of the beautiful days with my big sister. Just thinking about her made my heart hurt a little. I missed her so much. It had been three years and it felt like yesterday.

"How come you don't have a factory like that?" Lucy asked.

"Because we live in the real world." I laughed. "I don't think it's legal for me to employ Oompa Loompas."

"But it would be so much fun," she said with a grin.

"Sorry, kid, it's just me and my staff," I told her.

"Do I get to work there one day?" she asked.

The question struck me hard. She had asked me before and it was always a simple answer. If she wanted to, she could. Now, the answer was in jeopardy. If I took the money from Case, Lucy would never get to work in the family business. She would never get to know the joy of creating something so amazing. The chocolate factory was her family legacy. At least I hoped it would be.

"Alright," I told her halfway through. "It's time for bed. We'll come home tomorrow and finish the movie."

She was a smart girl and didn't put up a fight. I tucked her in and went back downstairs to have a glass of wine in front of the fireplace. I needed to unwind and think about my future. About Lucy's future. I sat in the dark with only the light from the gas fireplace bouncing around the room. My eyes, like they so often did, went to the albums on the coffee table. I had looked at them so many times, they were on their way to falling apart.

It was terrible, but I was glad Marie left me Lucy. She was all the family I had. I hated that she was orphaned at the age of two, but I was so glad I had her. I needed to come up with a decision about the offer. As much as I wanted to believe Case was gone for good, I knew that was unlikely. He was the kind of guy that wouldn't give up without a fight. He was also the kind of man that expected to win every fight he took on.

Did I want a fight? I shook it off. It pissed me off I was forced to even stress about this nonsense. Why couldn't they just leave me alone? I just wanted to make my chocolate and enjoy my life. I wasn't rich, but I didn't need to be. We were comfortable and that was what mattered. Millions would be great, but I had lived without it this long.

11

CASE

I walked into the gym and quickly spotted Edwin flirting with some girl. I shook my head at him. He loved the attention. He loved that women fell all over him. I walked past the two of them and kept going. I heard him make his excuses to leave.

"Have you ever heard the 'don't shit where you eat' phrase?" I asked him.

"I don't eat here." He winked.

"You better be careful," I warned. "Some of these ladies are tough. They will kick your ass."

He grinned. "I know."

I shook my head and stepped onto a treadmill with him taking the one beside me. "You're taking a huge risk."

"Speaking of risks," he started, and I knew exactly what was coming next.

"Don't start."

"Dad was mad," he said. "He called me at least three times."

"I know. He was waiting for me when I got home. Do we have any idea at what age we get to be big boys and make decisions without our father lecturing us?"

"I'm guessing when we're visiting his headstone." He laughed.

"So, what was the deal with that? Those pictures were pretty steamy. I've seen porn with less heat."

"It wasn't what it looked like," I said.

"It looked like you were pushing up on the woman you were supposed to be trying to work out a deal with," he said.

"I wasn't pushing up on her," I retorted. "We kissed. I don't know why everyone is making such a big deal out of it. I've seen worse on the subway."

"The sparks were fierce," he said. "I can't imagine what it was like being there. That was some serious fireworks."

"You can't possibly see all that in a picture."

"*Everyone* saw that." He laughed. "So, what's the deal with that?"

"Nothing," I said again. "There is no deal. We kissed in the hallway. Right after that picture was taken, she left. I went back to my hotel and she went home. That was it."

"You're talking to me, not our father," he said. "I know you and you never pull that shit. Were you drunk?"

"I was a little buzzed," I admitted.

"Still, that's not like you. You like this girl?"

"Actually, I do," I said. "I can't say I really know her, but I wouldn't mind getting to know her a little better."

"No shit?" he said with surprise.

"She's different than the women we meet around here," I said. "It's hard to explain."

"What about the deal?"

"I made her the offer," I answered. "In the meantime, I didn't think it would hurt to get to know her a little. We had fun."

"Are you going to see her again?" he asked.

"I don't know." I shook my head. "After the kiss, she took off pretty quick. When I went to see her the next day, she was acting like she'd never met me."

"She was probably embarrassed by the pictures," he said. "Not all women want to be in pictures."

"I think she has a kid," I said.

"Really?"

"Yes. She never mentioned the little girl."

He laughed as he started running at a steady clip. "You would make a good daddy."

"Fuck you."

He only laughed in response. Once we were off the treadmills and able to talk again, he got very serious. "You should call her," he said. "Seriously, if you like her, don't let dad hold you back."

"I'm not sure," I said. "Things might get very messy if I do convince her to sell her company. She might hate me. Hell, she might hate me if she doesn't sell. If we met at a party or something like that, things might be different."

"Shut up." He laughed. "Who are you?"

"I'm serious," I said. "I don't want to start something I can't finish."

"What the hell is wrong with you?" he asked, aghast. "You like this girl. Fuck dad and fuck Lyons. Call her and ask her on a real date. You don't need permission from anyone."

"She's in Pennsylvania," I reminded him.

"And you can easily use the jet," he said.

"She didn't know who I was," I told him. "She didn't seem to care about who I was. It was kind of weird in a good way."

"I get it," he said. "Just call her. Don't let dad stop you."

"I'll keep that in mind," I said.

We finished our workout and took advantage of the locker room before we each headed off to work. Once I was in the office, my demeanor changed. I was all about the job. I went directly to my office and sat down. A moment later, my assistant, Billy, was walking through the door.

"Is the deal going to fall apart?" he asked.

"What deal?" I asked like I didn't know what he was talking about.

When I had stepped off the elevator, I heard the whispers as I walked down the hall. Those stupid pictures were still making headlines. It was a simple fucking kiss. I didn't know what the big deal was. If they thought that kiss was newsworthy, they'd lose their shit at some of the other stuff I did when I wasn't in my stuffy suit and sitting behind a desk.

"James Lyons was here yesterday," he said. "He wasn't exactly quiet about the situation. I assured him everything was fine. Sheila and Cassie jumped in and tried to explain everything was just fine. This is a huge deal."

"I know," I said in a tight voice. "I don't know why everyone is freaking out. It's handled."

"Is there anything I can do?" he asked.

"I've got it handled," I said again.

He nodded and stopped at the door. "I'll get the reports for the week."

"Thanks," I said and turned my chair to look out the window.

I appreciated my position in the company. While I wasn't going to deny there was some nepotism involved with me getting my foot in the door, it was me and my skills that got me to the top. I had climbed the ladder on my own steam. I crunched numbers and filed tax returns for years. My job as one of the top CPAs was something I earned by proving my ability to make our clients wealthier. The Lyons account had been given to me three years ago. In that time, I had helped him acquire numerous businesses and sell others smoothly. This wasn't a big deal. It would get done.

Before I could fall too far down the rabbit hole, my phone rang. It was time to get my ass to work. I did have other clients that needed my attention. The day was busy as I played catch up after taking a couple of days off. When I got the invitation to go to the family home for dinner, I knew I was still in hot water. The invitation wasn't really optional. My presence was demanded.

When I arrived at the massive townhome my parents lived in, my brothers were already there. Edwin pulled me to the side. "Did you get your ass handed to you today?" he asked quietly.

"What are you talking about?"

"Dad? James? Aunt Anne? Victor?"

"Aunt Anne is somewhere tropical," I reminded him. "She's enjoying the freedom of being the CEO and having peons like me run the show. I didn't see Victor. I haven't talked to James or dad any more since they ripped me a new one."

"Good," he said and actually sounded relieved.

"Does everyone know?" I asked.

I could hear voices down the hall. My other brothers were in the study and talking about the big football game coming up. There were six of us in all, and we could get a little noisy when all together. Our poor mother had been blessed with all boys. I was the oldest, which made me the de facto leader of the group. Sometimes. There was really no leading a group of strong-willed, powerful men.

"There's Casanova!" Bram, number three in the line of brothers and the first to settle down, said as he walked into the small kitchen where we'd been hiding out.

"Don't start," I growled.

"Who's the girl?" he asked. "Did you make a baby?"

I rolled my eyes. "You're such an idiot. Are you five?"

He grinned and drank from the glass he was holding. I could hear footsteps coming down the hall and knew they were all coming to harass me. As each of them filed in, they all had a stupid comment.

"Is that how you got to the top?" Hans asked. He was just a year younger than I was and already in a serious relationship with Heather.

"Very funny," I said and knew I may as well suck it up and deal with whatever they were going to be dishing out for the next couple of hours. "Get it all out of your system, guys. Mom isn't going to let you talk shit at the table."

"We're just curious about this woman," Filip said.

"I don't know why you're all acting like this is the first woman I've ever kissed," I said. "If you're all confused, let me make it clear. I'm not a virgin. I'm not a saint. I'm very straight and I like women. I kiss women. This isn't the first time I've been caught with my tongue down a woman's throat. I'll remind all of you of your own scandals."

That seemed to slow down the teasing. Thankfully, our mom called us into the dining room for dinner. She had one rule at the table—no shenanigans. Dad acted normal. He didn't say anything about the situation. By the time I left that night, I felt like I was back on solid ground.

I went home to the apartment instead of going out to the house. Emma had been on my mind all day. Was she pissed at me? Did she see the pictures? That was a no-brainer. I was sure she had. She was probably pissed I'd put her in that position. If I wasn't who I was, that situation wouldn't have been worthy of a picture. It certainly wouldn't have made the rounds on social media.

The deal was in jeopardy. If she was pissed at me, it was going to be difficult to get her to talk to me. If I couldn't talk to her, I couldn't persuade her to sell the company to Lyons. Hindsight was twenty-twenty. But I didn't regret the kiss. Hell, I wanted more. If she hadn't pulled away, I would have kept going.

After changing and pouring myself a nightcap, I picked up my phone with the intention of sending her a text. A smile spread over my face when I saw I had a message from Emma.

Will you be back in town soon? Her message made me smile. Did she miss me?

I tapped my finger on the screen while I thought of a reply. "Fuck it," I said. *I'll be heading back tomorrow morning.*

It had not been my intention to go back quite yet, but if she was texting me, I still had an in. While I waited for her to reply, I quickly sent off an email to Billy and let him know I would be out of the office tomorrow. Then I found the first flight out.

She texted back. *Can we grab coffee when you get into town?*

I grinned. I was back in. *Absolutely. Text me the place and I'll be there at nine.*

With the date set, I headed to my room to pack for at least a few days. This was my last chance to close this deal. Closing the deal was a priority but seeing her again was what really had me excited. I hoped she was a little less frosty than during the meeting we had in her shop. If I was smart, I would hold back. I would put the business first and what I wanted last. But all I could think about was getting another one of those kisses.

12

EMMA

I didn't want to admit it, but I was actually very excited to see Case. I had gone back and forth on what to do with him. I wasn't entirely sure I had a choice in what I did with him. He was back in New York. Kissing a woman at a party was probably pretty damn common for him. It was just another Tuesday. For me, it rocked my world. I tried to deny it, but I couldn't. I was attracted to the man. It couldn't hurt to flirt a little.

I took a step back and checked out my outfit in the mirror. I wanted to look casual but hot. The goal was to look good without appearing like I tried to look good. I had put on three different outfits before I finally settled on the skinny jeans and black sweater with my favorite black booties. I fluffed my hair and added just a little more mascara.

"Lucy, are you ready?"

"I'm down here!" she called out.

I headed downstairs and found her sitting on the couch with her backpack by her foot. "Ready?"

"Yep."

I took her to school and headed for the coffee shop. I couldn't explain why I was nervous. It was silly. I was a grown woman. A single, grown woman. I could have coffee with a man without creating a scandal. This was what normal people did.

When I took Lucy into my home and became her fulltime and only guardian, I put myself in a bubble. I shut out the world. In many ways, I stopped living. I had been twenty-two and living life to the fullest when we got the news Marie was sick. Nothing prepared us for the hard year ahead of us. We assumed she would kick it. She was young and healthy, and twenty-somethings didn't die of cancer.

And then she did. I didn't know how to be a mommy. In my case, I also had to be a daddy. I was Lucy's entire world, which meant I needed to shut down my world and focus on her. But that was then. We had found a rhythm and I felt like I was ready to dip my toes in the dating pool.

I ordered my latte and took a seat to wait for Case. He walked through the door two minutes before nine. I didn't miss the looks he got from the other women in the coffee shop. His presence commanded the room. When he turned his eyes on me and smiled, I felt a shift. I was the one he was smiling at. I was the one he was there to see. All the women in their power suits and thousand-dollar hairstyles were not on his radar. It was just me.

Oh shit.

Now what? I hadn't thought past the part about seeing him. Now that I was seeing him, what did I do? Shaking his hand felt wrong, considering he had touched my breasts and his tongue had touched my tonsils. A hug felt too intimate.

"Hi," he said, and I realized he was feeling just as awkward.

I went with a side hug, which felt so stupid after I did it. "Did you just get in?" I asked.

"About an hour ago," he said. "Give me two minutes."

I watched him get in line and took a moment to size him up. He was wearing a suit again. His ass was fine. I would love to see him a little less stuffy again. I had never been super attracted to the suit guys. I loved a blue-collar man. I liked a man that didn't mind getting his hands dirty. The suit was window dressing and didn't make the man—I hoped.

He returned and sat down with that same sexy smile on his lips. "How are you?" he asked.

"Good. You?"

"Good." He nodded.

This was awkward. I really thought things would have been normal. I didn't think it was the kiss making things awkward. It was the way I ran away after the kiss that left me feeling like a total fool.

"I'm sorry," we both blurted out at the same time.

"You're sorry?" I asked.

"Yes." He nodded. "I'm sorry about the pictures. I swear I had no idea anyone was there. I should have been more aware. I shouldn't have—"

I stopped him. "No." I shook my head. "Don't apologize for the kiss."

"Why are you sorry?" he asked.

"For running out like that," I said. "I made you feel bad. That wasn't my intention. You don't have to apologize for the kiss. I think we both know I was a willing party."

He grinned with the cup halfway to his mouth. "I am sorry about the pictures, but I won't apologize for the kiss."

"Good. And don't worry about the pictures. It wasn't your fault. Does that happen to you a lot?"

He nodded and put the cup down. "It does. I thought I was relatively safe here. I didn't think anyone would recognize me."

"That must be hard," I said. "To live under a spotlight all the time."

"It's not as bad as A-list celebrities have it, but it can be a little annoying," he said with a shrug of one of those very broad shoulders. "I was brought up in the limelight. I'm used to it."

"Do you think people are taking pictures of us right now?" I asked.

"I don't know," he said as he looked around. "Possibly. People are sneaky. You think they're texting or looking at something on their screen and they're actually taking pictures of you. I usually try and go about my day like I'm being filmed. It helps to keep me on the straight and narrow, which brings me to something else we need to talk about."

"What would that be?"

"I had a great time the other night, but I think it's best we keep this about the business at hand," he said.

There was something about the way he said it that had me questioning the sincerity of his statement. "Okay."

"It's not that I'm not—"

I stopped him before he could finish that sentence. "This is all business," I said. "We are two professionals. No need to explain. Chalk it up to the bubbly. I have no desire to kiss you again." I offered a small smile before quickly sipping my coffee.

He grinned and held up his coffee. "Glad we got that settled."

"Are you doing anything today?" I asked him and moved right past the weird stuff.

"Besides trying to convince you to sell your company, no," he said with a small chuckle.

"Good, then I'd like to take you somewhere."

His brows raised. "I don't know if that's a good idea. The last time you took me somewhere, we got ourselves in a little trouble."

"Ah, but we've already agreed this is all business," I said with a hint of sauciness.

"You're right." He smiled again. "What did you have in mind?"

"Have you ever been to the Hershey factory?"

"No," he said and shook his head. "Never been on my radar."

"I'd like to go with you," I said.

"Why? Is this us spying on the competition?"

"It isn't really a tour of their real factory," I explained. "But when I was younger, my dad took me and my sister. I loved it. I fell in love with the process. It's a quick, free tour, but it's what gave me my inspiration."

"I'm up for anything," he said. "Show me the way."

We caught a cab and headed for Chocolate World. "I suppose you've seen Willy Wonka?" I asked conversationally.

"Of course." He nodded. "Another source of inspiration?"

"Yes." I smiled at the many memories that came to mind.

"Why chocolate?" he asked. "Whenever you talk about chocolate, you get a look on your face."

"A look?"

"Yes," he said and was staring just a little too hard. "You smile, but I also see sadness, or maybe I'm seeing fondness. I can't tell. It's like you disappear for a few seconds."

He was very astute. "I suppose it reminds me of happier times. Chocolate is a comfort food for so many. It reminds us of the good times when we were kids and our parents or grandparents gave us a treat. It reminds us of sitting next to a sibling and chowing down on a Hershey's bar. Chocolate is a reward. It's always been that way. Way back when, only the rich got to have it because it was that good. Now, we all get it, but we never forget that it's special."

He was smiling at me and I realized I had rambled a bit. I tended to do that when I was talking about chocolate. "You make me want to devour all the chocolate."

I laughed and looked away. "Lucky for you, you're headed to the right place. There is chocolate as far as the eye can see."

"I'm excited to see it," he said.

When we arrived, he reminded me a lot of myself the first time I came to the factory. We walked into the massive shop with chocolate for days arranged on tables and shelves. "I'll get our tickets," I said when he seemed cemented in place.

The place was busy but not as busy as I had seen it in the past. I purchased the tickets for the full package, including the cheesy little movie. I wanted him to have the total experience. When I found him, he was reading the label of one of the candy bars offered for sale.

"There is so much," he breathed. "I can't believe how big this place is. It's like being in a chocolate mall."

"Yes, it is," I told him and waved our tickets. "Do you want to do the movie or tour first?"

"Uh, tour," he said as if it were obvious.

"Then we better get in line," I told him.

We took our place in line and climbed into one of the little cars that would carry us around the fake factory. Our thighs touched as the car made its way through the factory. Memories flooded me but being here with him was going to change that. I knew when I came here again, which was inevitable, I would think about this moment with him.

"I had no idea it was such a complicated process," he said as we made our way around. "I see why it was so expensive in the olden days."

"Every detail counts," I told him. "From the very beginning to using the perfect milk and the right temperature. One little misstep and the chocolate is ruined."

"And coming here is what started you on your own chocolate journey?" he asked.

"Yes." I nodded. "Technically, I loved chocolate already, but when I learned how it was made, I became really intrigued."

"I bet you made more than one mess in the kitchen when you were little." He laughed.

I had to laugh. "Oh yes. More than one. Our old house had chocolate on the ceiling. It was stained."

"Do I want to know?" he asked with amusement.

"Like I said, temperature means everything." I remembered the first time the chocolate had boiled and splattered the kitchen. Marie had tried to help me clean up before our father got home, but neither of us could reach the ceiling. He didn't notice for weeks, but when he did, I was in big trouble.

We finished the tour and stepped back into the madhouse. "What next?" I asked him. "Are you hungry? Up for a milkshake or one of their amazing cupcakes?"

"Maybe we should save the sugar coma for the end," he suggested.

"Good plan. The trolley tour is a little over an hour."

"Let's do it," he said and clapped his hands together. "I'm your willing victim. Show me all the tourist traps."

13

CASE

I t had been a long time since I sat back and let someone else take the reins. I was used to being in charge. If I took a woman out, I usually picked the restaurant. I took care of ordering the wine and getting transportation.

While I was out, I was always very conscious of who I was and the fact that people would be interested in who I was out on a date with. They would want to know every detail of our date and it was inevitable our picture would be taken. It usually felt like I was on duty all the time.

Being with her like this was different. I got to be an average guy sightseeing with a beautiful lady. There might be some people who recognized me, but I didn't think I was the priority. Chocolate took precedence.

"How many times have you done this trolley tour?" I asked her.

"Only a couple of times," she answered. "I live here. It's not quite as exciting."

"Understood."

We made our way back into the store and got in line to make our very own chocolate bars. "Nuts?" she asked.

My first reaction was to make a dirty joke. Judging by the look on her face, that was what she was expecting. She was daring me to do it. I never backed down from a dare. "Do you like nuts?" I asked with a completely serious face.

I saw her fighting a smile. "Sometimes."

"Today?"

She gnawed on her lower lip. "I think I might like nuts today."

There was no stopping the reaction that happened in my pants. "Me too," I croaked.

We watched the bars slide along the conveyor belt and moved to wait for them to be cooled and ready for us to take. "How about that milkshake now?" she asked as we carried our bars.

"Sounds good to me."

We ordered our shakes along with some lunch that didn't contain sugar and headed out to sit down at one of the tables in the heated patio area. "Tell me more about your inspiration," I said.

"What do you mean?"

"You came here as a child, right?" I asked.

"Yes." She nodded.

"With?"

"My sister and my father," she answered, and just by the change in her demeanor, I could tell we were heading into territory she wasn't thrilled to be in.

A smart man would retreat. I didn't. I wanted to know more about her. If I could understand her, I would know where to go with my proposal. I had learned from experience with other clients, making it personal was the way in. This company was special to her. I couldn't approach her with an all-business proposition. I needed to appeal to her on a different level.

"Are they part of the business?" I asked. In the research I had done, I didn't see any other names on the paperwork.

"No," she said and looked down at the cheeseburger. "My sister was going to be a part of the business. She did help me out in the beginning."

"And now?"

"She passed away three years ago," she said.

I felt like I'd just stuck my giant foot in my giant mouth. "Oh, I'm sorry."

"It's fine," she said with a soft smile. "Not talking about her or her death doesn't make it not real."

"Can I ask how?"

"Breast cancer," she said.

"Ah, that explains the percentage of your profits going to cancer research." I nodded with understanding.

"Yes. I promised her I would do everything I could to find a cure. I'm not a science whiz, but I'm hoping all the people that are science whizzes will find a cure. The small amount of money we donate to the cause doesn't do much, but it does something."

"It's an amazing gift," I told her. "You're honoring your sister's memory."

"I'm trying." She smiled. "I owe it to Lucy."

"Lucy is your sister?" I questioned.

She smiled and slowly shook her head. "No, Lucy is Marie's daughter. Marie is my sister."

"Does Lucy live in town?" I asked casually.

She gave a small laugh. "Lucy lives with me. I'm her mom now. Her aunt but her mom. I have guardianship of her."

That explained the little girl I saw in the window. Oddly enough, I felt better. "How old is she?"

"Five." She smiled.

"Damn, she was only two when she lost her mom?"

"Yes." She nodded. "I think it's both a blessing and a curse. She doesn't really remember her, which means she doesn't miss her. I'm glad she doesn't have to feel that kind of pain, but I'm so sad she doesn't get to know how amazing her mother was."

"That's rough," I said. "What about her father?"

She let out a long sigh. "He died when Marie was pregnant with her."

"Shit," I muttered. "That's rough. It's a good thing she's got you."

"Thank you." She smiled. "It's just me and her."

"Your parents?" I questioned.

"Our mother died when we were little," she said. "I guess that makes me uniquely qualified to understand what Lucy is going through. Our father died when I was a senior in high school. Marie took care of me and kept me out of the foster system."

My heart hurt for her. She'd seen way too much death in her short life. "I feel like I should say sorry, but that feels really inadequate."

"Thanks." She smiled. "I don't mean to make you feel weird."

"I don't feel weird. I just feel like nothing I say is worth saying," I told her.

"I don't tell very many people about that stuff," she said. "It is a great way to kill a conversation. It makes people uncomfortable. All I can say is I'm okay. I'm not some broken woman."

"Your factory is what drives you," I said with a nod. I felt like I was getting to peek behind the curtain. Her defiance to accept a huge amount of money for a factory that was worth far less all made sense.

"It does," she said. "I know it's hard for you and your client to understand, but this factory isn't just a business. I don't just make chocolate. Some of the most popular products are the ones I created with my sister. Whenever I'm in the kitchen or boxing up chocolates, I'm thinking about her. I was remembering our many, many missteps. I think about how much we laughed together. The tears we shed when a recipe failed or I was denied yet another loan are all part of the factory. It's not just chocolate."

"I get it," I said. I didn't really get it, but I did understand a little more. "You're a pretty amazing woman."

She laughed and took a drink of her shake. "I don't know about that. I'm just a lady trying to get by. I wake up every morning and have to put my pants on just like everyone else. I put one foot in front of the other and just keep going."

"There are a lot—I imagine a strong majority of women—that

wouldn't be able to do what you have done," I said. "Not just do what you did but do it with a smile. You smile a lot."

"Is that a bad thing?" she asked.

"No." I shook my head. "Not at all. When I first met you, I figured you were this person that had it all. You had a thriving company and a good life."

"I do have a good life," she said somewhat defensively. "I have a great life. I have a little girl I love with all my heart. She's happy and healthy. My business is good. I have a nice home. I'm happy."

"That came out wrong. I meant you have a good life despite what you've been through."

She looked thoughtful for a few seconds. "I don't remember where I heard it or read it, but it's something that has always stuck with me. Happiness is a choice. I could choose to let the things that have happened in my life bring me down, or I can choose to be happy and live my life to the fullest."

"That's impressive," I said. "I'm in awe of your strength."

She snorted. "Don't be. I'm not special. I have plenty of bad moments. During Marie's last days, I was angry. I was furious with the world. She had very few moments of lucidity, but she reminded me about the 'happiness is a choice' saying. I had to remember it wasn't just me. If I was sad and pissed at the world, Lucy would suffer. If she hadn't been around, I think I probably would have given in to the anger. Instead, I chose to be happy most of the time. I cried in the bathroom on more than one occasion, but I didn't want her to feel my pain. She had the luxury of not understanding death."

She could tell me not to be, but I was very impressed. I was fascinated by her strength. She had so much wisdom and strength for someone who was still relatively young. "Lucy is a lucky girl," I said.

"I'm lucky I get to be her pseudo-mom," she answered with a bright smile. "Every day she makes me laugh. I'm always so amazed by how smart and kind she is. I firmly believe it was inherited from her mama."

"I'd like to meet her one day," I blurted out before I could stop and filter it. That probably sounded a little creepy.

"Are you busy tomorrow?" she asked.

"No," I answered.

"Will you be in town?"

"I think so," I said with a wink. "I'm working on a deal."

She laughed and didn't seem to be bothered by my reminder about why I was really in Pennsylvania. "Lucy and I will be going to the zoo tomorrow," she said. "You're welcome to tag along."

"Really?" I asked with genuine surprise.

"Sure." She shrugged. "It's small but Lucy loves it. It's fun and I don't have to walk for miles and miles."

"I'd love to," I said. "Thank you."

We finished our lunch and I was trying to think of an excuse to hang out with her a little longer. "I have to get to the factory, but I'll see you tomorrow?" she asked.

"I'll pick you up?" I offered.

"Or I can pick you up, considering I invited you," she said.

"How about I get a ride to your place and you drive us to the zoo?" I reasoned.

She grinned and put up her hand for a high-five. I would have preferred to seal the arrangement with a kiss, but I would worry about that later. I slapped her hand. "Thanks for today," I told her. "It was fun and informative. When do I get a tour of your factory?"

"We'll see," she said coyly.

I headed back to the hotel with a lot more than business on my mind. I was getting in deep. If my father found out about the extracurricular activities with the woman, he was going to be pissed. I was going to be in hot water once again. Then I remembered I was a big boy. I could go to lunch with anyone I wanted to. I could go to the zoo. If I got busted, I would tell him it was part of the plan.

I hated lying, but it seemed like the only way I was going to get to spend time with her. Hopefully, I could fly under the radar. If people would just mind their own business and let me enjoy the afternoon with her, it would be nice.

I could hear my mom's voice in the back of my mind. "You're the oldest son of one of the oldest families in Manhattan, you need to remember your privilege," she would always say. "You have to set the example. You aren't like other kids. Be smart. Make good choices and always remember everyone is watching."

More than once, I used to wish we could live somewhere else. Anywhere else. As I got older, I began to appreciate the benefits of my last name. Then there were times like this and it was a real drag.

14

EMMA

"Are you really going to go through with this?" Jennifer asked.

Her voice filled my bedroom. I had her on speakerphone while I got ready. "I am. I did. He'll be here soon."

"I'm so proud of you," she squealed. "I feel like you're growing up right before my very eyes."

"Ha, ha," I said. "It's just a trip to the zoo."

"With Lucy," she pointed out. "You must really trust this guy."

"Why do you say that?" I asked.

"This is the first guy you've brought around Lucy," she said.

"I take her to the factory all the time," I replied. "She's around lots of guys."

"Not like this and you know it."

She wasn't wrong. "Do you think I'm making a mistake?" I asked her. "Be honest."

"No, I don't. You deserve to have a little fun. You deserve to live your life. I think you're doing it right. You're easing back in."

"I think I might be using Lucy as a shield," I confessed.

"What? Why?"

"Because I'm a little nervous to be around him," I said. "If she's there, she's the buffer."

"You're overthinking it," she said. "Go. Have fun. Just enjoy yourself."

I groaned and shook my head. "Okay. You're right. I'm freaking out. I can't believe I asked him to go with us."

"You're going to have fun," she said. "Call me tonight when you get back."

"Good luck on your job," I told her.

Lucy was downstairs waiting to go. She was excited to go to the zoo. There was a knock on the door. Lucy jumped off the couch and practically ran through me to get to the door. I had told her we were going with my friend. Lucy was a bit of a social butterfly. She loved hanging out with people.

She pulled open the door. "Hi!" she exclaimed.

Case, handsome as usual, smiled at her. "Hello."

"I'm Lucy," she said. "Come in, please."

She was using her impeccable manners. Case walked into the house and smiled at me. He was wearing jeans and a hoodie. This was the casual look I had been hoping to see on him. As expected, it was hot as hell. He was sexy and dangerous.

"Thank you," he said. "I'm Case."

"Hi, Case," Lucy said. "Are you excited to go to the zoo?"

He looked at me and grinned. "I am. It's been a very long time since I've been to a zoo. I'm hoping you can tell me all about the animals we see."

Lucy looked at me, then him. "There are people that tell you," she said as if she didn't understand why he was asking her.

"Oh," he said and hid his smile. "I'll keep that in mind."

"I think we're ready to go," I said.

Lucy, in her very bold way, walked right up to Case and took his hand. To my surprise, he didn't flinch. He didn't get that panicked look in his eyes I had expected. Instead, he led her out to my SUV. I buckled her in before getting behind the wheel.

At the zoo, Lucy was in high spirits. She bounced around, pointing at this and that and chattering a million miles a minute. "Is she wearing on your nerves yet?" I asked him as we walked behind her.

"Not at all," he said. "She's a cool kid."

"She is full of energy."

"She's happy," he said. "What you told me yesterday about what she'd been through, you would never know. You've done great with her. I haven't been around a lot of kids, but she definitely seems smarter than the average kid."

I laughed at his assessment. "She is pretty smart."

"Case!" Lucy called out. "Look!"

He walked ahead and followed her to the lion enclosure. I stayed back to allow the other kids to get up front. Lucy was hopping up and down. I knew what she wanted but was too far back to help. Case figured it out and picked her up. My heart skipped a beat as I watched him hold her up high enough for her to see over the rail.

It was such a sweet gesture that probably didn't mean much to anyone else, but to me, it was amazing. It was thoughtful and kind. I could see them talking and pointing. My ovaries were singing at the sight of the two of them. I was sure there was something preprogrammed into a woman's DNA. It was instinct to look for a good, strong baby daddy. Case was checking all the boxes and that was dangerous. He was making me want things I had never wanted before.

Case turned around with Lucy still in his arms. She waved at me with the biggest grin on her face. She was eating it up. Once he cleared the crowd, he put her back on her feet. She wasn't about to let him go and kept a firm grip on his hand.

"Do you want to ride the carousel?" I asked her.

"Will you ride with me, Case?" she asked him.

He looked at me. "I will if Emma does."

"I'm game," I said.

We paid our tokens and picked our chosen animals. "Smile," Lucy said as the carousel began to turn and the camera snapped our picture.

Because I figured it was a good time to splurge, we ordered lunch at one of the overpriced food stands. Lucy barely ate. She was too excited to play with the other kids in the small play area.

"Thank you for coming with us today," I said. "She likes you. I'd love to tell you that's a rarity, but the truth is, she loves most people."

He laughed and didn't seem to be too insulted. "She's a good kid," he said. "I'm glad she likes me. I like her."

"I'm guessing this isn't your typical day," I teased.

"Not so much, but I like this change of pace. I could get used to doing stuff like this."

I wasn't sure if that was a hint he'd like me to invite him for more or a simple compliment. "She wasn't always like this," I told him.

"Like what?"

"Happy and bubbly. She used to be really shy. The last six months or so, she started to come out of her shell."

He watched her talking to another kid on the playground. "She's great," he said. "I really mean that."

"Thank you."

After letting her play for an hour, we packed up and started the drive back to my house. Lucy passed out in the back seat. When we got to the house, he picked her up and carried her into the house. "Where should I put her?" he whispered.

I hated to let her sleep this late in the afternoon, but she was exhausted after a very long day. "Follow me," I said and headed upstairs.

He gently laid her in bed and stepped back. I pulled her blanket over her and gestured for him to walk out with me. We didn't say a word until we were downstairs. "Would you like to stay for dinner?" I asked.

"Sure, if you don't mind," he said.

"She'll probably sleep for an hour or so. Do you want a beer?"

"Please," he said.

I opened two bottles and handed him one. We sat down on the couch and kicked our feet up. "Long day, huh?" I said with a sigh.

"It was, but it was a good day."

"Thank you again for hanging out with us," I told him. "I'm sure a city boy like you is used to golf clubs and Broadway shows."

"No on both." He laughed. "It was a new thing for me, but I'm serious. I liked it. I had fun. I wish my parents would have taken us out for things like this."

"You didn't go to the zoo?" I asked with surprise.

"We did, but usually it was with nannies," he said. "My parents were busy. My dad worked constantly. Mom was always ferrying one of us to a game or practice. There was always something happening with one of us."

"How many are there?" I asked. "I'm assuming you mean siblings."

"Yes, siblings." He laughed. "Although my mother used to call us jackals. Sometimes little monsters. She wasn't wrong. We were pretty awful. There are six of us in total."

"Six?" I gasped.

"Six brothers." He laughed. "I'm the oldest."

"Holy shit!" I exclaimed. "No wonder she was always running around."

"Yeah," he said and took a long drink from his beer. "Honestly though, it wasn't always us taking her time. She was on every board and charity organization she could squeeze into her schedule. I think she probably slept like four hours a night."

"I don't mean to sound insensitive, but is she still around?"

"Yes, she is," he said. "She's still just as busy."

"Do you get along with her?"

"Yes." He nodded. "I love her. I know she tried. Being a Manhattan wife is no joke. She had a standard to live up to. My dad is a tough man to be married to."

"I bet it's also tough to be his son," I said. "You must have some pretty high standards to live up to, especially being the oldest."

He looked at me and I was certain I saw his gratefulness. "It is. I don't hate it and I'll never complain about who I am because being me is pretty great. I was raised with everything I could ever want. I have a great family. We have our own issues and we argue, but we love each other. My extended family is all very close. I'm lucky. I have it all."

"But you wanted the little things money couldn't buy," I said softly.

"I survived." He laughed. "I don't mean to sound like a whiny bitch. My parents did the best they could to give us all a little attention."

"Is your family in Manhattan?" I asked.

"They are." He nodded.

"Are you close to your brothers?"

He shrugged. "Yes. We're pretty good friends. We hang out when we can. My brother Edwin and I spend the most time together. We try and meet up to go to the gym at least five days a week."

I couldn't resist teasing just a bit. I squeezed his bicep. "That explains these."

"Shit, they don't happen by themselves," he joked.

"Do you live in the city?" I asked. I was probably asking too many questions, but I wanted to know everything I could about him. He was nothing like I expected him to be when I met him. This was a lesson I needed to learn about judging people by what I saw and assumed.

"I have an apartment close to my office in the city," he answered. "I also have a house out in Great Neck. When I have a full schedule, I stay in the city. It's just easier. Have you been to Manhattan?"

"Once," I said. "Didn't stay long. It was a conference. As soon as it was over, I bailed."

"Too much for you?" he teased.

"It's pretty loud," I said.

"You get used to it. What else do you and Lucy do on the weekends?"

"Oh gosh," I sighed. "We go to the park a lot. When it's too cold, we go to one of the indoor playgrounds. We sometimes go to the factory. She likes to hang out there. It's nice because I can get some work done while teaching her the family business."

"She's a lucky kid," he said. "You sound like you're kicking ass at this whole mom thing."

I groaned. "Thanks, but it doesn't feel like it some days."

"Ah, I think that's how you know you're doing it right." He laughed. "From what I heard that is."

15

CASE

"Can I help?" I offered. "I feel like I'm a bum."

"You know how you can help?" she asked sweetly.

"Tell me. Anything you need, I'll do it."

She flashed me a grin. "Entertain my little helper," she said.

Lucy was buttering a loaf of French bread. It was a bit of a train wreck. I nodded with understanding. "Lucy, why don't you show me that game you were talking about?"

"You want to play with me?" she asked excitedly.

"Yes," I said. "We'll play while Emma finishes dinner."

"Is that okay?" Lucy asked.

"I'll be fine," Emma replied. "You guys play, and dinner will be ready in twenty minutes."

Lucy stepped off her little stool.

"Thank you," Emma mouthed.

I winked in response and followed Lucy into the den where there was a small table in the corner. A stack of board games was on a shelf. She grabbed the game and gestured for me to sit in one of the small chairs. I looked at it with a great deal of skepticism. "You know, I think I might be a little big for that chair," I told her. "I'll sit on the floor."

"Aunt Emma sits in the chairs," she pointed out.

"Your aunt is a lot smaller than I am."

"Do you know how to play this game?" she asked.

"No, but I think I can figure it out."

I listened to her tutorial and nodded along. I vaguely remembered the game from my childhood. It wasn't exactly rocket science. "Ready?" she asked.

"Let's do this." I nodded.

She was suddenly very serious about the game. It was a little intimidating. I was glad it wasn't poker. I had a feeling she would whoop my ass. We started playing. Lucy clapped on the good cards and offered me sympathy when I had to chute back down.

"How goes it in here?" Emma asked as she came into the room.

I gave her a dry look. "How do you think?"

She laughed softly. "Then I will save you. Dinner is ready."

"Five more minutes," Lucy begged.

"Sorry, kid, I'm starving," I said and got up. "We'll clean this up after dinner."

She didn't seem too thrilled with the idea, but she did what she was told. It was another testament to how amazing Emma was doing raising the little girl on her own. She was a woman of many talents. She ran a successful business and was singlehandedly raising a little girl that wasn't her own. From what I could see of her home, she was doing okay for herself. The home was comfortable, and Lucy was certainly not lacking for anything. In a way, I was a little jealous of the little girl. Then I remembered how much she had lost.

"It smells delicious," I said and took the seat Lucy indicated was mine.

"I love spaghetti," Lucy declared.

For a moment, I simply watched as Emma dished Lucy up. It was strange to sit down to a family dinner that was so quiet.

"Everything okay?" Emma asked.

"Yes." I nodded. "I was just taking it all in."

"What does that mean?"

"Family dinners when I was growing up looked a little different," I said.

"I imagine it was a lot louder," she said with a laugh. "I don't know how your mom managed six boys at her dinner table."

"She didn't," I said. "We had a couple of nannies and a cook. Mom and dad weren't home for dinner all that much. They are trying to make up for all those lost dinners now. They try and get us all together at least once a month."

"Does your mom cook?" she asked as she handed me a bowl with the slightly mangled French bread.

"She does now," I said. "She took cooking lessons after we were all out of the house."

"Little late to the party," she joked.

"Exactly what we said," I agreed. "But she suddenly decided she wanted to be the grandma that baked cookies and had the grandkids over for sleepovers. In some ways, it's pretty cool that she got to live two lives. She had her time as the busy socialite and now she wants to settle in and be a grandma."

"Do your brothers have children?"

"Not yet." I grinned. "Trust me, it hasn't slipped her notice. She reminds us every chance she gets but she has Bram who is settling down with Rachel so maybe soon she will."

"I don't have a grandma," Lucy announced, and it pretty much felt like I had my heart cut in two.

"I'm sorry," I said.

"I don't have a grandpa either," she said matter-of-factly.

I looked to Emma for her lead. I didn't know what I was supposed to say to that. "But you have Aunt Jennifer," she said. "And you have all the people at the factory that love you. Miss Dee always makes you cookies. She's like a grandma."

"I know." Lucy shrugged.

Emma looked at me. "The people at the factory have all been a part of her life since she was born. Most of them consider her to be family."

She didn't have to spell it out. She was letting me know once again the factory was worth a lot more than just a few million dollars. I knew what she was doing, but I wasn't sure what the goal was. Was she trying to get me to increase the offer? If that was the case, I was certain I could get James to do it. But now that I knew her just a little better and thought I had a better understanding about who she was, I didn't think that was her goal. She wasn't interested in money. It wasn't what motivated her.

"I see that," I said. "That's good."

"Can we watch a movie after dinner?" Lucy asked.

"You can have one hour," Emma said.

Lucy looked at me. "Do you want to watch Cinderella with me?" she asked with a bright smile.

I looked at Emma to see if that was okay. "If you want, but don't feel obligated," she said quietly.

"I would love to watch Cinderella with you," I said. "Is it the old Cinderella?"

Lucy looked confused. "Old Cinderella? She's not that old."

"It's the original," Emma clarified.

"Good," I said. "I've seen the advertisements. It seems like they like to make things over and over and it ruins it."

"Oh, you're a purist," she teased.

"I think I might be," I agreed.

"Me too," she said. "And Lucy will be if I have anything to say about it. I keep it to the original stuff."

After we finished eating, Emma insisted on doing the cleanup. "Are you sure I can't help you?" I asked.

"No," she insisted. "Go ahead and sit down. Lucy knows how to find the movie. Unless you don't want to watch? I understand if you don't. Please don't feel obligated."

"I don't feel obligated," I said. "I want to."

"Have you ever seen it before?" she asked.

I wrinkled my nose. "Maybe thirty years ago. I can't say I sat through all of it."

"Then you better get in there." She giggled and shooed me out of her kitchen.

Lucy was sitting on the couch with a fuzzy pink blanket pulled over her. "You can use that one," she pointed to a blue blanket on the other end.

"Thank you."

I settled in and Lucy started the movie. Emma joined us about ten minutes later. She sat in the middle with Lucy snuggled against her. I found myself looking at them more often than I was watching the movie. It was a strange feeling. It was a weird contentment.

I could honestly say I had never hung out with a woman and her kid before. I had dated a few women with kids, but I had never hung out with them. This felt very adult-like. It was then I realized I was growing up. Finally. Sitting here watching an old Disney movie was far more appealing than going out to a ritzy club. I was very happy to be hanging out with the two of them.

"Okay, little miss," Emma said after a bit. "Time for bed. No fussing."

Lucy pouted but slid off the couch.

"Goodnight, Lucy," I said. "I hope we can hang out again sometime."

"Goodnight, Case," she said with a wave.

"Should I go?" I asked.

"You don't have to," she said. "This will only take a few minutes."

I was eager to accept the invitation. "I'll be here."

"Help yourself to another beer or there's a bottle of wine," she said as she walked upstairs.

I had a feeling the wine was her preference. I poured two glasses and sat on the couch once again. I didn't miss the photo albums on the coffee table. I was tempted to look at them, but it felt like an invasion of privacy. I decided to mind my own business.

She came back downstairs. "I poured you a glass of wine," I told her.

"Thank you," she said and sat down. "I don't remember when I had that kind of energy."

"She's spunky," I said. "She's a really, really good kid."

"Thank you, but I don't know if I can take credit," she said.

"Sure, you can," I said. "You've had her more than half of her very short life. The first two years are all about learning how to walk and stuff like that. You've obviously taught her the rest. She's polite and smart. She's funny."

"Thank you. I sometimes feel like I'm making one mistake after another." She held up her wineglass. "This is my guilty pleasure. I try not to drink in front of her. But once she goes to bed, I reward myself with a glass. I sit down here in the dark and think about all the ways I'm screwing up. I usually look at the albums and talk to Marie."

"Those are pictures of her mom? Your sister?"

"Yes." She nodded and picked one up. "This is the one I often look at the most. It starts when Marie and I were really starting to put together the idea of a chocolate factory. There are pictures of her pregnant and right after Lucy was born."

I looked at the pictures as she flipped through the pages. "You haven't changed much over the years," I told her. I put my finger on a picture of her and her sister. They were both laughing. "I like this one."

She smiled and stared at the picture. "This was before she was pregnant with Lucy. We had just made a batch of chocolates and they were good. Really good. We were celebrating and might have gotten a little carried away. We're both pretty drunk there."

"You look happy," I said. "And you look a little like Lucy, or rather, she looks like you."

"People always say that," she said. "I think it makes Lucy feel good."

"She doesn't call you mom," I pointed out.

"She does when she wants to," she explained. "I've never told her she has to. I have told her who I am. I have noticed she says it more than she used to. It's something she's growing into."

"You're really the only mom she knows," I said. "Are you okay with her calling you mom?"

"Oh yes! Absolutely. It's just, well, this will sound silly, but I feel like I'm stealing that privilege from my sister."

"I bet she would be honored to have her little girl call you mommy," I told her.

"If she does, she does." She shrugged. "I'm good with whatever make her comfortable."

She closed the book and put it back on the table. I was amazed by her. Simply, truly amazed. She moved to sit back on the couch. I grabbed her and kissed her before she could sit back. She didn't pull away. Quite the opposite. She leaned into me and kissed me back. Her mouth was hot and tasted like the wine we were drinking.

I didn't want to spill my wine. I blindly reached out and put the glass on the table before putting my hands on her waist and pulling her closer. I slid one hand up, rubbing over her breast before sliding up her neck and into her hair. She broke the kiss and pulled away.

I was about to blurt out yet another apology when she got to her feet. "Come with me," she whispered and reached out her hand.

I took it and followed behind her. She led me up the stairs and into her bedroom. I was just a little too excited for this. It was not what I expected to happen, but I was happy it was going to.

16

EMMA

"Naked, now," I rasped as I attacked his clothing. I wanted him naked. I needed him naked. I had been semi-aroused since we kissed the other night. I didn't want to stop and think about what I was doing. I just wanted to do it.

He pulled his shirt off and tossed it over his head before fumbling with his pants. I stripped as fast as I could. It was a race to see who could get naked the fastest. Once we were both down to wearing just our skin, we paused.

"You're sure about this?" he asked in a deep voice.

"Yes," I answered.

He lunged for me with his mouth slamming against mine. I found myself pushed up against a wall with his naked body pressed against mine. My hands roamed over his hot skin, sliding down his back and massaging the muscles I felt bulging. He reached under my thigh and hiked one leg up.

"Damn, I want you," he growled. "I've made myself crazy thinking about this."

"Me too," I murmured against his mouth.

"I'm going to tell you something," he said with his mouth running over my jaw and down my neck.

"What is it?" I gasped when he sucked my flesh between his teeth.

"I've been having the wettest, hottest dreams about you since I almost flattened you in the store that day."

Heat flooded between my legs. "Really?"

"You doubt me?" he growled and grabbed my hand. He pushed it against the swollen cock rubbing against my belly. "I'm so hard right now my teeth hurt. I've been thinking about fucking you for days. I wanted to fuck you that night at the hotel. I would have if you wouldn't have stopped me."

His raw honesty was melting me from the inside out. "I'm not stopping you now," I said.

He released my hand and cupped my wet pussy. "You're wet," he said the words like they were causing him pain.

"I want you," I said. "Now, Case. Right fucking now!"

He pushed a finger inside me. "Like this?"

"Don't tease me," I groaned.

He pulled my lower lip between his teeth before opening wide and pushing his tongue inside. He reached his other hand into my hair and pulled as the finger inside me pushed higher. I nearly cried out before remembering there was a little girl sleeping in the next room. I turned my head and bit my fist as he teased at my clit. The orgasm was threatening to break free and I was suddenly worried about the power of it.

I tried to push him away before whipping my head around to grab his mouth with my own. He fingered faster and harder until I was whimpering with need. When the orgasm hit, my head went back, slamming against the wall.

He held the back of my neck while his fingers continued to work inside me. "That's it," he said against my lips. "Damn, woman, you're so fucking wet."

I slumped against the wall and slowly slid down. He gently lowered me to the floor, kissing me before pulling away. I looked up and came face to face with his rather large cock. The temptation was too strong to resist. I grabbed him and pulled him into my mouth. It was him who cried out before quickly shushing himself.

He bent forward with his arm pressed against the wall above me and his forehead resting against his forearm. He grunted, groaning as I sucked him deep into my throat. I moaned with unexpected pleasure. It was like I could feel how good it was for him. I was aroused all over again. I sucked harder while my hand massaged his balls.

One second, I had his cock halfway down my throat, and the next, he was jerking me up and spinning me around. "Don't move," he ordered. "Stay just like that."

I leaned my cheek against the wall with my chest heaving up and down. I heard the condom wrapper open before he was back against me once again. He kissed over my shoulder while using his knee to open my legs. His hand slid up my inner thigh and gently spread my folds. The head of his cock probed at my opening and a moment later he was pushing inside.

I gasped and slapped against the wall. "Shh," he whispered. "Give it a second. You're so tight. Relax."

I moaned and arched my back, inadvertently taking him deeper. It was his turn to suck in a breath and let out a loud groan. "Oh damn," he said. "Oh shit."

"Don't stop," I begged as he pushed in deeper.

"You feel so good," he said in a voice thick with desire.

I could barely think straight. All my attention was focused on him inside me. It was making me crazy. Driving my need to heights I didn't think possible. Although I had just enjoyed one very nice orgasm, another one was already building. I murmured something to the effect I was close. I didn't know if the words actually came out or were just more moans.

He leaned back and grabbed my hips. He rocked into me over and over. My head bounced off the wall once. I pulled away and put my hands flat against the wall. I knew I looked like a woman ready to be frisked. My fingers curled as he hit the right spot over and over. There was no stopping the orgasm that crashed over me.

I let out a soft cry, conscientious of a sleeping Lucy.

"Oh fuck, again?" he said and moved faster.

I felt my body growing limp with my hands sliding down the wall once again. He pulled out and practically dragged me to the bed. I fell back with my legs open as I reached for him once again. I felt drunk with need. He pulled me to the edge of the bed and lifted my hips as he drove into me once again.

Another moan escaped my lips. I felt like a limp noodle and tried to participate but he had fucked me into sweet oblivion.

"Just like that," he said through heavy breathing.

"Don't stop," I begged. I felt greedy but I wanted more.

"You want another?" he asked in a gruff, slightly cocky voice.

I opened my eyes and looked at him. "Yes," I replied clear as day. "Another."

He smirked and grabbed a pillow, shoving it under my ass. He pushed deep inside me and gently pushed his hand on my lower stomach. I nearly came off the bed. My body bucked and thrashed as he continued to slide in and out of me. I didn't know what he was doing to me, but it was the most intense experience I ever had.

"Oh god," I groaned and reached for something. Anything to anchor me.

"Now, Emma, now," he gasped and pushed a little harder.

That was all it took. I exploded around him. I was certain I saw stars. His body pumped once, then again before he fell forward with his face planting between my breasts. I felt his body spasming and reached up to try and soothe him. My hands rubbed up and down his back as my own body went through a series of brilliant aftershocks.

He stood and pulled away. I couldn't move while I watched him walk into the bathroom. My legs no longer felt attached to my body. My arms were limp. Everything was in a weird state of limbo. I was and I wasn't at the same time.

"Are you okay?" he asked.

I could only smile. "Yes."

"Should I go?" he asked.

"No," I replied. "It's late. Stay."

I made no effort to move. Well, I tried but it was useless. He chuckled and pulled me up before pulling back the blankets. I crawled under them and waited. He slid in beside me and tucked me against his chest.

"That was—"

I couldn't finish the sentence. I didn't have a word to describe what that was. It was everything. It was all the adjectives. The good ones, that was.

"Yeah, I agree," he said and kissed the top of my head. "That was a first for me."

I scoffed. "Bullshit."

"Not my first time having sex." He laughed. "My first time giving a woman three orgasms. I'm feeling like I should climb on the roof and beat my chest."

"While I won't knock your ability, there should be a small disclaimer."

"What would that be?" he asked. "Those weren't even ribbed condoms."

I slapped at his chest. "You're the first guy I've been with in a couple of years. There might have been some pent-up stuff there."

"Shh, don't burst my bubble."

"You were very good," I assured him.

"Good? I was fucking amazing." He laughed. "You were pretty hot. Hot, wet, and tight. Definitely better than my dreams."

"Did you really dream about sex with me?" I asked.

"Yep. I have my sheets as proof it was a lot more than just a dream. It was very real."

I had to laugh. He was very open. It had to be the age thing. He was old enough and secure enough in his manhood to be very blunt. It was very refreshing. "I'm so tired," I said. "I'm not sure I'll be able to walk tomorrow."

"You keep talking like that and I'm going to be messing up your sheets," he teased. "You're making me feel about ten feet tall."

I smiled and snuggled against his chest. In my mind, he was ten feet tall. I was going to have a hard time not wanting to do this with him again. He was pretty damn incredible and hanging out with him was fun. It was the total package.

17

CASE

I woke up, and for the first three seconds of being conscious, I was confused. I was not in my bed. I was not at the hotel. I turned to look at the mess of brown hair spread over my arm and chest. Then it all came back in a hurry. It was her. Emma. I was in bed with Emma.

She was sound asleep, judging by the steady breathing I heard. I would love to stay right here with her and maybe even enjoy a little morning delight, but I couldn't. There was a little girl in the house. One thing I did remember was my little brothers getting up very early. It was like little kids had an aversion to sleeping past seven in the morning.

Emma deserved to sleep in. I very carefully extracted myself from under her and grabbed my clothes to quickly dress. No way was I going to run around half-naked in the house with Lucy around. I popped my head into Lucy's room and discovered she was still sleeping.

I walked downstairs and started coffee first. Then I did a little snooping and found a box of pancake mix. I wasn't exactly a gourmet, but I could add water to a mix. While I sipped coffee, I cooked pancakes, creating a nice big stack. The bacon I found in the fridge was sizzling in the pan on the stove.

"Case?" I heard Emma say.

"Good morning," I said with a smile. "I hope you don't mind."

"You made breakfast?" she asked with surprise.

"I did," I said. "Let me pour you a cup of coffee."

"I can't believe you made breakfast," she said as I handed her the cup.

"You made dinner last night," I said with a shrug.

"I don't usually sleep in this late," she said. "Neither does Lucy."

"You guys had a long day. Besides, I'm guessing you needed to sleep in."

"It did feel good." She smiled. "Thanks for that."

It wasn't long before we heard little footsteps coming down the stairs. Lucy bounced into the kitchen full of energy. "Pancakes!" she exclaimed.

"Sit down," Emma said. "Case made breakfast."

Lucy grinned at me. "Thank you."

"You're very welcome."

"What are your plans for the day?" Emma asked.

I didn't dare invite myself to hang out with them another day. I didn't want to overstay my welcome. "I have some work to catch up on."

"Are you going to be staying in town?" she asked casually.

"I can," I said without saying too much in front of the little girl.

She looked down. "Oh."

"I can easily work from here," I said. "I mean from my hotel."

"That might not be a terrible idea."

It took some effort to keep from jumping up from the table and celebrating. Her soft-spoken words were essentially an invitation to stay in town. Staying in town meant there was a pretty good chance I could see her again. That was worth scrapping the meetings I had for the coming week. They could be rescheduled or handled by someone else at the office.

"I'll make it happen," I said.

Lucy was blissfully unaware of what was really happening. I stared at Emma until she looked at me. Her eyes met mine and we exchanged a look. I was glad she wasn't blushing and looking away. She wasn't throwing me out of the house. I wasn't sure what it meant for us, but I hoped like hell she would see me again. See as in get naked.

"Why don't you go wash up and get dressed?" Emma said to Lucy.

She headed upstairs with Emma and me still sitting at the table. "I'll go," I said.

"I need to spend time with her today, but maybe you can call me later?" she said.

I smiled and nodded. "I will absolutely call you later."

"Thanks for making breakfast," she said as we got up and started clearing the table.

"You're welcome. I really had a lot of fun with you two. More fun than I've had in a long time. I really appreciate you guys letting me hang out with you."

"Thank you for tagging along." She laughed. "I know it wasn't exactly your idea of a good time."

I pulled her into my arms and put one hand on her face. "I had a very good time," I said in a husky voice before I kissed her.

She turned her face. "Lucy might come down."

I was disappointed but I understood. I wasn't going to push her. "I'll call later," I said and walked out of the kitchen.

Lucy came downstairs just as I was leaving. "Are you leaving?" she asked.

"I am. I have things to do. Thank you for hanging out with me. I'll see you later."

To my surprise, she threw her arms around me and hugged me. "Goodbye, Case."

I patted her back. "Bye, Lucy."

The Uber was outside waiting. I headed back to the hotel with way too many thoughts running through my head. I took a shower, but it didn't ease the angsty feeling I had. There was only one thing that would work. I changed into my workout gear and went down to the hotel gym.

I got right to work. Sweat started to drip down my back. I mulled over the day before. Every detail flashed through my mind. When I was in the moment, it was like being in a fog. Now that I was out of the fog and I could step back and look at everything that went down, I had a clearer recollection. I could process my feelings. There were a lot.

Most importantly, I had to figure out my next move. She didn't really seem all that interested in selling her business, but she did seem interested in me. I could stop the pitch and focus on the relationship.

But my father's face loomed in the back of my mind. I could practically feel him glaring at me. I would be letting him down and disappointing a valuable client. If I screwed this deal up, James Lyons might just pull his account from the accounting firm. He would pull his legal needs as well. I could end up costing the family businesses millions. It wasn't just about the money for them. It would be the hit to our reputation that would really sting.

The decision was a big one and I didn't think I could pump my way through it. I needed help to figure this shit out. I finished the workout and headed back up to my room. After another quick shower, I sat down and prepared myself to make the phone call.

Edwin answered on the second ring. "What's up?" he asked. "Did you get it done? Are you the super kid again? Making the rest of us look bad."

"No," I said. "I'm in trouble."

"Trouble?" he asked. "What happened?"

"I don't know how to do this," I told him.

"Do what?"

"I spent the day with Emma and Lucy yesterday," I said.

He laughed. "Two women? I can see why you're trying to figure out how to do this."

"Lucy is five," I said dryly. "She's Emma's niece. Emma is raising her. We spent the day together yesterday. And I spent the night."

"Oh shit," he said. "Is that part of the plan?"

"No. That fucked up my plan. I agreed to spend the day with her because I thought it would help soften her toward selling the business."

"And now?"

"And now I'm screwed," I groaned. "Her company isn't just a company. It's her extended family. I could drop this whole thing and I'm pretty certain she and I could have a relationship. If I keep pushing, she's going to get pissed. She won't want to see me anymore. But if I drop it and don't try to persuade her to sell, dad is going to lose his shit. Lyons is going to yank his business. My reputation will be ruined. Lyons has the power to fuck with the family businesses. He's connected. It will start a ripple effect. When we lose money and accounts, everyone is going to point to me."

"That's a little dramatic," he joked.

"Is it? What happens if he yanks his business from my firm? You've seen his temper tantrums before. He destroyed that furniture store that screwed up his order. That was furniture. It isn't just Lyons. It's dad. Dad will be disappointed."

The more I talked it out, the clearer my decision became. There was no guarantee this thing with Emma and me was serious. It might be over in a minute and I would have exploded my career and relationship with my father for nothing. I needed to be logical.

"Dad will get over it," Edwin said.

"What?" I was expecting him to tell me to use my head and not my dick to make decisions.

"When have you ever done anything just for you?" he asked. "You've been a good soldier. You've busted ass and filled the family coffers. You've made James Lyons richer than he could have imagined. You get to have one thing in your life that's just for you."

"You're advising me to blow up the deal?" I asked incredulously.

"I can tell you like this girl," he said. "When is the last time you liked someone like this?"

"I don't know that I ever have," I answered honestly.

"Why is she different?"

I tried to think of a succinct answer. "She's special. She's never had an advantage, but she's overcome and persevered. Her business is thriving because she cares about it on a level I've never seen before. It isn't just her business—it's her life. She's raising her niece on her own after her sister died. She is patient, kind, and funny. She could have kicked me out of her business and that would be that, but she didn't. She welcomed me in. She's trying to show me why her company is special."

"Is she doing it because she wants more money?" he asked.

"I considered that, but no," I answered. "I don't think so. She isn't like that. Obviously, she could use the money, but I don't think it would make her happy. Her chocolate factory makes her happy. Honestly, I don't know if I could take that away from Lucy."

"I can't believe you were hanging out with a kid." He laughed.

"I did and it was awesome," I said. "We went to the zoo and then made dinner."

"Go for it," he said. "I'm serious. You've been looking for love for a long time. How often do you come across someone that makes you think about blowing up your life?"

I scoffed. "Never."

"Exactly. Business comes and goes. It's not like Lyons is the only game in town. He's not going to pull his accounts. He knows where his bread is buttered. Dad will be pissed but he'll get over it. You can't live your life for them. Live it for you. You're not getting any younger."

"Thanks," I said. "I'm not exactly over the hill."

"No, but you're headed that way, and if you keep putting dad, James, and everyone else ahead of what makes you happy, you're going to be miserable. Fuck them. You do you."

"Brave words for a guy that isn't putting his career on the line," I joked.

"Shit, your career is safe. You know it and I know it. Even if you fuck up so bad they fire your ass, big deal. It's not like you'll be broke. Do you really need the job?"

He made a very good point. "Thanks, Edwin. I guess I have a lot to think about."

"Don't think too hard," he warned. "You'll get yourself twisted up. Are you going to see her again?"

"I'm sure I will. She hinted at it."

"That means you'll be staying there for a bit?" he asked.

"I think for at least the next couple of days," I said, making the decision on the fly.

"Good for you, and good luck."

18

EMMA

I carried boxes to the back door in preparation to be picked up by the shipping company. There were boxes stacked all over the area. It was probably a fire hazard. These were the last of the orders to go out. Valentine's Day was two days away. We were all scrambling to get the last of the orders filled.

"You need more coffee," one of the employees said.

I fought off the yawn. "It's been a long morning."

"I just checked the sheets and we've completed the orders," she said with a big smile. "We did it."

"We're actually done?" I repeated.

"For now." She laughed. "The most pressing orders have been filled."

I finally let out the breath I'd been holding for the last month. "We did it. Wow. I'm impressed. You guys never cease to amaze me. I think we all know what this means."

Her face lit up. "Really?"

"Absolutely! If I had one of those horns, I would blow it. I'll go talk to them. We're done for the day. I want to personally thank you for coming in early. I wasn't sure we'd get done by the pickup time."

I walked to the factory floor where the machines were pumping and my staff was chatting as they inspected and packaged. "Everyone, can I have your attention?" I shouted to be heard.

When I was certain everyone saw me and heard me, I began clapping. "You did it. We've filled the Valentine's orders. For those of you that came in early, you are free to go for the day. I want to personally thank everyone for working so hard. We beat our deadline by three hours! You guys are awesome! Tomorrow, lunch is on me. We'll get that taco bar we all voted on. Thank you again! Now, go home! Get some sleep and come back tomorrow ready to rock!"

There was a round of cheers. I was done for the day and I was taking full advantage of it. We worked our asses off and I was ready to have a little retail therapy to recover from the busy month. I grabbed my phone and called Jennifer to see if she wanted to do a little shopping. We agreed to meet in thirty minutes.

I found her sitting at one of the outdoor tables in the shopping district. "Are you actually done for the day?" she asked when I took my seat.

"Done. Valentine's is in the books."

"Damn, you're getting a lot better at this whole business thing." She laughed.

"Thanks. Practice makes perfect. Before we shop until I drop, I need food. I'm craving carbs and sugar."

"How about pizza?" she suggested.

"Perfect," I answered.

We ordered personal pan pizzas and extra-large drinks before finding a table to sit at. "How was your weekend?" she asked.

I had not told her about the time I spent with Case. I couldn't explain why, but I almost felt guilty. Like I had done something bad. I knew it wasn't bad. It just felt that way. She was my best friend in the world. She would give me good advice.

"Good. I think. I don't know. Case stayed the night."

She frowned with the pizza halfway to her mouth. "Case. Manhattan Case?"

I nodded. "Technically Case Manhattan, but yes."

"Wow."

She didn't say anything which made me nervous. Maybe I was right to feel bad. "Wow," I repeated. "Like wow what a slut and I can't believe you did that?"

"Stop." She laughed. "As if I would ever think that. I'm shocked but in a good way. What's going on there?"

"I don't know," I said. "I have no idea what I'm doing. Am I totally screwing up?"

"I don't know," she said. "What did you do?"

"Are you seriously asking me that?"

She burst into laughter. "I have to. I'm not sure we're talking about the same thing here."

"We went to the zoo and Lucy passed out on the way home. He was so sweet and carried her upstairs so she could nap. We talked a bit and then I invited him to dinner. Then Lucy wanted him to watch a movie with her. She went to bed and we were just kind of hanging out. I told him about Marie, and we looked at one of the photo albums."

"You really let him in," she commented.

"I did. I can't even claim I was drunk. I kissed him. Or he kissed me. I don't know. I could have stopped it with the kiss but not me. I got up and took him to bed."

She grinned and held up her hand. I rolled my eyes and gave her the high-five she was looking for. "That's my girl. I wouldn't have been able to last that long. I would have been crawling all over the man after the first date."

"Now what do I do?" I asked her. "It wasn't like a one-night stand. He stayed and cooked breakfast for us. I told him to call me, and he did. I don't know what I'm doing with him. I feel like I'm falling into something I'm not ready for. I don't even know if it's what he wants. What if this is part of the game for him?"

"Why do you think it's a game?" she asked.

"Because look at him!" I exclaimed. "He's a wealthy celebrity in his own right. I'm just me. I'm nobody."

"Uh, that's not true," she said. "You are somebody. You are my best friend and Lucy's aunt slash mommy. You own a business."

"Exactly!" I said and jabbed my pizza in the air to punctuate my point. "What if that's what he's doing?"

"What is he doing?"

"Getting close to me to convince me to sell my business," I said. "Maybe I'm just a little jaded, but why would a man like him be interested in a girl like me?"

"Because you're gorgeous," she said. "I told you I saw the way he was looking at you. He wanted to throw you against the wall that night he picked you up. I know the look of a man that wants a woman. He wanted you."

"I'm sure he wanted me for a quick roll in the hay, and that's what he got," I said. "What if that's all he wanted? He's here on business and figured why not get his rocks off while he's attempting to close the deal. Why not try and woo the country bumpkin with a little sex?"

"I understand why you might think that, but I think you're wrong," she said. "Maybe you should ask him what he wants."

"I know what he wants," I spat. "He wants Miller's Chocolates. Once he gets what he wants, he goes back to New York and that's that. I'll have no man, no dignity, and no company."

"You've got plenty of dignity," she said. "Have you thought about whether you want to sell? Are you actually considering it?"

I groaned again. "I don't know. At first, I wasn't. Then I was. Now, I feel like I'm choosing between the man and my business."

"Why in the world do you think you're choosing between them?" she asked with confusion.

"What if we actually like each other?" I said. "I don't want to get too far ahead of myself, but it does feel like there could be something between us. I like him. I don't know if it's just because he's the first man I've let myself be with in years, but it feels like it could be a thing. I want to believe he likes me. Yes, there's a little voice in the back of my head telling me he's only trying to get me to like him to get my company. If I like him, can I really ruin his career?"

She held up a hand and shook her head. "I think I missed something. Why would you ruin his career?"

"Not ruin his career, but if he doesn't close this deal, I can't imagine it would be good for him," I explained. "He's spent a lot of time here. I'm sure he has other clients but he's devoting his time to pleasing this one client, which tells me the guy is a VIP. If I say no to the sale, it's not going to look good for Case."

She snorted and picked up her pizza again. "Trust me, Case is going to be just fine. He's a Manhattan. It wouldn't hurt for him to lose once or twice. It builds character."

"How do you know he doesn't lose all the time?"

"Because look at him," she said. "He comes from success. I bet he's never been told no."

I didn't like the way she was categorizing him. "He's not like that," I defended. "He's very down to earth. I think that's why I like him. He could easily be a stuck-up prick, but he's not. He's so good with Lucy. They played together. He held her up so she could see the animals. If he was one of those guys that walks around like he's some kind of god, I wouldn't be interested in him. He's not like that."

She was smiling as I talked. "Sounds like you got it bad for this guy."

"I don't know if I got it bad, but I am very interested in seeing him again, which is why I'm stuck."

"I think you're looking at this situation like it's an either/or," she said. "It's not. You can say no and still have him. If you reject his offer and he gets pissed and doesn't want to see you again, then he wasn't worth your time in the first place. If he knows you and respects you, he'll know how important Miller's is to you. He wouldn't ask you to sell. He would tell his client you rejected the very generous offer and still want to see you."

I sighed and wanted to believe that was true, but I didn't see it going down like that. "He lives in New York. I live here. I don't want to move and there is no way he would move. Even if he did want to see me after I turned him down, how would that work?"

"You could make it work if you both really wanted it," she replied. "He's got the means to fly here whenever he wants. You could go there and visit him on the weekends. You're not all that far away."

"This is stupid," I muttered.

"What's stupid?"

"I'm borrowing trouble," I said with a shake of my head. "I'm already trying to figure out a relationship that doesn't exist."

She laughed. "That's who you are. You analyze and prepare. That's not a terrible quality. Talk to him. This will be a good test. If he gets pissed you don't want to sell, then he's not worth your time."

"I'm not even sure I don't want to sell," I said.

She cocked her head to the side. "Yes, you are. You can't sell Miller's. It's your life's blood. Maybe one day you can walk away, but we both know you aren't there yet. That place is special to you. I don't think you want to give up something that means that much to you. Certainly, don't give it up to please a man."

"You're probably right."

"I know I'm right," she said with a wink.

That night after I put Lucy to bed, I poured my glass of wine and grabbed the photo album off the coffee table once again. I wished Marie was there to tell me what to do. Sitting on the edge of the table was the picture from the zoo. The three of us were smiling as the camera snapped while we were on the carousel. The smile on Lucy's face touched my heart. Case was grinning as well. When I looked at the picture, I saw happiness. Bliss. I wanted more pictures like that.

I realized I wanted more pictures with Case like that.

19

CASE

I couldn't hide. I refused to hide. That was not my style. James Lyons was going to try and intimidate me. It would usually work but not today. Normally, he'd shout and make some thinly veiled threats about what would happen if I didn't give him what he wanted. I would quickly jump through hoops, and ultimately, he would walk away a satisfied client. I had used my powers of persuasion on more than one occasion to get him what he wanted.

I was having a crisis of conscience. I hated the idea of taking her company from her. From Lucy. I'd been up all damn night trying to think of a solution that would satisfy both sides with no one feeling like they were losing. I was drawing a blank.

When the phone rang, I knew it was time. I had to face the music. "James," I answered. "I was just getting ready to call you."

"I wish you would have called earlier," he said. "I don't like waiting."

"I'm in Pennsylvania," I told him.

"Has she agreed to my deal?" he asked.

"I'm going to have the deal done within the next week," I said and almost puked as I said the words. There was a bitterness on my tongue.

"You're sure about that?" he asked.

"I've got it handled," I said. "Have I ever let you down?"

"I'll wait for your call," he said. "And I will expect a call. Don't make me call you again."

I wanted to tell the man to kiss my ass, but I held my tongue. He was a client after all. I had to be professional, even if it was making me ill. After the call was over, I pulled up the contract I had been working on for the purchase of Miller's Chocolates. It was a good deal. She would be able to literally walk away from the factory. It would be all turnkey. She handed over the keys and got a fat check.

To anyone else, this deal would be amazing. She wasn't going to be asked to provide financial statements or justify spending. But Emma wasn't just anyone else. She was different. Her company was different. It wasn't just a paycheck for her. She would be selling a piece of her soul. I wasn't sure that was what I wanted for her. This decision was hers to make, but I already knew what I wanted for her, even if it did contradict what was right for me.

A text came through. I checked it and found myself smiling. Emma wanted to go hiking. I quickly agreed to meet her. Spending a few hours with her was much better than sitting around crunching numbers and trying to make rich spoiled men happy.

After changing into a pair of joggers and a hoodie, I took an Uber to the park she wanted to meet at. She was already there. Damn, I was a lucky guy. She was wearing a pair of black spandex yoga pants with a pink hoodie. Her hair was pulled back in a ponytail. She looked very serious about her hiking. I was thinking she meant a walk.

"Hi," I greeted her and gave her a quick kiss.

"You might get a little warm," she said as she looked me up and down.

"Nah." I shrugged. "I'll be fine."

"Okay," she said with a grin.

"Do you hike up here a lot?" I asked as we started down a trail.

"Maybe once a week," she said. "I love coming out here. I used to do a lot more hiking before I became Lucy's fulltime guardian. This is a mild hike, but it's a bit much for Lucy. She can only handle about halfway before she starts whining."

It was a testament to her devotion to the little girl. She gave up something she loved because it was better for Lucy. "I bet in another year she'll be racing ahead of you."

"She's gotten a lot better." She laughed. "I tried one of those backpack things when she was little, but it didn't end well. I figured it was best to call mercy and wait until she was older."

"Ah, so I get to be your victim," I teased.

"I was thinking you would be able to keep up with all your big, strong muscles," she joked.

"If you need me to carry you, just let me know," I said.

"Yeah, I'll keep that in mind."

The climb got a little steeper. I was actually working up a sweat. It was a pretty good cardio workout. I followed behind her, enjoying the view as she moved in the tight pants. It was a cool day, maybe high forties, but it felt like it was much hotter. I was regretting the hoodie.

I wiped my arm across my brow and stepped up the pace. "Still back there?" she asked.

"I'm just waiting for you to actually start moving." I laughed.

"You sound like you're out of breath," she teased.

"Not a chance," I said.

We reached a flat area with a pretty amazing lookout. She turned to me and burst into laughter. "You're sweating."

"I'm a little warm."

"Told you." She laughed.

I pulled off the hoodie and debated leaving it hanging on a tree. "I'm used to sweating but usually it's a temperature-controlled gym. There are fans."

"Ah, you're a gym rat."

"There's not a lot of time to find a mountain to hike in Manhattan," I said. "Central Park is great for jogging but not exactly hiking."

"City boy," she teased.

"I think you're right," I said. "I guess I'm going to have to get down here and hike some of your trails."

"Yes, you will."

We started walking again. She took it easy on me. I liked the fresh air. I liked hanging out with her in the fresh air. "Are you one of those people that hangs off the side of a cliff while dangling from a rope?"

"No," she replied. "I like hiking with both feet on the ground. When I was younger and far more naïve, I used to think I wanted to do the Appalachian Trail."

"No kidding?" I asked with surprise.

"I love being outside," she said.

"Do you like camping and stuff?"

"I don't particularly love to camp, which is one of the reasons I decided I wasn't cut out for the extensive trail hikes. I have done it but I'm kind of a chicken."

"Afraid of the big bad wolf?" I joked. "Lions, tigers, and bears."

"I'm afraid of the big bad man," she replied. "I'm not exactly tough. I'm very murderable. I could carry pepper spray and that stuff, but honestly, I don't think it's going to do me a lot of good."

"You could learn some self-defense moves," I offered.

"I'm good," she said. "I can't be heading off into the wilderness when I'm responsible for a little girl. That's not exactly making a smart decision. I can't let her lose another parent."

"I get it," I said, even if I didn't truly get it. "But this kind of thing is safe, right?"

"I think so," she said. "It's why I do it whenever I can. Lately, I haven't had a lot of time to do much of anything."

"Because of the business?" I asked. I saw an opening to broach the subject of the sale.

"Because of adulting." She laughed. "There's work and Lucy's needs on top of the general stuff. I keep busy."

"Have you thought any more about the offer?" I asked.

We were heading back down the trail and it was a little easier to talk. "I've thought about it," she said.

"Have you made a decision?" I pushed.

"No."

"I'm not trying to pressure you," I said. "If you have any questions about the offer, I can try and answer them for you. I know the offer came out of left field and you weren't prepared for it."

"It was a little bit of a surprise," she said. "I've had other people ask if I was interested in selling, but no one has offered me the money your client did."

"I can tell you that's why he made the offer as high as he did," I said. "He wanted to eliminate the doubt and concern by swamping you with cash."

"There was definitely some swamping." She laughed.

"But you still have reservations," I said.

"I do. It's not just about the money. I think I've made that clear. My company isn't just the thing that pays my bills. It's a legacy. It's a future for Lucy. It's a connection to something her mother had a part in building."

"Do you see her taking over the company one day?" I asked.

"I do, but not if she doesn't want it," she answered. "I don't want to pressure her into doing something she doesn't want to do. If she decides she wants to be a doctor or a dancer or a teacher, I'll support it. If she doesn't have chocolate in her veins, that's okay."

"But you do," I said. "Have chocolate in your veins."

"I do." She laughed. "I always have. I know I'm a different breed and I won't pressure her to do anything."

"I think she might have a little chocolate in her veins," I teased.

"Maybe a little."

"If you come up with a decision, no matter which way you go, let me know, please," I said. "I won't keep asking. I don't want to hound you. I know this is a huge decision for you."

"It is and I appreciate you giving me some time to think it over," she said. "Is your client pressuring you?"

"No more than usual." I laughed.

We made it back to the parking lot with a few benches. "Do you have anything to get back to?" she asked.

"Nope. Nothing is more important than this."

"You're very smooth." She grinned and sat down.

I sat down beside her. "How is work?" I asked. "You're here in the middle of the day. Is that good or bad?"

"Good," she said. "We finished our orders yesterday. I went in this morning and handled some business before deciding I wanted to take the rest of the day off."

"Perks of being the boss," I joked.

"Definitely. I put in more than enough hours. I'm glad I get to take this time off. It makes all the hard work worth it."

"Does business drop off after Valentine's?" I asked.

"Are you asking as a friend or as a man looking to negotiate a contract to buy my business?" She grinned.

"A curious friend," I said. "The chocolate business is a new one to me. I've helped negotiate many buyouts but never a chocolate factory."

"What does your client want to do with my company?" she asked.

"I honestly don't know the details," I told her. "I think his goal is to grow it."

She looked thoughtful as she looked out at the trees. "I'm thinking about it," she said.

"I know." I nodded. "That works."

"Are you going to be in town tomorrow?" she questioned.

"I will. Do you have plans?"

She scoffed. "No."

"Are you not a fan of Cupid?" I teased.

"Cupid is a pain in my ass," she said. "I love the sales but not a fan of the day."

"Too commercial?" I asked.

"Come on, you're talking to the owner of a chocolate factory." She laughed. "I have to like the fact it's too commercial. But on a personal level, it's never been my favorite holiday. There's so much pressure on a couple, and when you're single, it's like you're walking around with a flashing sign above your head."

"I agree." I nodded. "I don't much care for it either."

We sat for a bit longer before she had to go pick up Lucy. Once again, we didn't commit to seeing each other again. I had learned she preferred to keep things open. I would go back to the hotel and text her tonight after Lucy went to bed.

20

EMMA

I took Lucy to school and headed back home to find a bouquet of red roses on my doorstep. I looked around the neighborhood. I was certain they were delivered to the wrong house. I felt like I was invading someone's privacy by checking the card, but I wanted the intended person to get their flowers.

"Happy Valentine's Day," I read the card that was signed by Case.

My cheeks burned and my smile was so big it almost hurt. I carried the vase inside and put the flowers on the kitchen table. I couldn't remember the last time I had gotten flowers. I did remember. It was when Marie died. I had been overwhelmed with white flower bouquets. Getting red roses was a welcome change.

I grabbed my phone and sent Case a text. *The flowers are beautiful. Thank you.*

I took a picture of the flowers for my own benefit. I wanted to look back at the picture and remember how amazing it was to be the beneficiary of such a special gift. I checked the time and headed upstairs to change into my workout clothes. I was meeting Jennifer for a spin class. Something I wished I could do more often.

Case texted back. *Have dinner with me tonight. No need for us both to be alone.*

I got butterflies in my stomach thinking about it. Could I? Dinner meant date. Did I want to date him? Would that be dangerous?

After our hike yesterday, I knew he was still here because he needed an answer about the sale. I almost felt guilty for leading him on. I wasn't sure what I wanted to do with my business, but I knew which way I was leaning. Going out with him again was giving him the impression I was seriously thinking about it.

But if Jennifer was right, this might be more than just him pursuing a business deal. "Fuck it," I growled. I texted him back. *Yes. When and where?*

After some back and forth, we established he would be picking me up. Now I had another problem to deal with. What was I going to wear? This was an emergency. After spin class, I was going to have to buy a dress.

I walked into the gym and found Jennifer flirting with some jock. I didn't want to interrupt her and walked to the locker room to drop off my bag. "Ready?" I asked Jennifer when she walked in. "I don't want to interrupt your flirting."

"I got his number." She grinned.

"I'm sure you did," I said. "We have to make this quick. I have an emergency shopping need."

"That sounds dire," she said as we walked to the spin bikes.

"I need a dress."

"Right now?" she questioned.

"I have a date," I said and couldn't help but squeal as I said it. I was excited about it. More excited than I thought I would be but saying it out loud made it real.

"With Manhattan?" She grinned.

"His name is Case," I said. "And yes, with Case."

"On Valentine's Day," she said with a smile. "That's big. That's like *the* day."

"He sent me roses this morning," I said.

"No way!" she gasped. "This man is smooth. He is sweeping you off your feet in a big way. You're not going to know which end is up if he keeps going at this pace."

"I know," I said. "I'm a little overwhelmed by him. He's coming on strong. Is this normal?"

"Yes." She laughed. "He's not proposing marriage. If he did, that would be too strong. I think he's a man on a mission. He wants you and he's pulling out all the stops. That's what they're supposed to do. How are you feeling about it? Are you thinking about keeping him around?"

"I'm not sure that's a choice I have right now," I told her. "We're going on a date. Nothing more."

"Keep telling yourself that." She laughed. "He wants more. You want more."

"I kinda do," I whispered.

"Go with it," she said. "Don't get in your head and start thinking about all the things that might happen. Enjoy the ride for what it is. This is dating. This is what us single ladies do. We date and feel a guy out. Are they worth our time? Could there be more to this thing? While you're figuring that out, you enjoy some of the perks."

"Sex," I said. "That's the perks you speak of?"

"Not just sex," she said. "Although that's a big part of it. You enjoy companionship. When you're having a bad day, that guy is the one you call and vent to. When something good happens, you call him, and he celebrates with you."

"I have you for that." I grinned.

"I love you, dear, but I'm not playing for the other team to satisfy your other needs."

"Dirty." I laughed.

"I'm free tonight," she said. "I'll watch Lucy."

"Are you sure?" I asked. "I can get one of the girls from work to watch her."

"Trust me, I would love to hang out with her," she said. "That way I will have a valid excuse for not having a date."

"Thank you," I said. "I appreciate it."

"Anything I can do to get your ass out of the house," she teased.

After the gym, we headed out to find a new dress. I refused to do red. I didn't want to look like everyone else. "This one," she said. "It's perfect. The color will make your eyes pop."

"It's short," I said.

"It's hot. Black strappy heels. It's perfect. He's not going to be able to resist you."

"I'm not trying to get him to jump my bones." I laughed.

"Sure, you are." She shrugged. "That's the goal. You want him to want to jump your bones."

"I'll try it on."

It wasn't my usual style, but Jennifer was a model. She knew fashion. She knew how to dress. I tried it on and stepped out of the dressing room. "Well?" I asked.

She let out a low whistle. "Hot. So hot. You have to get it."

Ten minutes later, I was walking out of the store with a new dress and heels. Really steep heels. I just hoped I didn't break a leg.

"I'll be at your house at four," she said.

After picking up Lucy and getting home, it was time to get ready for my date. I was nervous and anxious at the same time. I wanted to look good for him. I hoped he looked at me and thought he was a lucky man to get to be out with me.

When Jennifer showed up, she was carrying a bag. "What's that?" I asked.

"My overnight bag. You don't have a curfew tonight. If you decide to go back to his hotel, do it without worrying about whether we'll be okay. We will."

"I'm not a heathen," I said. "I'll be home tonight."

"We'll see," she said with a wink.

I headed back upstairs to finish getting ready. "You're not going to work," Jennifer said as she walked into the room.

"I know."

"Then slap some paint on that face," she said. "Don't be afraid to go bold. Knock his socks off."

"I don't want to overdo it."

"Sit," she ordered.

She grabbed a towel and put it across my chest and shoulders.

"I'm not going to be in front of a camera," I reminded her. "I don't need to look like I'm in a photo shoot. Light. Don't you dare put that heavy-hand on me."

"Stop, I've got this," she said and used her years of sitting in the makeup chair to do my face.

I tried to sit still. Lucy came into the room. "You look very pretty," she said.

"Thank you, sweetie," I said.

"Are you going to go dancing?" she asked.

The girl loved princess movies. She was likely imagining me on a dance floor doing swirls and twirls. "I don't think so," I said. "We're just going to have dinner."

"Done," Jennifer declared and stepped back.

"I'm afraid to look," I said.

"Oh stop, you look amazing."

I turned to look in the mirror. "Wow, it felt like you were packing it on," I said. "It doesn't look like much at all."

"That's the goal," she said. "Go get the dress on. You only have twenty minutes before he's here."

Nerves were making me jittery. I put on my dress and sat down to put on the heels before stepping into the bedroom. Lucy started jumping up and down while clapping. "I love it!"

"Gorgeous," Jennifer declared with a discerning eye. She stepped forward and tugged here and there. She did a full circle around me while adjusting the skirt.

"It feels so short," I said again.

"It's perfect," she said. "Just don't bend over."

I groaned and turned to look in the mirror. It was short but not scandalous. I was so used to wearing jeans to work and lounging around in my sweats at home. It had been a long time since I dressed up. The heels were dangerous, but they made the look. I smoothed my hands down the dark fabric and tried to push it down a few more inches.

"You look pretty," Lucy said.

I turned to her and gave her a hug. "Thank you. I love you."

"I love you," she said and gave me a good squeeze.

"Why don't you go downstairs and pick our movie?" Jennifer said. "Our heart-shaped pizza will be here soon."

Lucy bounced out of the room. Jennifer turned to look at me. "I'm serious about staying out tonight," she said. "You don't need to rush home. Go be free for the night."

"I can't do that," I said.

"You can," she insisted. "Play it by ear, but don't think you need to come home. I want you to live it up. That dress deserves to be taken off by a man."

I laughed and rolled my eyes. "You better call the guy from the gym. You sound like you need to get laid."

"I do, but that's not what this is about," she said. "His mouth is going to be watering when he sees you."

"I hope so."

"Did you guys talk about the business any more?" she asked.

I shook my head. "No. He says he's not going to pressure me."

"Good man."

The doorbell rang a minute later. We exchanged a look before she rushed out the door. "I cannot wait to see the look on his face when he lays eyes on your hotness!"

I paused and took one more look in the mirror. I didn't know why I cared if he was impressed. I was trying to tell myself I needed to keep him at arm's length. I didn't want to let myself fall madly in love with a man I probably wouldn't see again after I rejected his offer. I was having fun. I was dating. This was what people did. I could enjoy a nice dinner with a man that was funny and smart.

21

CASE

I waited for someone to open the door. The car I hired was idling on the street. I didn't want either of us to have to worry about driving. I wanted to give her my full attention and I wanted her full attention. Lucy was the one to open the door. She smiled up at me. "Hi, Case."

"Hi, Lucy."

"Are you going on a date?" she asked.

I slowly nodded. "I am."

"She looks really pretty," she said. "You're going to love her new dress."

I stepped inside the living room. Her friend Jennifer came downstairs and flashed me a smile. "She'll be down in just a minute."

"Thank you."

She always made me feel like she was inspecting me. It was a little disturbing. "Hello." I nodded when she stepped in front of me.

"I think I need to ask you what your intentions are," she said.

"My intentions?"

"Yes, what do you intend to do with my best friend?" she asked.

"I intend to take her to dinner," I said.

She opened her mouth and I thought maybe she was about to lay into me, but she didn't get the chance. "Jennifer, leave him alone," I heard Emma say.

"Keep her out too late," she whispered and flashed a wink before stepping away.

That was a slightly confusing message. I got the impression she didn't like me but yet was encouraging me to stay out with Emma. When Emma walked into the room, I no longer cared what her friend thought. Lucy said Emma looked pretty, but that was a gross understatement. Emma looked incredible. I was certain my tongue was hanging out with my jaw on the floor.

"Hi," she said with a sheepish smile.

"Hi," I croaked the word. I cleared my throat. "You look—" I couldn't find the right word. "Gorgeous."

"Thank you," she said and looked away. I watched her give Lucy another hug before collecting a sheer black shawl and her purse.

"Ready?" I asked.

I was still somewhat shellshocked. She looked different but the same. I thought she was beautiful in her jeans and company T-shirts, but this look was hot. If it wasn't a special day, I would invite her back to my hotel room and get her out of that dress.

"I am," she said and waved goodbye to Lucy.

I opened the car door and let her slide in the backseat before following her in. "You really do look incredible," I said.

"Thank you," she said and tugged at the hem of the dress. When she sat, the hem had ridden up to mid-thigh. All that skin on display was making me hard.

"Do you have to work tomorrow morning?" I asked.

"Not on the line," she said. "I need to go in and take care of some things."

"Got any plans for a hike anytime soon?" I teased.

"Maybe." She laughed. "I'm not sure you could survive another hike."

"Given the right attire, I know I would do just fine."

"I don't know," she said and gestured to the luxury car. "Is this how you always travel?"

"What do you mean?" I asked.

"Do you drive?"

"I can." I nodded. "I don't do a lot of driving in the city though. It's too much of a pain in the ass to find parking. And I don't have the patience to deal with the traffic. It's easier to hire experts to ferry me around."

"Ah, I see." She smiled.

"And tonight, I hired a driver because I didn't want to be distracted."

"Distracted?"

"By you," I said. "Seeing you in that dress makes me very glad I did hire a car. There's no way I could pay attention to the road if you're sitting beside me in that dress."

She smiled and rolled her eyes. "You are very smooth tonight."

"I'm smooth every night."

She laughed again. "Is this the city version of Case Manhattan?"

I flashed her a smile. "This is me."

"So, how did you spend your day today?" she asked.

I shrugged and tried to think of what to tell her. I didn't think she would appreciate knowing I spent time putting the offer into writing. I didn't think she wanted to talk about that. I knew I didn't. "I worked for a while and then hit the gym. I even did a little sightseeing."

"So, can I ask you about your work?" she asked.

"What about it?"

"You said it's the family business," she said. "Does that mean you work with your whole family?"

"Why don't I explain it to you over dinner?" I said. "It can be just a little confusing."

"I'd like that." She smiled.

I reached over and grabbed her hand. I was happy she wanted to know more about me. That had to be a good sign. She wasn't in it just for the sex. Okay, that was a given, but I liked that she wasn't all about who I was because of my name.

Once we were seated at the table and had ordered wine, it was time to fill her in. "Alright, so my family is huge."

"You said that."

"I told you I am one of six," I said. "My father is a direct descendent of the Manhattan family that basically built the city. He is one of four siblings. Each of them has six kids."

"Damn, you guys really like to procreate." She laughed.

"We're good at it." I grinned. "Anyway, my dad and his siblings all have their niche in the business world. My father manages the law firm my family owns. He also manages the insurance agency."

"And you work at neither?" she questioned.

"Nope. I work at the accounting firm that my aunt runs."

"Do your brothers work at the accounting firm?" she asked.

"No," I answered. "They are spread out in the other family businesses."

"There are more?"

"Tech firm, property management, and real estate as well," I said.

She sipped her wine. "There's more, isn't there?" She laughed.

I nodded. "A few different investment firms."

"Your family really does run Manhattan," she exclaimed. "I had no idea. Are you groomed from an early age to go into the family businesses?"

I shrugged. "Yes and no," I answered. "It's encouraged and we've all went that way, but it's not a demand."

"Did you feel pressured to become a CPA?"

I knew why she was asking. She was worried about Lucy. This was one subject I felt like I had enough experience to provide some sound advice. "No," I answered. "None. I think for us, it's a little easier than most kids dealing with a family business. We had a variety of options. We were never pushed into any one field."

"Did you have to start at the bottom?"

"Yep." I nodded.

"Did you go to school?" she asked.

It was beginning to feel like an interview. "I did. I have a bachelor's degree."

"Smart and handsome." She grinned.

"I'm more than just a pretty face," I teased.

"Yes, you are." She laughed.

"Now that you've got Valentine's behind you, what's your next big thing?" I asked.

"We pretty much skate by on normal business until about October. Then we have to gear up for Christmas."

"Damn, that's back-to-back holidays," I commented.

"Yeah, from October until February it's pretty nonstop," she said. "I love it, but it's also very stressful."

"I bet. Do you ever get to go on a vacation?"

"I try and take a couple of days but it's hard to leave for a full week or two," she said.

"I suppose people tell you that you work too hard all the time, right?" I asked.

She burst into laughter. "I have heard that once or twice."

"My family has a home in the Hamptons," I said. "I'd love to take you and Lucy out there sometime."

She smiled again. "Of course, you have a home in the Hamptons."

"Sorry, did that sound like I was bragging?" I asked with a grimace. "I didn't mean to."

"No, you weren't bragging," she said. "It's just, I've never met anyone like you."

"How so?"

"You're obviously wealthy, but you don't really act like it," she said. "You seem very normal."

I had to laugh at her assessment. "I'm glad I'm normal."

"I was expecting something different from you," she said. "That first day you were in my shop I thought you were a douchebag."

I almost choked on my wine. "When I bowled you over?"

"Yes!" She giggled. "You were like a linebacker coming in hot. You nearly took me down. I was glad it was just the chocolates that hit the floor."

"I'm so, so sorry," I said. "I felt like a douchebag."

"Why didn't you help me clean up?" she asked. "Or see if I was okay?"

I dropped my head. "I'm sorry. I went into the shop to check out the business. Then I saw you, and to be perfectly honest, I kind of lost my shit. I turned into a gawky twelve-year-old boy. When I slammed into you, I felt like such an idiot. I was too embarrassed to stick around. I ran out like a coward. I swear, I'm not usually quite so uncool."

She was smiling. "You are forgiven. I was pretty pissed at you, but I think you've made up for it."

"We'll have one hell of a story to tell our grandkids about how we met," I said the words and then froze. I couldn't believe I just said that out loud. That was supposed to be an inside thought. "I mean—"

"It's fine," she said. "It would be a funny story."

We ate our dinner, enjoying the atmosphere. There were happy couples all around us. The quiet hum of conversation was barely heard over the soft string music pumping through the speakers. It was all very romantic.

"Should we order dessert?" I asked her once our meals were cleared away.

"Actually, there is an ice-cream shop a few doors down," she said. "It is seriously some of the best you'll ever have."

"You have a real sweet tooth, don't you?" I teased.

"Oh, you have no idea." She laughed. "I can sniff out chocolate better than a German Shepherd can sniff out drugs."

"Good to know." I nodded.

I paid the check and we decided to walk the block to the ice-cream shop. I held her hand as we walked. We weren't the only couple out and about on the day for lovers. We each ordered a scoop and sat down at one of the tiny tables.

"This is pretty damn good ice cream," I said.

"Told you," she said as her tongue slid across the ice cream. "If I had the space and the capital, I would love to go into the ice-cream business."

"Boozy ice cream?" I asked.

Her eyes lit up. "That's a very good idea."

"Uh oh, did I just spark an idea in the mad scientist's beautiful brain?" I joked.

"Oh, you know you did," she said. "I'm going to work out some recipes."

"Since it was my idea, I get to be the official taste tester," I volunteered.

"It's going to have to be you." She giggled. "Can't be Lucy and I don't want to get smashed."

"You say that like it's happened before."

Her expression changed. I knew a memory had been triggered. "It has. Marie and I ended up drinking the tequila we were supposed to be putting in the chocolate. The chocolates kept failing and we ended up getting stupid drunk. The kitchen was a mess."

"I take it you eventually worked out the recipe," I said.

"We did with the promise we weren't going to be drinking and cooking anymore," she replied. "It was a learning lesson. I'm glad I got to learn it with her."

"Sorry if I brought up a bad memory," I said quietly when I noticed the tears shimmering in her eyes.

"No, no." She shook her head. "It's a great memory. I never want to quash the memories. I live in them. When they hurt, I ride it out. I'm never going to forget her."

"Good." I nodded.

We went back to our ice cream. I wasn't ready for the night to end. "Feel like taking a dip in the hot tub?" I asked.

She raised a brow. "Where is this hot tub?"

"My room, that's not too far from here," I replied.

She didn't immediately answer. "I didn't bring my suit."

I gave her a look. "Who said anything about suits?"

"Alright, but I can't be out too late."

That was contrary to what her friend said.

22

EMMA

"I need to let Jennifer know I'll be late," I told him and pulled the phone from my purse. I shot off a text and let her know I was going to be another hour, possibly two.

He led me up to his room, which was one of the suites. I wasn't surprised. A man of his wealth would want the best. "Champagne?" he asked.

"Yes, please," I answered. I walked to the large windows and stared out at the city below. I could see him moving around the room in the reflection in the glass.

Getting naked and in the hot tub was likely only going to lead to one thing. I knew what I was agreeing to when I came up with him.

"Here you go," he said and handed me a glass. He had taken off the black suit jacket. The blue shirt sleeves were rolled up to his elbows.

"This is a nice view," I commented.

"I think I have a better view."

I turned to look up at him and found him staring at me. "Is that another one of your very smooth lines?"

He brushed a piece of hair away from my face. "It's not a line. It's true." He bent down and gave me a kiss. "I'll get the hot tub fired up."

There was a bowl of strawberries sitting next to the bottle of champagne. I didn't think that was an accident. I wasn't going to be mad about it. He had been hoping to bring me back to his room. Again, I was pretty sure we both knew this was how the night was going to end. We wanted this.

"The strawberries are a nice touch," I said and picked one up from the bowl.

"Are you mad?"

"Why would I be mad?" I asked.

"It might seem a little presumptuous." He shrugged. "I swear I wasn't planning to seduce you, but I wanted to be prepared."

"I appreciate the gesture," I said. "I love strawberries and champagne."

He pulled his shirt from his pants and began to unbutton it one little button at a time. "Hot tub is ready."

I could be demure and pretend I didn't want this, but that was a waste of time. I had to be home soon. I didn't have time to play hard to get. I put my glass down and turned to give him my back. I pulled my hair to the side. He got the message. I shuddered when his hands touched my back and slowly slid the zipper down.

The bodice fell forward, revealing the black lace bra I had picked out for the night. I stepped out of the dress and draped it over the back of a chair. I turned toward him wearing nothing but the black lace thong and bra.

"You're overdressed," I said and bent down to take off one heel, then the other. I walked to the edge of the hot tub and was about to climb in when he stopped me.

"It would be a shame to get those sexy panties wet. You know there's a lot of chlorine in that water."

I looked down at the bra. "You're probably right." I reached up to unhook the bra, but he stopped me.

"Allow me," he growled.

I climbed into the hot tub in nothing but my birthday suit. I turned and folded my arms on the edge. "You're still very dressed."

"I'm enjoying the view," he said.

"I'm enjoying the water," I said and sank neck deep into the bubbling water. "I thought about getting one of these at my house but worried Lucy would somehow find her way in. This feels so good."

He put our glasses of champagne on the edge of the tub. I saw his foot first, followed by the length of one of his very long muscular legs. He sank into the water beside me.

"I have a hot tub at my house," he said. "It's the best thing after a long, shitty week."

"I'm not sure I would ever get out," I murmured with my eyes closed.

He slid close to me and kissed my temple with his arm wrapping around my shoulders. "If I had your naked body in the hot tub with me, I don't think I would let you out."

I turned to look up and kissed him back. He kissed me with his hand sliding into my hair. I couldn't get close enough. I slid closer until I was in his lap with his arms around me. My breasts rubbed against his chest with our tongues dueling. I could feel his erection growing. I twisted around and straddled him with my hands on his face. I held his head steady and kissed him until things were getting dangerously close to crossing a line.

"My condoms are in the nightstand," he murmured against my lips.

"That's not going to do us much good in here," I replied.

He stood, water sluicing off us. I wrapped my legs around his waist and held on as he carried us to his bed. When he very unceremoniously dropped me on the bed, I gasped. "Sorry," he said, and it was pretty clear he was not sorry.

He reached for the box of condoms he had on the nightstand. "Do you always come prepared?" I asked.

"I come hoping I will need to be prepared," he replied.

He slid the condom down his full length before staring at me with a fire in his eyes I hadn't seen before. "Roll over," he ordered.

I flashed him a cocky smile and did as he asked. He jerked my hips up, bringing me to all fours. His hand slid over my ass before slapping once. I jumped at the sting that was quickly soothed by his lips. He slipped his hand between my legs and pushed a finger inside me.

My head rolled back and forth between my shoulders.

"Like that?" he asked in a husky voice.

"Yes," I answered honestly. "There's something else I like more."

He chuckled and continued to probe and stroke over my clit. "I know. I think I'll go for four this time."

"I don't think I would survive four," I answered on a breath.

"I guess we're going to find out."

He pushed a second finger inside. I could feel myself moving right up to the edge of an orgasm. I had no doubt he could give me four if he put his mind to it. He continued stroking in and out until I was rocking back and forth on my hands and knees. I rocked and pushed down, taking his fingers deeper inside me.

"Keep going," he said, stilling his fingers. "Do it. Make yourself come."

I moaned and moved faster until I was crying out. He pulled his fingers away and gently pushed me down. I rolled to my side and looked up at him. He bent over me and kissed me with one hand massaging my breast with his other gently massaging my hip. I moved to lie on my back, but he shook his head.

"Stay just like that," he whispered. He slipped in behind me and pushed one leg forward. His hand pushed between my legs once again. He rose up to his knees behind me and pinched one nipple. I gasped, pleasure ripping through me.

I tried to lift my leg to give him a wide opening, but he pushed my thigh down. "No," he said.

One finger found my opening and he pushed inside. The single finger felt like three with him gently pressing down on my thigh to keep my legs tightly closed. He moved in a second finger, and I was certain the pleasure would kill me.

He began to move my leg back and forth just a few inches while his fingers worked inside me. I didn't even have time to prepare myself for what was to come. My body erupted. I didn't hold back. I cried out over and over as he continued to massage my thigh.

"Two," he whispered as he lay on his side beside me.

"Oh lord," I groaned. "I don't think I can have another."

He kissed the back of my neck and ran his hands up and down my body. The tightness I had felt in my muscles with the last orgasm eased. His gentle touch and wet kisses were so good. He rose over me and pushed me onto my back.

He moved over me, using a knee to open my legs. His entry was smooth with no resistance. He took his time filling me before going perfectly still once again. I watched him take several deep breaths.

"Ready?" he asked with his blue eyes flashing.

I licked my lips. "Do it."

He proceeded to tease and tantalize until he reached his goal of giving me all four of those orgasms. When he stretched out beside me, both of us were breathing hard. I turned to face him. "Feel better?" I asked him.

"Me?" He grinned. "I should ask you that."

"Oh, I'm beyond better," I said. "I'm boneless. I don't think I'm going to be able to move."

"Don't move," he said. "Stay the night."

I wanted to argue and claim I had to go home, but I didn't. "I need to let Jennifer know."

Neither of us made an effort to move. I gave myself a little pep talk and extracted myself from under him. I grabbed my cell and fired off a text.

Turns out I'm a very dirty heathen. Are you cool staying the night with her?

I waited for her response and eyed the minibar. I was absolutely in need of water. I didn't know if multiple orgasms could dehydrate you, but I was certain that was the problem. "Can I get a water from the mini-fridge?" I asked.

"Go for it," he said from the bathroom. "Get me one too."

My phone vibrated. *Have fun you dirty girl. She's fine. Get some!*

I laughed and put the phone away. I opened the water and sucked it down in a very unladylike fashion. "All good?" he asked and crossed the room.

He walked like a cat. He was sleek and sexy, and despite feeling a little sore between the legs, I wanted him again. "All good," I said.

He guzzled his water before wiping his mouth with the back of his hand. "Ready for round two?" He grinned.

"I'll die," I groaned. "Tempting but I'm certain I'll die. I need to rehydrate."

"Say the word and I'll be ready to go." He winked.

I finished the water and together we walked back to the bed. Once again, I found myself snuggling against him. "You always leave me feeling completely sated."

"Woman, if you're trying to get me to beat my chest, it's working," he said.

"Going caveman on me?"

"If you want me to," he offered. "I could give you a gentle club and carry you back to my bed."

"No clubbing necessary," I said. "All you have to do is crook your finger and I'll probably come right there."

He groaned and hugged me tighter. "You always make me feel good and I don't just mean physically. Thank you for not being a bashful Betty. I like a woman that can tell me what she likes. I love giving you pleasure. I love hearing you reach your peak. I feel like I could conquer the world when I'm with you."

23

CASE

I pulled her against me and inhaled the scent of her hair. She was so perfect. She moaned softly. "I don't want to get up," she murmured.

"Then don't," I said. "I don't want to get up either."

"I have to."

"But do you?" I replied. "I mean, we can lay here for another thirty minutes, right?"

"I should check on Lucy."

"Do you think she's even up yet?" I asked.

"She's probably on her way to school," she answered.

"Oh shit, I forgot about that," I said. "Then there is definitely no reason to get out of bed. We have all day."

"Actually, I have to go into work today," she said.

I groaned and tugged her closer. "No. Stay with me."

"As much as I enjoy laying in bed with you and doing the other things we do in bed, I can't."

"I like spending time with you," I told her. "I've had a good time in Pennsylvania."

"I've liked spending time with you," she said and kissed my chest. "I honestly thought you would be a much bigger prick."

I laughed at her bluntness. "Tell me how you really feel."

"That was before I got to know you. Now I know you're a pretty cool guy. I like hanging out with you and I hope we can do it again, but today I have plans."

"What kind of plans?" I asked. "Going to work on that boozy ice cream?"

"After the rush of the holiday season, I throw a big party for my employees," she said.

"That's cool."

"You're welcome to come if you'd like to," she offered.

"Really?"

"I don't think it will be anything like your fancy New York parties, but we have fun," she said.

"If you don't mind, I will absolutely go."

"There's just one more thing," she said.

"I'm not dressing as Cupid."

She burst into laughter and sat up. "That's a good idea, but that's not what I was going to say. I have to get over there and set up. This is my gift to my staff, which means I have to do this for them. Your ticket in is you have to help me set up."

"Deal," I agreed. "I'm down for it."

"Have you ever had to blow up a balloon in your life?" she teased.

I sat up and grabbed her face. "I've blown up a balloon." I kissed her and then pulled her back down with me. "Let me hire someone to deal with the decorating. We can stay in bed all day."

"I don't think so," she said. "Part of the thank-you package is me doing this for them. I want to do it. It's good for me to do it."

"Alright, I'll blow up some balloons," I said.

"And I have to stop at the store to get the cake," she said and climbed out of bed. "Then I have to go get the rest of the decorations. But before I do any of that, I get to do the walk of shame. This should be fun."

"You could wear a pair of my sweats," I offered.

She laughed as she walked her naked ass out of the room. "I'm not sure which would be worse."

I got up and found some clothes to put on. I felt guilty she was going to have to wear the dress out of the hotel, but it wasn't like she was the first person to ever leave a hotel wearing the same clothes she came in with.

"I've got a car waiting," I told her as I walked into the room.

She turned around, and once again, I was staring at her back. I zipped up the dress and kissed the back of her neck before stepping away. We got into the waiting car and headed for her house. Jennifer had left a note on the counter.

"Am I a terrible mom?" Emma asked with a frown.

"I don't think you're a terrible mom," I told her. "Is this the first night you've been away from her?"

"Second," she said. "Two years ago, there was a problem with the factory. I stayed all night to try and fix things. I had a nanny that stayed with her. I felt so bad for leaving her."

I put my hands on her shoulders. "Emma, listen to me. You have to know you are a good mom. Parents leave their kids sometimes. What about parents in the military or cops and firefighters? They're not bad parents. You have set a very high standard for yourself, which is admirable, but I think you have to give yourself a break. You are still a young woman who needs to take care of herself too. What do they call it, me-time?"

"I have me-time every night after she goes to bed," she insisted.

"Fine, but don't feel guilty about last night," I said and swatted her ass. "Go change. We've got balloons to blow up."

She was laughing as she climbed the stairs. I amused myself by checking out all the pictures on the walls. It was like watching a story in pictures. I loved the family pictures. Our house growing up only had professional pictures and paintings. The candid photos that were framed and hanging on her walls were more real life. It was a testament to the life she had lived.

"I hate that picture," she said, coming downstairs.

"It's cute," I said. "Is that your dad?"

"It is."

"How old are you in the picture?"

"I think ten or eleven," she answered. "The super awkward phase."

"I think it's cute," I said. "Ready?"

"I am." She nodded. "I'll have to shower before the party."

I enjoyed sitting shotgun as we ran her errands before heading to the factory. "The party is going to be held upstairs in the conference room we never use. The staff knows they have to stay away while I decorate. Every year I try to do a different theme."

"Isn't it Valentine's?" I asked.

"Yes, but last year I did all red roses," she said.

"And this year?"

She grinned and looked at me. "You're going to love it."

"Now you're freaking me out," I said.

"Cupid." She grinned.

"Cupid?"

"Yep, arrows and a little man wearing a diaper. The whole shebang."

"You're serious?" I asked.

"I swear it was already decided before you expressed your distaste for the little guy." She giggled.

I shook my head. "The shit I get myself into."

She handed me numerous bags to carry up while she carried the cake inside. We walked into a fairly large room that looked like it was used for storage more than meetings. I put everything down and looked around the space.

"Tell me what to do," I said. "I'm your willing servant. If you want me to give you a little extra something to help you through the day, just holler."

She tossed a roll of red streamers at me. "Very funny. We are not getting naked in my conference room."

"Baby, I don't need to get naked to get you off."

She blushed and tossed a package of balloons at me. "Stop!"

"Alright, alright," I said. "What should I do?"

"Start blowing up the balloons," she said. "I've got to go to my office and get the tacks and tape. And I have to find my speaker. Where is that thing?"

"That?" I pointed to a sound bar stashed under a table pushed against a wall.

"Yes, thank you," she said. "I always get so scattered when I know I have a lot to do."

"Take a deep breath," I said. "We've got this."

She smiled and nodded. "Thank you."

She dashed out of the room. I started the tedious process of blowing up balloons.

She returned a few minutes later. "Got it."

"Keep blowing?" I asked, feeling a little lightheaded.

"Yes," she said. "I've got to figure out how to hook up the speaker. I've done it before."

I watched her fiddle with the speaker. A moment later, an old eighties ballad came over the speaker. "Dang, this is the good stuff," I said.

"I like to cheese it up a little."

I finished blowing up the entire bag of balloons and got to my feet. I swayed a little.

"Are you okay?" she asked.

"I'm good," I said. "What's next?"

"I want to hang the streamers from the ceiling," she said.

I did as she asked under her very detailed direction. I hung them and then added the balloons. While I did that, she was taping large hearts and cutouts of Cupid on the walls. The room was really starting to look festive. She was walking by when I reached out and grabbed her around the waist. "Dance with me," I said.

"You're crazy." She laughed.

We swayed back and forth to the music. "This is going to be a great party," I told her.

"Not if we don't get back to decorating," she said. "Help me with the tablecloths."

I loved sharing a dance with her, but this was important to her. I helped her spread the tablecloths out. I watched her arrange some of her chocolates on the various plates. The cake was put in the center. "Hand me the rose petals please," she asked.

I handed her the bag of silk petals. It was fun watching her in action. It took about two hours total for us to transform the room completely. "You are a woman of many talents," I told her when we took a step back and drank it all in.

"This is nothing," she said. "You should have seen Lucy's fifth birthday party. She wanted princesses. I decked it all out. For her sixth birthday, she wants a unicorn party."

"Are you going to get her a real unicorn?" I teased.

"If there is one to be found, I'm going to make sure she has it," she said with a laugh.

If I was around, I was absolutely going to find her a unicorn. It couldn't be that hard to put a horn on a white horse. "Where is Lucy going to be tonight?" I asked. "While you're at the party."

"I have a sitter for her," she said. "I will be going home tonight."

I pouted a little. "Alone?" I asked gently.

She grinned. "We'll see. I need to get home and shower and change. You're going to come tonight?"

"I'd love to if you'll have me."

"I would love for you to be here," she said.

"Then I would love to be here," I said and gave her another quick kiss. "I'll call a ride back to the hotel."

"I can take you," she offered.

"No, you've got stuff to do. Go home. I'll see you in a few hours."

I left the factory and headed back to the hotel. On my way, I got a call from my father. The urge to ignore it was strong. It would have made me very happy, but he wasn't one to just let it go. He would keep calling.

"Hello, dad," I answered.

"I haven't seen the paperwork cross my desk," he said.

"What paperwork would that be?"

"You know what I'm talking about," he said. "You've been there for almost two weeks. When is this deal going to be done?"

"I'm working on it," I said.

"I've got James breathing down my neck," he said. "He doesn't think you're going to make this happen. He's got some very big concerns. Why haven't you updated us?"

"Because there is nothing to update you with," I said. "It's not like there is a step-by-step process here. She knows the offer. She's considering it. If I push, she's going to go in the opposite direction."

"If she doesn't say yes by the end of the week, it's done. You've got other clients here that need your attention. You need to get back here. Admit defeat and let James move on."

"I'll let you know," I said and hung up.

I would worry about all of that later. I had another night with Emma, and I was going to enjoy it.

24

EMMA

I buttoned the blouse and made sure it was untucked evenly around the slacks I was wearing. My team could wear whatever they wanted, but I felt like I needed to step it up just a little. When I went downstairs, Lucy was sitting in front of the TV. The sitter was next to her and working on her laptop.

"I'm headed out," I said. "Lucy, I might be home after you go to bed. I'll make sure to come in and give you a kiss."

"Have fun!" She waved.

My guilt about not coming home last night had been assuaged when I picked her up from school. She chattered on about watching a movie and eating pizza with Jennifer. She was none the worse for wear because I went out and had a little adult fun.

When I arrived at the factory, I was the first one there. Things had been shut down early for the day to give the employees time to go home and change. I turned on the lights and the punch fountain. Then I turned on the music in preparation for everyone.

As the employees trickled in, I personally thanked each and every one of them for their part in making it another successful season. I kept looking for Case. I was beginning to think he might not show. I couldn't really blame him. He didn't know anyone here.

I was sipping sparkling cider when I noticed him walk in. Everyone noticed him.

He was wearing jeans and his usual dress shirt. Even when he was trying to look casual, he looked hot. I walked to the door to greet him. "I wasn't sure you would show," I said.

"Sorry, got caught up with a client."

"No worries," I said and patted his arm. "We've got champagne, beer, or sparkling cider."

"I'll take a beer," he said.

I grabbed one from the bucket of ice and handed it to him. "I'll introduce you to everyone."

We made our way around the room. He shook hands and made small talk with everyone. It was like he'd known them all for years instead of minutes. I chalked it up to his frequent parties in Manhattan. He'd been brought up to do this exact thing. He knew how to schmooze. I could admit it was a very valuable skill.

"I need to do my little spiel," I told him.

"I'll be right here," he said and gave me a soft kiss on my cheek.

It was nice to have him there. It was like having a real partner. He made me feel supported. This was dangerous. I was beginning to wonder if this could actually work between us. The more time I spent with him, the more I wanted to be with him. He wasn't going to be in Pennsylvania forever. He was going to be going home soon. Then what? What happened then?

I couldn't think about that right then. I needed to focus on my people. "Everyone, can I have your attention please?" I said from the front of the room.

I waited until everyone ended their conversations and gave me their attention. "I want to thank you all for coming tonight," I said. "I wish I could give you all million-dollar bonuses. Unfortunately, that isn't possible. All I can do is try and show you all how much I appreciate every single one of you. Every one of you has brought something special to this business. Every single one of you is important. I never want anyone to feel like they are just another cog in the wheel. Without you, there would be a lot of very unhappy Valentines out there. You guys helped some very lucky guys and gals get lucky last night!"

There was laughter and applause. "You guys are all amazing. Drink up. Eat up. Enjoy the fruits of your labor! Thank you, thank you, thank you all!"

Another round of applause and everyone went back to their drinks and desserts spread out over the table. Case found me and wrapped an arm around my waist. "They love you," he said.

"I hope so, because I love them," I said. "They are all important to me. I know some bosses say that, but I mean it."

"I bet you have low turnover," he said.

"I've only had to hire three people in the last year, and that was just to keep up with the increase in demand."

"If I haven't said it today, let me say it now," he said before bending down to brush his lips over my ear. "You're amazing."

"Thank you," I said. "Have you tried some of the chocolates?"

"I've tried a few," he replied.

"Eat up," I said with a grin. "Free boozy chocolates doesn't happen often."

"No, it doesn't."

Thankfully for me, he was very comfortable being left alone while I talked with my employees. Once again, I felt like I had a partner. This was what life was about. It was programmed into our DNA to find that one person we could split the burden of life with. It was all about sharing the ups and downs. When I put Lucy to bed at night, I wanted to sit back and share my day with my partner.

He caught me staring at him and walked over to me. "Is everything okay?" he asked and touched my elbow.

It was such a simple but intimate gesture. "I'm great," I said with a smile.

"Are you upset that I was talking to them?"

"No, not at all," I said.

He tilted his head and studied me. When he looked at me like that, I felt like he was staring into my soul. "Something is on your mind."

"I was just thinking about how awesome you are," I said. "You fit in wherever you go, it seems like. Everyone here is smitten with you. They think you are pretty badass. More than one of them has come to me to tell me congratulations for snaring such a good guy."

"Really?" He flashed that cocky smile.

"Yes, really."

"How long until this thing is over?" he asked in that husky voice that was becoming very familiar.

"Not long." I winked.

Thankfully, my crew was not exactly the partying type. Not to mention, most of them had to work in the morning. The party started to wind down with people quietly exiting. I couldn't leave until the last one was gone. I had to lock up. With the crew gone, I locked the doors and headed back upstairs. Case was sitting at one of the tables with a beer in his hand.

"Is this the part where we have to clean up?" he asked.

I looked around the room. "*We* don't have to do anything. I'm going to leave the bulk of it for tomorrow. I just need to put away the cake and chocolates."

"I'll help," he offered.

"You have already done so much," I said. "You don't have to do that."

"I do. I want to. Anything that gets me a little more time with you."

I bent down and kissed him. "There you go with those smooth ways again."

"I can't help it." He laughed. "Did I tell you how many brothers and cousins I have? Us Manhattan men ooze charm. We are smooth from the moment we take our first breath. It's impossible to ignore it."

I rolled my eyes. "You're laying it on pretty thick."

He grabbed me when I moved to walk away. "Thick enough for a quickie?"

I smiled and kissed him before stepping away from him. "Quickie wouldn't be quick enough."

I started to pack up the chocolates and the rest of the food. I put the booze in my office to keep from violating any laws. "This is the last of it," he said and carried a bucket in.

"Thank you," I said. "You've saved me a lot of time."

"Then there's enough time for a little bit of fun," he said and pushed me against my desk.

His mouth slammed against mine. It was the same hunger I had been feeling since he walked through the door earlier. My hands roamed over his shoulders and down his back. His hands were all over me. He tugged my shirt up and slid his hand underneath to cup my breast through my bra. He groaned and squeezed harder.

I arched my back, pressing my breasts against him. The need was driving me crazy. I wanted him. Judging by the erection I felt pressed against my belly, he was feeling the same thing. If I didn't stop now, I was going to end up having sex with him on my desk.

"We can't," I breathed.

He groaned and rested his head against mine. "Okay," he said. "I'm sorry."

"Don't be sorry," I whispered with my hand resting against his cheek.

"Come to New York with me," he said.

"What?" I asked and leaned back to look him in the eyes.

"Come to New York with me for a few days," he said again. "You're not needed here. Things have slowed down. Come with me."

"I can't just up and leave," I said.

"I've spent time with you here and gotten to know your life," he reasoned. "Come learn about me. I want to show you Manhattan. I want to show you who I really am."

"I have Lucy," I said.

"Can she stay with Jennifer?" he asked. "I know you don't really trust me. You think I'm doing all this to persuade you into selling your company. The deal is separate from this. I want us to get to spend more time together."

I wanted to see him in his natural habitat. He was right about me being just a little suspicious about why he was spending so much time with me. This could be good. It could help me make a decision based on the offer and not what I was feeling for him.

"I can ask Jennifer if she can watch her for a couple of days," I said. "When are you thinking?"

"I need to head back tomorrow," I said. "I've got a lot of people counting on me."

"To close this deal?" I asked.

"Not just that," he answered. "I've got other clients. I just need to check in and touch base with my staff. Then I can give you the tour."

"You are very tempting," I said.

He kissed me again and showed me just how tempting he could be.

"Okay, let me make a call." I stepped away and grabbed my phone to call Jennifer. "Hey," I said in a low voice. "Are you busy?"

"Nope, what's up?"

"Do you have any jobs lined up over the next few days?" I asked.

"No, why?" she asked. "Are you okay?"

"I'm fine,' I said. "I was just wondering if you could watch Lucy for a few days. Case has invited me to New York."

She shouted before composing herself. "I'd love to. Is this really happening?"

"We'll talk later," I said without getting into too many details with him right behind me.

I hung up and turned back to Case. "She'll watch her."

"I'll book the flights." He grinned.

I couldn't resist walking into his arms. "I bet you are used to getting what you want, aren't you?"

"Not always."

"But most of the time." I laughed.

He pulled me against him and kissed me until I forgot why I was a little irritated with him for being spoiled.

25

CASE

This was big. This was bringing her home to meet the family. I never did that.

The women I had dated in the past might have known my family, but I didn't bring anyone around if I didn't have to. I was hoping I could show Emma I wasn't just some rich asshole trying to disrupt her life by buying her company. She needed to be able to trust me and I was certain the way to do that was to bring her into my life.

What we had was very one-sided. I invaded her space. It was time for her to take a step away from the day to day at her company and give her a chance to see what life could be like without the restraints ownership brought.

I tossed my bag in the back of the cab and headed for her place. I was assuming she was going to stay with me at my place, but if that made her nervous, I would happily get her a room. "Give me three minutes," I said to the cabbie as I climbed out.

I jogged up to the front stoop and knocked on her door. She opened it with a smile on her face. "Hi," she said.

"Hi. Ready?"

"I am." She nodded. "I can't believe I'm doing this."

"She's going to be fine," I assured her.

"I know," she replied. "She's very excited to hang out with Jennifer."

I picked up the suitcase by the door and waited for her to collect the last of her things. On the way to the airport, I held her hand. I could feel her nervousness. I felt a little bad that I was pulling her out of her comfort zone, but I was certain this would be good for her in the end. She worked too hard. She never took time for herself.

"So, I should ask this now before we get to the city," I started.

"Uh oh, that doesn't sound good," she said with a nervous laugh.

"Would you like to stay at my apartment, or do you want to get a hotel?" I asked her.

She answered my question with one of her own. "Do *you* want me at your place?"

I leaned over and kissed her. "I do, but I don't want to pressure you to do something you don't feel comfortable with."

"I don't think it makes sense to get a hotel," she answered. "I would like to spend time with you. I know you can afford it, but I don't think there's any reason to waste money on a room."

"Good!" I grinned. "I want you at my place. I want you in my bed."

"What else do you have planned for me?" she asked with a sly smile. "Please tell me it's more than just being in your bed."

"Would it be so terrible to be in my bed for the next three days?" I teased.

"No, but I've seen the city from a window." She laughed. "I was hoping to actually see it."

"We will," I promised. "The first thing we're doing when we land is get pizza. Real New York pizza."

"Is there really a difference?" she asked with a laugh.

My eyes widened and I pretended to be horrified. "Woman! That's blasphemous!"

She laughed again. "My bad. Will we be meeting your family?"

"Possibly," I said without committing to anything.

"I'm not asking to meet them," she said. "I don't want you to think I'm butting into your life."

"No," I corrected. "I want you to meet them."

"Tell me more about them," she said.

"I'm not sure where my brothers will be, but I imagine you'll meet Edwin for sure. He works in real estate. My brother Bram is a lawyer and I would imagine he will be around if he is not with his girlfriend, Rachel. Hans is iffy. He's a banker and his schedule can be a little wild along with he has a new girlfriend, Heather. Filip works with Edwin in real estate. Then there is Isac, who works at the investment firm. He's also hard to nail down. Lastly, there's the youngest, Gerrit. He's a tech guy and speaks a different language most of the time. If you ever want to feel old, talk to Gerrit."

She laughed and nodded. "I doubt I'll remember all those names, but I'll try."

"My mom is pretty easygoing now, but she does tend to default back into the prim and proper socialite," I explained. "I'm sure you'll get along with her."

"And your dad?" she asked.

I blew out a breath. "That one is a little different."

Thankfully, I didn't have to get into the story just yet. We arrived at the airport and went through security. The flight was short and uneventful. There was a car waiting to take us to my apartment. We walked in and I gave her the two-cent tour.

"Ready for that pizza?" I asked her.

"You were serious." She smiled.

"Very. I'm craving a pie. A good New York pie."

"Let's do this," she said. "I would hate to deprive a man."

I couldn't help but grab her ass as we headed for the elevator in my building once again. I took her to my favorite pizza place.

"Well?" I asked after she had taken a few bites.

"It's good," she said.

"Good? It's amazing! It's the best pizza ever. You can't deny that."

"I think you're very enthusiastic," she countered.

"Have you ever been to Times Square?" I asked.

She shook her head and wiped her mouth. "Nope. Never."

"Been to a Broadway show?"

"Nope," she answered.

"Any interest in seeing a Broadway show?" I asked.

"Can you get tickets on such short notice?" she questioned.

I smiled and pointed at my chest. "Case Manhattan here. I can get tickets."

She burst into laughter. "Of course, you can. I forget I'm eating pizza with royalty."

"What show do you want to see?" I asked and pulled out my phone.

"I've always heard great things about The Lion King," she said. "But I'm good with anything. I'm sure it's sold out."

I grinned and was already texting my hookup. After some back and forth, I secured two premium tickets. "Done," I said. "Seven o'clock."

"Seriously?"

"Of course," I said. "We'll roam around Times Square, go back to my place and change, and then go to dinner. We'll catch the show and I'm sure we'll both be spent, but if you want to get a drink, we can."

"Wow." She shook her head. "I guess that's the perks of living in the big city. You can plan a full day and still not even scrape the bucket of things to do."

"It's a loud, somewhat abrasive place to live, but you'll never be bored," I told her.

We finished our pizza and headed to the square. It wasn't all that exciting for someone who saw it all the time, but I knew how overwhelming it could be to those who had never seen it. We wandered around for hours.

"I think this is what you should wear tonight," I said and pointed to a mannequin in a store window.

"You do, huh?" She laughed.

"Let me buy it for you," I said.

"No! You are not buying me a dress."

"It's for me, not you," I argued. "I see that dress and all I can think about is taking it off."

"If that's the case, I could just be naked," she countered.

I slowly shook my head and grabbed her hand as I led her into the store. "Not the same. The thrill is taking it off. Please let me buy it for you."

"This is one of those situations that I'm sure you are used to getting what you want," she said.

I was barely listening. I talked to the salesgirl who was already moving to get the correct size. I handed the dress to her. "Try it on," I said. "If you don't like it, I'll drop it."

"Case, it's beautiful, but I can't let you buy me a dress."

"Yes, you can," I said and ushered her toward the changing room.

I waited and looked around the shop. When she came out of the dressing room, she was wearing her jeans. "You don't like it?" I asked with disappointment.

"I love it, but you're going to have to wait to see it," she said with a saucy smile.

The anticipation was going to kill me. We went back to my place to get ready for our night on the town. It was damn near impossible to keep my hands off her. I wanted her. It was insane how badly I wanted her. I had never wanted a woman as badly as I wanted her.

She stepped out of the bedroom wearing the blue dress that hugged her curves. It was perfect. I knew she was going to look amazing, but this was so much more than I could have imagined. "Stunning," I breathed.

"You have excellent taste." She laughed. "You and Jennifer would get along very well. She's an amazing shopper as well."

I couldn't resist and pulled her into my arms. I kissed her, but because I wasn't an animal, I was very careful not to muss up her hair or makeup. "Ready?" I asked somewhat breathlessly.

"Ready," she replied.

Dinner followed by the show had been fun. I would never claim to love Broadway but watching a show with her made it better. I had sat through the show before and had been unimpressed. It wasn't my jam. But with her, I was bummed when it was over.

"Amazing," she gasped. "That was so much better than I could have dreamed of. I'm so moved. I felt the music in my soul."

"I'm glad you liked it," I said as we climbed into the waiting car.

When we got back to my place, we changed and settled in on the couch with a glass of wine. "You live such a different life than I do," she said.

"What do you mean?"

"You go to Broadway shows and get around in cabs or hired drivers," she said. "You have a hundred different restaurants at your fingertips. There's so much life here."

"True, but like I said, it can be a bit much, which is why I have the house. Sometimes I need to get away. Being in the city means any of my brothers or even my father can stop by anytime. We don't work side by side, but the buildings we work in are all on the same block. It gets a little crowded. I don't always want to be under my father's thumb."

"Does he keep a close eye on you?" she asked.

I rolled my eyes. "Yes. I'm thirty-two but he seems to think I'm twelve. We don't even work in the same office, but he has his hands in my business. He's always telling me what I need to do. He's so worried I'm going to fail and embarrass him."

"Is there more focus on you because you're the oldest?" she asked.

I nodded and sipped my wine. "Definitely. He's hard on my brothers, but I feel like he rides me the hardest."

"Was it like that when you were younger?"

"Oh yes." I nodded. "Absolutely. My dad is one of those guys that could win the lottery eight times without trying. Shit just happens for him. He closes deals with little effort. People just like him. He walks into a room and people behave like he's the sun. He casts a long shadow."

"I think you've certainly risen to the occasion," she said gently. "You are successful. You definitely inherited the sun thing. My staff was enamored with you. You walked into the room, and it was a total shift in the atmosphere. I know what it's like to feel like you haven't lived up to expectations, but I've learned no one else gets to use their measuring stick on you."

I looked at her and was thoroughly impressed. "Did your parents do that to you?"

She looked into her glass of wine. "My mom died early, so I don't think so. My dad, well honestly, I just don't think he cared."

"He didn't care?" I asked.

"My dad was never in the running for father of the year," she said. "He didn't want kids. He made sure we knew that. Marie pretty much raised me. He was never around. If we'd had relatives, I know he would have shipped us off. He said as much. We were an albatross around his neck."

"I'm sorry," I said.

"Don't be." She shrugged. "It's weird, but I don't care. I never felt like I was lacking for anything. He wasn't hateful, but he wasn't loving. He was there. He kept food on the table, and we lived an okay life. It was just me and Marie."

"Losing her had to have been devastating," I said gently.

She sighed. "It would have killed me if I didn't have to pull my shit together to take care of Lucy. Marie, even in her last months, was so strong. It's weird, but she helped me grieve before she was even gone. When she did pass, it's terrible to say, but it was almost a relief. Those last few weeks were rough. She was ready, which made me ready."

"And now you're out here kicking ass and taking names," I said with a small laugh.

She flashed a grin. "You know it. What doesn't kill you makes you stronger and all that."

"Absolutely."

I watched her drink and realized I was falling hard. There was so much about her that impressed me. I was in awe of her. I wanted to be with her more and more.

"I know I've said it before, but you really are incredible," I said. "I've never met anyone like you. Being with you makes me feel like

I'm on solid ground. I couldn't quite put my finger on what I was feeling, but now I get it. I've been drifting and you're my life raft."

Her warm smile hit me square in the belly. "That's a very good
way to put it. I feel the same. At the party, I felt like I had a partner.
I've been alone for a long time and it's never bothered me, but when
you were there, it was nice. It felt good to look around the room and
see you."

We were on the same page. My heart felt fuller. I put down my
wine glass and took hers and got to my feet before leading her to the
bedroom.

26

EMMA

When I woke up, I knew immediately he wasn't there. I sat up and looked around the room. There was a note on his pillow. I picked it up and read the short note aloud. "I had to go into the office. We've got plans tonight. Be ready by six. See you soon."

The blinds were closed, keeping the room fairly dark. I wondered what time it was. I reached for my phone and damn near choked. "Holy shit!"

It was ten o'clock. I couldn't even remember the last time I slept so late. Despite being in what I had decided yesterday was one of the nosiest cities in the world, his apartment was quiet. I didn't hear birds, lawnmowers, or traffic. I didn't hear the footsteps of a little girl looking for breakfast or wondering if she could play with her slime. Whoever created slime was not a mom and never had to clean the crap out of a little girl's clothing or carpet.

Just then, I would have loved to get the slime and played with her. I missed her. I had planned to call her before she went to school. Mom fail. Aunt fail. I failed. To try and alleviate my guilt, I called Jennifer. I knew she would have called me if anything happened, but I still felt terribly guilty.

"Hey," I said when she answered. "I'm so sorry I didn't call earlier. How is she?"

"She's fine and don't be sorry," she said.

"Did she ask about me?"

"I told her you were having a lot of fun with Case and you would call her after school," she said. "Don't worry about her forgetting you. You are her entire world."

"I feel so bad I didn't call her before school," I said with a groan.

"Stop. You're allowed to have fun. What were you doing that you didn't call? Getting a little something-something from your hot hunk of a man?"

I laughed and walked out to the kitchen. There was a sticky note on his coffee machine with an arrow pointing to a rack with what looked like every kind of coffee under the sky. "No, I was passed out cold."

"You were sleeping?" she asked with obvious surprise.

"Yep. Alone. He went to work."

"Damn, I bet that felt good," she said.

"It did," I said. "How was last night? Did she go to bed without fussing?"

"She did great," she insisted. "We had fun. Today I'm picking her up and we're going to McDonald's for a treat."

"You're spoiling her." I laughed.

"Yes, I am and I'm not ashamed," she replied. "What did you do on your first night in the big city?"

"Oh my gosh," I gushed. "We went to Times Square and had an amazing dinner at a fancy restaurant. He got tickets to The Lion King. It was so fun."

"Good! I'm glad you're enjoying yourself. How are things going with you and Case?"

I sipped the coffee before carrying it to the living room, flooded in natural light. I sat down and stared out the window. "I'm almost afraid to say it."

"Say what?" she asked, and I could hear the concern in her voice.

"I think—" I stopped. The words caught in my throat.

"You think what?" she asked. "Did something happen?"

"No," I said. "It's just, I don't know what to call this feeling. Love feels too strong, but I think I might actually be falling for him. Is that stupid? Crazy? Dangerous?"

"I think it's awesome," she said. "It's not stupid. Why would you think it's stupid?"

"Because I barely know him," I said. "He's so different from me. How could this ever work?"

"Love conquers all!" She laughed.

"Funny."

"Are you really falling in love?" she asked.

"I think so," I sighed. "He likes Lucy, and she is crazy about him. He's a good man. We have so much fun together. I know it sounds cheesy, but he makes me feel whole. I feel like I'm not alone in life. I know I have you and Lucy but having him at my side is different."

"I get it," she said. "I want you to have that. From what I've seen, he's a good guy. If he makes you happy, go for it. Don't try and talk yourself out of this. You're in New York with him. Live it up. Don't hold back. Have fun with him and follow your heart."

"I'm terrified to fall in love with this man," I told her.

"Why?"

"I don't know," I said. "I don't want a broken heart. I know he is probably one of the few people on this planet that can break my heart."

"You're borrowing trouble," she warned.

"I know, I know."

"Just let yourself go," she said. "Put down the walls and get out there and really live. You can play it safe forever and never experience the highs or the lows or dare to love. Dare to put yourself out there and reap the rewards."

"You're always very philosophical when it comes to me, but when the shoe is on the other foot, you're far less prone to the peace and love vibe."

"That's because I've had my heart smashed a few times." She laughed. "I put myself out there all the time."

"He left me a note," I said. "He's got plans for us again tonight."

"That's exciting."

"I think I'm going to venture out and do a little shopping," I told her. "Although I need to find the part of town I can afford. He lives in a luxury apartment in a neighborhood with limos lining the street."

"I'm sure you'll find something," she said. "Now go and enjoy your day. Don't worry about anything here. Lucy and I are having fun. This is good practice for me."

"Uh, do you have something to tell me?" I asked.

"No, but one day I want one of these little gremlins," she said. "I need to see if I can hang."

"You'll hang just fine," I assured her.

We hung up and I finished a leisurely cup of coffee before going to shower. His apartment was impressive. I wondered what his house would be like. He said he lived by the water and had a private dock, but he never really said much more about the place. I dressed in my jeans and a pretty chenille sweater before heading out. The doorman offered to get me a cab, but I insisted on walking.

I wanted to see as much of the city as I could. I meandered in and out of several shops in search of another dress for tonight. I finally found one I was certain he would like. I wanted to look good for him. I didn't know where we were going, but I wanted to impress him. I knew he was a big shot around the city. Last night there had been more than one person that wanted to shake his hand. I was certain I had caught a few people trying to take our picture as well. I remembered what happened at the hotel at home. I did not want to be caught looking frumpy and undeserving of his attention.

I suspected that might have also been a motivating factor in his decision to buy me the dress yesterday. I was on the arm of one of the wealthiest and most eligible bachelors in the city. Hell, the state. I needed to look the part. I didn't want to read a headline about why I was so undeserving of his attention. He was a ten. I had to be at least a seven.

He called when I was on my way back to the apartment. "Good morning, gorgeous," he said.

"I think it's afternoon," I replied.

"Are you enjoying a leisurely day?"

"I'm shopping," I told him. "I'm actually on my way back to the apartment now."

"What are you shopping for?" he asked.

"I bought a dress for tonight," I answered. "Want to give me a hint about where we're going?"

"It's a surprise," he said, and I could hear the smile in his voice. "Is it a sexy dress?"

"It's a surprise," I said, throwing his own words back at him.

"I can't wait to see you," he said.

"How long will you be?"

"Not long," he said. "I'm trying to get out of here. I'm sorry it's taking me so long. I was hoping to be in and out of here quickly."

"It's okay," I assured him. "I'm going to go back to your luxury apartment and take a long, hot bath in that massive tub. I bought some bubble bath."

He groaned. "You're teasing me."

"Hurry home," I said.

We ended the call and I followed through with my promise. The walking last night and again today had left my feet sore. It wasn't the same as hiking. It felt far more intense. I took my time getting dressed and doing my makeup.

"Emma?" I heard Case call out.

"In here," I said.

He walked into his bathroom. I was just finishing up my makeup. "Hi," I said.

"You're killing me," he groaned. "You're so fucking hot."

"Thank you."

"I'm going to take a quick shower and we'll go," he said.

"Where are we going?"

He dropped a kiss on my forehead before he started to strip in front of me. "You'll find out soon."

I watched him step into the shower and was very tempted to follow him in. He wasn't kidding about taking a quick shower. He was out and dressed within fifteen minutes. I was a moth to a flame. I kissed his neck, inhaling the scent of his soap and shampoo. A hint of musky cologne clung to him. It was so good I was tempted to climb him and beg him to forget all his plans.

"Are you going to tell me where we're going yet?" I asked with my tongue trailing down the side of his neck.

"If you don't stop that, we're going to be going to the bedroom," he growled.

"Would that really be a bad thing?"

He put his hands on my hips and pushed me away. "We're going to be late, and trust me, we don't want to be late."

"Late for?"

"Dinner," he answered with a sexy grin.

As usual, there was a car waiting for us when we stepped into the cool February air. The car started down the road and I found myself watching him. I was trying to figure out just what it was I felt for him. It was confusing.

He reached over and took my hand with his lips brushing over the back of my knuckles. "We're going to a family dinner."

I froze. "What?"

"My parents would like to meet you," he said. "A few of my brothers are free and will be there as well."

"Case, this is kind of a lot to spring on me," I complained.

"Just be you," he said. "There's no pressure to be anything but who you are. They've been hounding me to bring you over. I'd like you to meet them."

I licked my lips. It did little to appease the dry mouth I suddenly had. This was a big step. I wasn't sure how to act. It was like meeting the queen. Did I curtsy? Were there going to be eleven forks at dinner that I could embarrass myself with? I wasn't fancy. I didn't hang out with billionaires. This was so far out of my league.

"If I do anything wrong, please tell me," I said. "Don't let me make an ass of myself."

"Relax." He chuckled. "We're normal people. They are going to love you. Just be you."

That was a lot easier said than done.

27

CASE

It was a risk taking her to meet the family so soon into our relationship, but I had to do it. My family knew I had been seeing her, and if I didn't bring her to them, they would show up at an inopportune time. It was better to get it over with. It was a lot like pulling a band-aid off. I wanted to rip it off and suffer three seconds of pain rather than hours of agony.

"Ready?" I asked when the car pulled to a stop.

"If I say no, can we go back to your place?"

I kissed her. "I promise it will be fine. If you're really uncomfortable, say the word and we'll go."

We climbed out of the car and headed up the stairs to the front door of my parents' home. I rang the bell and waited. Bram opened it with a big grin on his face. "I thought you were out of town?" I asked.

He pulled me in for a hug and slapped my back. "I had to be here for this."

I stepped back and pulled Emma beside me. "Emma, this is Bram."

"Bram." She nodded. "You're number two or three?"

Bram looked at me with amusement. "Three," he answered. "You told her about us?"

"I warned her about you guys," I corrected.

"Come in," he said. "Mom's still cooking. Hans and Edwin are in the den. We were just having a drink."

"Is dad here?" I asked as we stepped into the foyer.

"He was on the phone," Bram said.

I was doing my best to hide my nervousness. I had no idea what to expect from my father after our meeting earlier today. Things had been contentious. He was pissed at me for being out of town for so long. My work didn't suffer, but he was convinced I was fucking around and not living up to the family name. By his standards, I probably wasn't.

I had told him about Emma. I let him know there were feelings there and things were a little complicated. What started as me trying to get to know her to find a way in, had transformed. It started out as a tactic. As a way to get the deal closed, but it had changed. His response had been about what I expected. His first concern was the deal. I assured him the deal might still happen, but my top priority was Emma. I was certain I was falling in love with her. He didn't seem interested in giving me advice. He didn't congratulate me on finding the one. His only words had been to bring her to dinner.

I didn't tell Emma because I didn't want to put that kind of pressure on her. I didn't want her to know my father was going to be sizing her up. He could be a fair man, but he was discerning. When he met someone, it was up to that person to prove to him they weren't an asshole. He was a "guilty until proven innocent" kind of man.

"Do you want a drink?" I asked Emma.

"Yes, please."

Hans came to stand beside myself and Emma. "Hello," he said, and I heard the flirting in his voice.

I shot him a look. "Hans, this is Emma."

Emma looked at him. "Number two." She nodded.

"You numbered us?" Hans asked with amusement.

"Made it easier." I shrugged.

"Hi, Emma," Hans said and was once again turning on his charm.

I put my arm around her and pulled her close while shooting him a warning look. He grinned in return. "It's nice to meet you, Emma," he said and took his drink back to the chair he'd been in.

"Do I sense some healthy competition between you guys?" she asked quietly.

"Yes." I laughed. "Always has been. We used to race downstairs to see who could get to the table first. We competed in sports. If there was anything to compete for, we did it."

"Including women?" she asked with a smile.

I grimaced and nodded. "There was more than one fistfight over a girl."

"Your poor parents," she said. "I can't imagine trying to keep you all in line."

"They didn't," Bram said.

"They tried," Hans chimed in.

Edwin finished his phone call and finally made his way over to introduce himself. "So, you're Emma," he said and shook her hand. "I've heard a lot about you."

"Is that good or bad?" she asked with a small laugh.

"All good," Edwin said before giving me a slight nod. That was essentially his approval.

"Dinner is ready." Mom appeared in the doorway. She paused when she saw Emma. She walked in and directly to Emma. "Hello," she said.

"Mom, this is Emma," I said. "Emma, this is my mother, Nina."

"Hello, Mrs. Manhattan," Emma said and shook her hand. "Thank you for having me tonight."

"Of course," mom said and turned to walk out.

The rest of us fell in line and headed for the dining room. Our father was already seated at the head of the table. He watched me pull out the chair for Emma. "Dad, this is Emma," I said. "Emma, Britt Manhattan, my father."

"Hello," Emma said.

"It's nice to meet you," he muttered.

Dinner was served and it was mom who got the conversation started. "Tell us what you do, Emma."

"I own a chocolate factory," she answered.

"A chocolate factory!" mom exclaimed. "Oh my. Where?"

"Harrisburg, Pennsylvania," Emma answered.

"Oh, you're the reason my son has been in Pennsylvania this whole time," mom said.

Emma blushed. "I suppose."

"What kind of chocolate?" Hans asked. "Case said it was boozy?"

Emma laughed softly. "It is chocolate infused with liquor. We have a wide variety."

"I think I've had those before," mom said. "We have some friends that always give us a box at Christmas. You remember, Britt. The ones with the brandy you like."

"I remember," dad said without looking up from his plate.

"You own the company?" mom asked.

I felt like we were heading into some pretty dangerous territory. The last thing I needed was dad to start talking about James and his desire to buy the business. I could practically feel the tension growing thicker by the second.

"I do," Emma said. "I started it a few years ago. It's slowly growing."

"This is really good, mom," I said when it looked like my dad was going to chime in.

"Thank you." She smiled. "I'm putting those cooking lessons to good use."

"Yes, you are." I nodded.

"What's the name of your company?" Hans asked.

"Miller's Chocolates," Emma answered.

"I'm going to have to look it up," he replied.

"I wouldn't bother," dad said.

I felt the turning point like a dagger in my heart. "Dad, don't," I warned.

"I'm sorry, why wouldn't he look it up?" Emma asked. I felt her prickling beside me. She wasn't an imposing woman, but I knew her and what she'd gone through. She might not be big, and she didn't look tough, but I knew otherwise.

"You won't own it much longer and I happen to know the buyer will be changing the name," dad answered nonchalantly.

"Dad!" I warned again.

"I have not agreed to sell it," Emma said in a tight voice. "I'm considering the offer, but nothing is a done deal. I believe your buyer might be jumping the gun a bit."

"From what I understand, my son has been doing his best to convince you to sell," dad said and folded his hands. "You're here on his dime. He's wined you and dined you and he's pretty sure you're going to accept the offer."

She cleared her throat. "Excuse me?

"Dad," I warned.

"No, I'd like to hear what he has to say," she said with her hand on my forearm.

"It's nothing personal," dad said. "Case is very good at his job. The client he is working for is a longtime family friend and client. Case is doing whatever it takes to make the client happy. That's why we gave him so much leeway with this particular situation. He explained you were having some doubts and he needed to convince you it was the right decision. This little fake romance was his ticket to closing the deal."

"Dad, stop!"

"I see," Emma said.

Everyone at the table was dead silent. No one was chiming in. They all knew better. When dad was on one of these rolls, the best thing to do was sit back and stay out of the way.

"You've done a great job building your company," dad said as if his compliment was going to mean anything now. "You've caught the eye of a man that will take the company to the next level. Be proud of what you've accomplished. From what I understand, the offer is extremely generous. You can do anything you want and never have to worry about working another day in your life."

Emma dabbed at her mouth with the cloth napkin before putting it on her plate. "Mrs. Manhattan, the meal, what I was able to eat of it, was delicious. Thank you." She got to her feet. "It was a pleasure to meet all of you."

"Emma, wait!" I called out as she rushed out of the dining room. She was making long strides toward the door. "Emma, stop! Let me explain!"

She jerked open the front door and headed for the sidewalk. "Leave me alone, Case."

"He was out of line," I said.

"Yes, he was," she said with her hand raised in an attempt to flag down a cab.

"I didn't tell him this was fake," I said. "He made that part up."

She spun around. Her eyes were flashing with anger. "That part?" she seethed. "You were working me. All of this was exactly what I thought it was. You were playing me from the beginning. I should have known."

"I'm not playing you," I said and tried to take her hand.

She jerked away from me. "Don't," she hissed. "Don't touch me. You can drop the act. Let me make it very clear to you and your client and your daddy. I'm not selling Miller's to you or anyone else. Ever. Hear me? Don't you dare show your face in my store again. I don't want to see you ever again. Tell your doorman to let me into your apartment so I can get my things."

"What are you going to do?" I asked.

"I'm getting the hell out of here! I'm getting away from you!"

"Emma, please," I said. "My dad was way out of line."

A cab pulled to a stop at the curb. The one time I didn't actually want a cab, one showed up. She got in before I could say a word. I watched the taillights fade away. She was leaving. That was that.

"Are you okay?" Edwin asked as he came to stand beside me.

"Honestly, no," I said.

He put a hand on my shoulder. "I'm sorry. Why don't you go after her?"

"She is not in the mood to talk," I said dryly.

"I'm sorry," he said again.

"Whatever," I sighed. "I'm going to go. I just need to give her time to get her stuff from my apartment. She doesn't want to see me right now."

"Are you going to talk to dad?"

"Hell no," I said. "I don't trust myself not to say something I can't take back. Right now, I'm pissed. I need to cool down."

"That's probably a good idea," he said. "For what it's worth, I like her."

"You knew her for five minutes," I snapped.

"But what I got to know, I liked."

"Doesn't really matter now though, does it?" I said. "He just torpedoed the deal as well as the relationship. There is no way in hell she's going to sell that company now. Not to me. I wouldn't be surprised if she sought out another buyer just to keep it out of our hands."

"She's pissed," he said. "Dad was pretty hurtful. Mom is in there giving him a sound scolding. I have no doubt you'll be able to fix this. She's into you."

"Was," I said. "She was into me. You don't know her like I do. This just destroyed everything. I don't know if there is any coming back from this. She's guarded. She's lost so much in her life. This is a lot more than just some asshole being rude."

He nodded and patted my shoulder. "Sorry, man."

28

EMMA

I tossed my shit in my bag without bothering to fold it. I would worry about wrinkles later. The dress he bought me was hanging on the back of the door. The temptation to slash it was strong. I resisted and left it where it was. I didn't even have a flight booked as I headed to the airport. I didn't want to be at his apartment when he got home. I didn't want to talk to him. My heart was crushed. I was afraid I would bawl my eyes out. I didn't want him to know how bad he had hurt me.

Lucky for me, I got a flight out and was home by ten.

"What the hell are you doing here?" Jennifer asked with shock. "You scared the shit out of me."

"Sorry," I said. "It was a last-minute thing. I didn't have time to call."

"What the hell is going on?" she asked.

I couldn't stop it. The tears were rolling down my cheeks. "Is she in bed?"

"Yes, an hour ago," she said and patted the couch beside her. "Come sit."

I kicked off my shoes and hung my jacket up before taking her up on the offer. "I need tequila."

"Sit tight," she said and hopped up. She came back in with the bottle and a glass. She poured me a shot and handed it to me. "Whenever you're ready."

I took the shot and held out the glass for a refill. She poured it and I slammed another one. "I was right," I said.

"You were right about what?"

"It was all bullshit. He played me. I'm an idiot and actually fell for it."

"What do you mean he played you?" she asked.

"We went to dinner with his family tonight," I said. "We had just sat down when his father was so kind to point out that the relationship was fake. He was only pretending to like me to get me to sell. His father said Case was notorious for being able to close deals. That's all I am. He was playing me. The whole time I thought we were actually developing a relationship, he was working me. He was gently pushing me into selling and I didn't even see it."

"Are you sure?" she asked. "That seems pretty manipulative. The couple times I met him, I didn't get that vibe from him."

"Me either," I said. "That's why he's so good at his job. He wasn't interested in me. He was interested in closing the deal. He only wanted my factory."

"I'm so sorry," she said. "What a dick. What a total complete asshole. I'm sorry I encouraged you to go for it. He fooled me as well."

"I just can't believe he was going to walk away after he got my company," I said. "I just keep replaying every conversation we've ever had about the company. I didn't see it at the time, but he was feeling me out. He was trying to figure out how much longer he had to keep pretending to want me."

"He wasn't pretending," she said.

"Yes, he was," I said. "Don't defend him."

"I saw the way he looked at you," she insisted.

"Yeah, he wanted to fuck me," I snapped. "He wanted in my pants and I welcomed him. I'm not doubting he didn't enjoy the time we spent in bed, but it wasn't what I thought it was. He gave me some bullshit line about having feelings for me and all that crap. It was all bullshit. I feel so stupid."

"Don't feel stupid," she said. "What did he say about it?"

"I didn't give him the chance to say anything," I said. "What was there for him *to* say? It was all true. He didn't deny it. He said he wanted to explain it."

"Maybe he told his dad one thing but felt another?" she offered. "He could be stuck between a rock and a hard place. He's trying to please the both of you."

"So, he told his dad he was only pretending to like me?" I snorted. "Gee, that's so much better."

"I know you're hurting right now," she said gently. "I just think it might be a good idea to hear him out."

As if on cue, my phone started vibrating. His name was on the screen. It was like being slapped in the face. I declined the call. "I don't want to talk to him. I have nothing to say to him. He used me. I feel like such an idiot. I should have known a man like him would never truly be interested in someone like me. He's used to dating women in his social circle. He probably told his dad and brothers all about the sacrifice he was making for the company."

"You are not a sacrifice," she said.

"Was it all fake?" I asked. "What about Lucy? Did he fake that?"

"I doubt it," she said with a smile. "There's no faking love for Lucy. She's a great kid and very easy to love."

"I shouldn't have introduced him to her," I said. "That's on me. I have held back on dating because I didn't want to involve her in stuff like this. What am I supposed to tell her when she asks about him? 'Gee, Lucy, he didn't really like hanging out with us, he just wanted our family business.'"

"You don't need to tell her anything," she said. "If she asks, you tell her he lives far away. She'll forget him soon enough."

"I hope so," I muttered. "I hope I can forget about him soon too. There were so many red flags and I ignored them. He turned that charm on and I turned into a bumbling idiot. I fell for his bullshit hook, line, and sinker. I was an easy mark."

My phone vibrated again. It was a text message from him. I didn't even bother to open it. I didn't care what he said.

"You are not an easy mark," she said. "He obviously saw something in you he liked. He didn't have to spend time with you. He did that because he wanted to."

"It was part of his game!" I shrieked. "He played me. The deal was going to make him shine in his daddy's eyes. He's the oldest of six boys. He told me his dad holds him to a higher standard and that it can be a lot of pressure to live up to that standard. So here I come along and give him the perfect play. He got to show his daddy just how good he was. He was getting the tough deal done. He was using all that Manhattan charm to close the deal just like his daddy. All the things he told me are just more proof his father wasn't lying. I just didn't see it."

She was quiet for several seconds. "I don't know what to say," she murmured. "He fooled me as well and I'm usually a pretty good judge of assholes."

"I guess he's just got a lot more practice than we do," I muttered. "He probably looked at me and laughed. I was easy pickings. He knew a little flattery and hot sex and he would be in. He didn't have to do anything more than send me some roses and take me to dinner. This is what happens when you've been out of the game for so long. I was so hungry for a man's attention I didn't listen to the warnings the logical side of me was shouting."

"I'm so sorry," she said again and gave me a hug.

"I'm humiliated," I said with fresh tears rolling down my cheeks. "They were all looking at me like I was a moron. They all knew. They knew I wasn't one of them. I can't believe I actually thought he was taking me to meet his family because we were getting serious. It was nothing like that."

"He's an asshole," she said like a true best friend. "If he calls again, I'll give him a piece of my mind."

"Thanks, but there's no point. He's out of my life. He got his fun in. He can go back to his client and tell him he failed. There is no way in hell I would ever consider his offer. Ever. He can fuck off. All of them can. I don't need their money. I am doing just fine on my own. We might not live in a massive brownstone or drive Ferraris but we're happy."

"That's right," she said. "You are a good woman and the right man is out there. You kissed a frog and he turned out to be a snake. You'll find your prince."

"I don't want to kiss any more frogs," I pouted.

She patted my leg. "You will. Give it time. You put yourself out there and got burned. You'll heal and be ready to get out there again."

I sighed and felt defeated. So defeated and tired. "I'm going to go to bed. Are you going to stay in the guest room?"

"I think I'll go home," she said. "If you're okay?"

"I'm fine," I said. "I just need to sleep. I'll be good as new tomorrow."

"I hope so," she said and gave me another hug. "Call me if you need anything."

"Thank you. And thanks for staying with her. I really appreciate it. Despite how the day ended, I did have fun today. I'm just going to pretend he never walked into my life."

After locking up, I headed to bed. My mind was spinning while my heart broke over and over. His father's words were on repeat in my head. What would ever make someone be so cruel? There were so many other ways he could have gone about making this deal happen. Why did he have to worm his way into my life? Into Lucy's life? That was what pissed me off the most. He didn't have to bring her into it. That was a low blow.

My phone was still vibrating. I had to give it to the guy, he was persistent. But I wasn't going to be swayed. I should have been firm in my rejection of the offer. It was the money. He had dazzled me with the money and that was his intention. As much as I blamed him for what he did, I had to shoulder some of the blame. I was the one blinded by the good looks and sexy smile.

"Never again," I said with a conviction that reached down to my toes.

I was never going to let anyone take advantage of me like that again. It wasn't just me. It was Lucy. I couldn't have a revolving door of men waltzing in and out of her life. It wasn't fair to her.

29

CASE

I had not slept all night. I certainly tried to, but every time I closed my eyes, I saw the hurt on her face. She wasn't answering my calls or texts. I didn't really blame her. My dad had crossed a line. He knew I had feelings for Emma. He knew it was much more than just a deal. I told him as much. I assumed he did what he did because he was pissed I wasn't solely focused on the deal.

Before I could attempt to fix things with Emma, I needed to clear the air with my father. I wasn't going to let this fester. Festering led to blowups and that would lead to a family rift. We'd had our fair share of arguments and there were hurt feelings on occasion, but we were tightknit. I didn't want to destroy that closeness.

I climbed out of the cab in front of my parents' house and headed up the stairs. I rang the bell and waited. Mom answered the door. "Hi," she said with a soft smile. "How are you?"

"Fine. Is he here?"

"He's in his office," she said. "Can I get you a drink? A snack?"

"No thank you."

"Did you talk to her?" she asked as we walked down the hall together.

"No," I answered. "She isn't taking my calls."

"Give her some time," she said. "She was hurt and embarrassed. I'm sure she'll calm down."

"I doubt it," I muttered and knocked on his office door before pushing it open.

He looked up at me when I walked through the door. "Son," he said.

"We need to talk," I told him.

"Sit." He gestured to a chair. "Can I pour you a drink?"

"No. This won't take long. I've got things to do."

"Pennsylvania?"

"Yes," I said and took a moment to gather my thoughts. I'd been reciting what I would say to him all morning. "Last night was not okay. I don't know why you felt the need to say what you did, but it was wrong. You hurt her."

"My intention was never to hurt anyone," he said.

"You did. I'll take some responsibility. I wasn't totally honest with you. Emma isn't just the owner of a company I was trying to buy for James. Yes, it started that way, but it evolved. I have genuine feelings for her. I thought if I got to know her and let her get to know me, she would be more open to selling her company. She didn't outright reject my offer. I thought there was a way to soften her up. As it turned out, we got to know each other, and I realized I really liked her. Hell, dad, I told you yesterday that I think I'm falling in love with her."

He leaned back in his chair and slowly nodded. "I see."

"I need you to understand something," I said. "Emma is more important than the deal. James Lyons is way too used to getting what he wants. I should have questioned his intentions. Why her company? Why did he want to buy Miller's? Is it another one of his stupid vanity projects? I'm going to lose the deal and I don't care. She doesn't want to sell, and I understand why. It's not just a company for her. It's important to her. James wants it because he's a bored, wealthy man. He doesn't know the first thing about running a chocolate factory. I won't do it."

"You really love her?" he asked.

"I think so. I don't know. I don't know if it matters after what happened last night."

"I didn't really think you cared about her," he said. "I thought she was just another one of your passing flings."

"She's not," I said. "I want you to understand that if I can get her to forgive me, she will be a part of my life. I will be spending more time with her. If you can't accept that, we have nothing more to talk about."

"Son, I didn't know," he said.

"Now you do. I know James is your friend, but I can't work with him."

He nodded. "That's fine. I get it. The guy can be a real prick sometimes. He keeps us busy at the law firm because he's always getting his big mouth in trouble. You do what you have to do. If you love this girl, or think you love her, then I want you to be happy. I would never stop you from finding love. All I want for any of you is to be happy. That's it."

It wasn't how I expected the conversation to go. I was pleasantly surprised he was being so accepting. "Thank you, dad."

"I take it you'll be gone for a few days?"

I grinned as I got to my feet. "I hope so."

We stood and shook hands. I called a cab and waited outside. While I waited for my ride home, I called James Lyons. It was going to be a good feeling to tell him to fuck off.

"Case," he answered. "I've been expecting your call. Do you have the banking info? Where do I need to wire the money?"

"You don't need to wire it anywhere," I said. "She isn't selling."

"Dammit, Case," he growled. "You were supposed to be getting this done."

"She said no."

"I don't care what she said," he said. "Make it happen."

"What are you going to do with the place?" I asked him.

"That's not your problem," he shot back. "I'll go up to six million, but not a penny more. I want it done by the end of the week. I'm done waiting."

"Sorry, James. You'll be waiting a long time. I'm not going to ask her to sell. In fact, I'm not going to get any company to sell to you again. I'm done. You'll need to find yourself a new CPA."

"What the hell are you saying?" he snapped.

"I'm saying I can't work with you anymore," I said. "I can't be a part of destroying companies. You see something you want, and I jump to do your bidding. You don't care about the people that make those companies so appealing to you. You don't take the time to understand the companies. You buy them and destroy what makes them special."

"Don't you tell me how to run my business!" he spat. "You're not paid to worry about what I do. You're paid to get the job done. Period."

"Yep, you're right," I said. "Good luck to you."

I ended the call with him shouting. The cab pulled up. I hopped in and headed back to my place. I tried calling Emma one more time. She wasn't answering. I hoped she would give me a chance. Clearly, that door was slammed shut pretty hard. I didn't know how to get her to open it. I didn't think it was a good idea for me to show up at her door. It would just piss her off even more.

Edwin called while I was moping at my place. I was thinking about heading out to my home in Great Neck. I wanted to get out of the city for a few days. I needed to retreat and lick my wounds.

"Did you talk to dad?" he asked.

"I did."

"Is he at the hospital?" he joked.

"No," I answered. "It actually went very well. I told him I had real feelings for Emma. When I explained it was a lot more than just me trying to close a deal, he gave me the green light. I fired James Lyons. I'm done with him. I'm done being his little bitch."

"No shit!" he exclaimed. "Dad knows you did that?"

"He does," I said. "He told me to do it."

"Damn, I didn't know the old man had it in him."

"Me either," I said.

"Now what?" he asked.

"Now what, what?"

"Did you talk to Emma?" he questioned.

"Nope. She won't answer my calls. She's pissed. I think that is done."

"Please." He scoffed. "You're not a quitter. If you really think you love her, you need to get your ass to her house and beg for forgiveness. Tell her how you really feel."

"She's not going to believe it," I said. "Not after what happened last night. She thinks I played her."

"You need to tell her otherwise," he said.

"I don't know." I sighed. "I think that ship has sailed. I fucked that up."

"Quit being a little bitch," he said. "You are not a quitter. Pack a bag, get on a plane, and go to her. Buy her flowers. I would say chocolate, but I'm not sure that would have the same effect as it would with most women. Maybe jewelry."

"I don't think she's going to be open to bribery."

"Won't know until you try," he said.

"And if she doesn't want to accept my apology?"

"You keep trying until she does. I saw you two together. Briefly, but what I saw and what you told me about her says you're crazy about her. You can't let that slip away. I don't know if you'll ever find another woman that you care that much about."

He was right. I was certain I would never find anyone like her again. From this moment forward, every woman I looked at would be measured against her. Every woman would pale in comparison to her. "Okay," I said. "I'm going to do it."

"I knew it!" He laughed. "Good luck. Buy some kneepads. You're going to need them with the amount of groveling you're going to be doing."

I laughed. "Thanks," I said. "I'll call you later. If you don't hear from me, take it as a good sign she let me in the door."

"Got it."

As soon as I hung up with him, I got online and found a ticket. Then it was a mad dash to pack enough for a couple of days. I hoped to stay longer, but I didn't want to get ahead of myself. I might be on the next plane home if she told me it was over. I didn't want to be a quitter, but I also didn't want to harass the woman.

On the way to the airport, I thought about what I would say to her. There was a lot I needed to say. For one, I knew for certain I was in love with her. It wasn't an almost sure thing. It wasn't maybe. I knew definitively. I loved her and the only future I could envision for myself was one with her and Lucy in it. She was the woman I wanted. She was the only woman I would ever want.

I would give up everything in New York to be with her. I should have packed more clothes. I was going to stay until she took me back. I wasn't going to let her push me away. I knew she cared about me. She was pissed, but we could work on that.

"I'm coming home," I whispered as I took my seat on the plane.

30

EMMA

I walked in the house and tossed my purse on the couch. Initially I had planned on going to work, but after dropping Lucy off, I decided I was taking a personal day. I needed to get caught up around the house. And truthfully, I just wasn't in the mood. I was sad. My heart hurt. I had told myself to avoid falling for him because I didn't want to know a broken heart.

And yet, here I was. I knew he would be the one man that would have the power to break my heart. I was a stalwart person. I took shit on the chin and kept going. This one was going to take a little more effort to push through. The thought of going to work was just too much. I didn't have the energy to put on a happy face. My staff would ask me about the hot guy I was with at the party. They would want to know all about him. I couldn't deal with that right now.

Cleaning was all I had the strength for. I wanted to clean from top to bottom. I wanted to tackle the junk drawer that had gotten away from me. I wanted to do it all. I turned on some music and got started in the kitchen. After cleaning the dishwasher, I loaded it before turning my attention to giving the stovetop a thorough scrubbing.

I ended up getting gross and needing a shower. After my shower, I put on my robe and nothing else. My strength was zapped. I walked downstairs to make myself a cup of tea when the doorbell rang. It was probably one of the many deliveries from Amazon. I made sure the robe was closed before going to answer it.

"Case!" I gasped and pulled the robe tighter around my neck. "What are you doing here?"

"I was hoping we could talk," he said.

"I don't want to talk to you," I said and tried to close the door.

He put his hand out to stop it. "Please hear me out. Five minutes. That's all I need. Please, Emma."

I shot him a dirty look. "Two minutes."

"Can I come in?"

"No."

"Emma, please," he said. The emotion in his voice was nearly my undoing. I hated that I couldn't resist the man.

"Fine," I sighed. "Two minutes."

He walked in and turned around to face me. I folded my arms over my chest and stared him down. I was trying to tell myself not to look at him. I had to see past his good looks. I couldn't let myself remember how good things were. That would weaken my resolve to hate him. I had to hate him, or it would hurt too bad.

"You're wasting your two minutes," I said.

"I'm sorry," he said. "My dad was out of line. He was wrong. He didn't know what he was talking about."

I rolled my eyes. "He got that idea from somewhere."

"I know," he said. "When I first came here, it was about getting the deal done. All of that was forgotten after our first day together. It was never about the deal. I got to know you because I wanted to find out who you were. I thought if I could know you better, I would understand the best way to convince you to sell."

"Asshole," I muttered. "You pig. Get out."

"Emma, my goal changed when I realized how much you loved your company," he said. "That was your goal, right. You wanted me to see how special it was to you. You showed me the pictures and told me the stories. It worked."

"I don't care if it did or not," I spat. "I don't give a shit if it changed your mind."

"I love you," he said. "I fell in love with you with every story. Every picture. Every minute we spent together made me fall in love with you even more. I would do anything for you. My dad didn't know how I felt even though I tried to tell him. I wasn't sure how he would take it. I'm so used to living under his thumb, I didn't realize I didn't have to be there. He gave me his blessing. He wants me to be happy and he knows that can only happen with you."

As he spoke, tears rolled down my cheeks. The logical side of me was screaming at me to throw him out. I couldn't fall for it again. I couldn't let myself get hurt again. "Case—"

"Please, Emma," he whispered. "I love you. I want you in my life. I want you and Lucy to be a part of my life. Whatever you need me to do to believe me, I'll do it. I fired my client."

"You what?" I choked and furiously wiped my cheeks.

"I fired him," I said. "I told him I couldn't keep working for him. He's been using me to buy companies for him and I'm not going to do it anymore. You showed me that every small company has a story. Every company was someone's dream. I hate that I went in and destroyed those dreams for a little cash. I'm not going to do it again. I understand you're angry with me, but know this, no matter what happens from here on out, I will never buy another company that doesn't want to sell."

The tears were falling in earnest. I felt like I knew him well enough to trust he was being sincere. I saw it in his eyes. I heard it in his voice. He was sorry. I walked up to him and kissed him. It was a sloppy, emotional kiss.

"I'm sorry," he murmured. "I'm so, so sorry."

"Shh," I whispered. "Take me to bed. Let's do this right."

He grabbed my hand and we rushed upstairs. He pulled the belt on my robe. It fell open. He groaned and dropped to his knees in front of me. He kissed over my belly button and between my legs. My hands moved through his hair as he kissed over my folds. I groaned and dropped my head back. His tongue slid over my clit with his hands holding my ass firmly in place.

My knees threatened to buckle, but he wasn't about to let me fall. He held on and continued using his tongue until I was crying out with my release. He kissed over my stomach and slowly got to his feet. His tongue lapped over my nipple before he sucked it into his mouth. My head dropped forward with my arms wrapping around his head and holding him close to me.

I reached down to pull his shirt up. He lifted his arms and let me pull it over his head. I tossed it on the floor and pulled him to his feet. My hands immediately went to the button on his jeans. I jerked them open and stuck my hand down his underwear to wrap my hand around his cock. I gently squeezed while he showered my face with kisses.

"I love you," he whispered. "I'm sorry I didn't say it before. It took me a minute to realize it."

"I love you," I told him. "I should have told you sooner. I didn't know what it was. I do now. I want this."

"You have this," he said.

I pushed his pants down and moved to sit on my bed. I gestured for him to join me. "Show me," I said.

"Baby, I want this, but I didn't think this was going to happen," he said with regret. "Give me ten minutes and I'll run to the store."

"Case?"

"Yes?"

"Do we really need that?" I asked. "I think it's pretty clear I've not been with anyone. Only you."

"You're okay with that?" he asked and stepped forward. He touched my cheek. "What about getting knocked up? I'm not sure I'm ready for that."

I laughed softly. "I've stayed on the pill, just in case."

"Just in case a man like me came along?" He smirked.

"Maybe." I grinned and slid back on the bed before very slowly opening my legs. "Come to me, Case. I want you. I want every last inch of you. I want to know what it's like to have you inside me with no barriers."

He crawled onto the bed and over me. I lay back and welcomed him between my legs. His body was held just above mine. Every breath I took scraped my nipples across his hard chest. He held himself up on his elbows with his face above mine. His thumbs rubbed over my cheeks as he stared into my eyes.

"I'm not leaving you," he said. "This thing we've got right here is the real deal."

I was overcome with emotion. I could only nod as he slipped inside me. Neither of us talked or even breathed as he pushed deep inside. Our eyes were locked together. The bond between us was sealed. I knew there would never be another man for me. This was it for me. He was it.

My arms wrapped around him and pulled him onto my body. I needed to feel the weight of him. "I don't want to hurt you," he murmured.

"You won't. I'm good. Feel me. Let me feel you."

He let out a breath and gave into what his body was demanding. He held me, unmoving as we both relished in the moment of being completely joined together. He didn't even have to move. I felt the orgasm spiraling through my body. It started as a warm heat in my toes that flooded through me.

"Emma," he whispered my name as his body stiffened.

"Case," I answered the call.

My body exploded slowly in gradual increments that intensified by the second. He groaned and dropped his mouth to mine. We kissed through the orgasm until he lay limp on top of me.

31

CASE

I slid off her and draped my arm across her chest. This was better than I could have expected. I was prepared for her to kick my ass out and demand I never return. Ending up in bed with her had not been on my radar. I would have remembered condoms. Then again, I was glad I didn't. Being inside her was probably the best thing I had ever experienced. It was far better than I could have ever dreamed of.

Being with her like this was right. I had never felt anything so right in my life. It was like I had been traveling aimlessly down a dirt road for years. Then I found her. I wasn't letting her go. This was where I was supposed to be. Manhattan was my home, but here with her felt like my real home.

"I know this might sound cheesy, but I have never felt like this. Never. I want to do whatever it takes to make you happy. You tell me what you want, and I'm there."

"I think you've done plenty," she said.

"My brother told me to bring kneepads."

"What? Why?"

I rolled to my side and looked down at her. "To properly grovel. I was prepared to go down on my knees."

"If I remember right, you were on your knees." She grinned.

"I was and I would love to do it again," I offered.

"As much as I would love to do nothing more than lay here in bed with you all day, I did promise Lucy I would make cookies for her after-school snack," she said. "I can't let her down."

"I'll help," I offered.

"Have you ever made cookies before in your life?" she teased.

"No, but there are a lot of things I haven't done that I want to do with you," I replied.

"Then we can make cookies," she said. "But before we do that, I have to put my oven back together."

"Put your oven back together?" I questioned.

"Yeah, long story," she said and got out of bed. "I should also put the couch back together."

"The couch?" I asked with surprise. "What the hell happened?"

She pulled on a pair of panties while I watched. I was stretched out naked on the bed as I looked at her. She pulled on jeans and then a bra before she finally turned to look at me. "I was doing a little spring cleaning," she answered.

"Which requires you to take apart your appliances and furniture?"

"Oh shit," she muttered. "I think I forgot to put the milk back in the fridge."

"You took the fridge apart?"

"When I get a little stressed, I clean," she said with a shrug. "You might want to get some clothes on. I'd hate for certain body parts to get burnt."

"That would be a crying shame." I chuckled and climbed out of bed.

I quickly dressed and followed her downstairs. That was when I realized the kitchen was a bit of a wreck. I felt a little guilty for bringing the cleaning frenzy on. "I would say ignore the mess, but I think that's impossible."

I walked to her and wrapped my arms around her from behind. "I'm sorry," I said. "I did this."

"You didn't do anything," she said. "You don't need to apologize. I just needed to stay busy."

"Because of what happened last night."

"I won't lie, it shook me," she replied. "I was humiliated. I don't blame you. Not really. I don't know if I'll ever be able to look your brothers or your mother in the eyes again."

"No," I said and spun her around. "You did nothing wrong. I'll make sure they all know what was really going on between us. I'll make my father apologize. I don't want you to feel like you can't be a part of my family. They will welcome you with open arms. I know my mom is going to be thrilled I made this right."

"I'm so embarrassed that I stormed out," she groaned.

"You didn't storm out," I told her. "You were very eloquent in your departure. You were far calmer than I would have been. You have style and grace. Trust me, you impressed the family."

"Thanks," she said. "We better get started on the cookies."

She directed me in the kitchen after we'd put it back together like she'd been doing it all her life. I supposed running a factory gave her plenty of experience bossing people around. She gave me detailed instructions on how to make the cookies but kept a close eye on me.

"Do I get to sample the goods?" I asked.

"Maybe if you're a good boy," she teased.

After making the cookies, she left me alone in the kitchen while she put on some makeup. "Do you want to go with me?" she asked.

"Do you mind?" I asked. "I understand if you want to talk to Lucy without me there."

"She doesn't know anything about what happened last night," she said. "She will be very happy to see you here."

"Can I broach another subject before we get little ears around us?" I asked.

"Sure, what's up?"

"What do you want me to do here?" I asked. "Do I stay? Do I go back? Do you need time? I don't want to overstay."

"You're not overstaying," she said. "If you want to stay, I would be more than happy to have you here. But you're right, we do need to talk about a few things. This isn't just me and you. Lucy is my priority. I can't have her be stuck in a back and forth."

"I'm all in," I said. "All in. If you're not okay with me staying here, that's okay. I'll get a hotel."

"I would love for you to be here." She smiled. "We'll talk to Lucy and do our best to explain the situation to a five-year-old."

"Okay," I said. "I'll follow your lead."

"Alright, then let's do this." She clapped her hands together. "I need to get a few groceries before we pick her up."

I felt like a lost puppy dog as I followed her around the grocery store. It was another new experience for me. "Is this seriously your first time grocery shopping?" she teased.

"Yes," I answered.

"How do you get food?" she asked with total confusion.

"Delivery service," I said with a shrug. "I have a housekeeper that keeps things stocked for me."

"Oh, sweetie, welcome to how the other half lives." She laughed.

"It's like being in a different world."

I loaded the groceries into the back of her SUV and off we went to pick up Lucy. I waited in the car while Emma went in to get her. When she saw me in the car, she started jumping up and down. I got out to give her a big hug.

"Hi, Lucy," I greeted.

"You're back!" she exclaimed.

"I'm back," I said and helped her into her seat.

"Are you going to our house?" she asked as Emma got into the driver's seat.

I looked to Emma, who gave a slight nod. "I am," I answered. "Is that okay with you?"

"We can play another game," she suggested.

"I'd like that."

When we got back to the house, I carried in groceries while Emma got Lucy set up at the table with her box of art stuff. "Ready for your cookies?" Emma asked Lucy.

"I helped make them," I said.

"You did?" she asked with surprise.

"I did. Emma helped me."

"I like to make cookies too," she said. "Do you want to paint a picture with me?"

"Sure," I said.

She opened the box and pointed out every little thing. It was a very well-stocked case. Markers, crayons, and paints with a couple of different sketch pads. "Do you like to draw a lot?" I asked her.

"Yep." She nodded and handed me one of the sketchbooks. "You can draw anything you want."

"What are you going to draw?" I asked her.

"You'll see." She grinned before taking a bite of her cookie.

To my surprise, she slid out of her chair and went to the opposite end of the table to make her picture. Emma was leaning against the wall and watching us. I picked up a crayon and drew the only thing I knew how to. No one was going to call me an artist. Kindergarten was the last time I had picked up a crayon. It all felt very childish and freeing at the same time. I could be me. I didn't have to act like I was the eldest son of Britt Manhattan. I didn't have to be the oldest brother setting an example. I got to be totally free.

"Are you done with your picture?" Lucy asked.

"Just about," I murmured and found I was really immersed in the coloring. I swore I took off ten years from my life in the last fifteen minutes. I added a sun to my scene and put the crayon back. "Done."

"Do you want to see my picture?" she asked.

"I do," I said.

She slipped out of the chair and walked to my side. Emma had been busying herself in the kitchen but was trying to watch without watching. Lucy presented the picture and I was pretty sure my heart had grown by ten sizes. I actually felt tears burning the backs of my eyes.

"Who's that?" I asked and pointed to the stick figures on the page. There were three figures with each of them holding hands.

"That's me and mommy and you," she said.

I heard Emma suck in a breath and knew she was just as touched by the picture as I was. I swallowed the lump in my throat. "It's perfect," I said.

"What did you draw?" she asked.

I showed her my very rudimentary picture. "It's a cabin in the woods," I said.

"Do you have a cabin in the woods?" she asked.

"Not yet," I replied. "But I think I'm going to find one."

"We went to a cabin one time," she said. "We went hiking and got our feet in the water. Then we had a little campfire and made s'mores."

"You did?" I asked with wide eyes. "That sounds like a lot of fun."

"Do you like s'mores?" she asked.

"It's been a long time, but I remember they were good," I said.

"Maybe we can get a cabin together," Lucy suggested.

I looked at Emma and smiled. "I think that sounds like a very good idea. What do you think?"

"I think that would be a lot of fun," she said. "Maybe for spring break."

"I know a really cool place in upstate New York," I volunteered. "I can make a reservation."

Emma smiled and looked at Lucy. "What do you think?" she asked. "Should we go on a special trip with Case?"

Lucy jumped up and down and clapped her hands. "Yes!"

"I'll finish dinner," Emma said and drifted into the kitchen once again.

Lucy and I hung out, drawing and talking about the trip to the cabin. I didn't know who was more excited, me or her. We ate dinner together and then watched a little TV before Lucy had to go to bed. "Are you going to be here tomorrow?" she asked me.

I nodded. "I am. We'll have breakfast together."

"Goodnight," she said and threw her arms around me.

I hugged her back and watched Emma take her upstairs to bed. While she was upstairs, I opened the bottle of wine we picked up before we got Lucy. I poured two glasses and turned on the gas fireplace. Emma returned a few minutes later.

"You know me well." She laughed as she sat down.

I handed her the glass. "You took care of dinner. The least I can do is pour you a glass of wine."

"I appreciate it," she said. "So, were you serious about the cabin?"

"I'm seriously thinking about buying one." I laughed. "We'll do a little cabin shopping."

She groaned and shook her head. "I'm not sure I can get used to someone just buying a cabin whenever they feel like it."

"Get used to it," I told her. "Whatever you want, I got it."

"Let's just worry about today and the right now," she said.

"Works for me," I said and pulled her close.

I stared at the dancing flames and let myself travel down a path I had never ventured down before. I saw a future with a family. I imagined us together as a family. We weren't the typical family. We were a tapestry patched together. I was determined to make it work.

32

EMMA

I looked over at the empty spot in my bed. I had grown very used to having him beside me. I missed him. He was back in New York. We spent several days together, but he did have a career to get back to. We were going to work out the logistics of our relationship together, but he had to take care of things there while we figured it out.

I waited in my car. Jennifer was supposed to be meeting me for a walk. I felt a little guilty for abandoning her this last week. She'd been scarce, giving me plenty of time with Case. I saw her car pull up and got out.

"Sorry," she said. "I was on the phone with my agent."

"Book another gig?" I asked her.

"Yep." She grinned "Which is why I need to get this walk in and then it's off to the gym."

"You know you're gorgeous," I teased.

We started down the path that wound through trees and around the park. "So, what's the deal?" she asked. "You've been very evasive. Are you guys a thing?"

"We are officially a thing." I nodded.

"Congratulations," she said with a smile. "I'm so glad it worked out for you."

"Thanks," I said. "And thank you for talking me off the ledge that night."

"I take it his explanation was a good one?"

"Very good." I nodded. "He wants us to go to New York soon to meet his family."

"Again?"

"Yes, again." I laughed. "I'm hoping the second time will be much better than the first."

"Do you guys know what you're going to do?" she asked. "I mean with the distance."

"We don't know yet," I said. "We haven't really worked it out. He's got a business and a career. I don't know how it works. We know we want to be together."

"I guess that's all that really matters, right?"

"I hate being away from him, but it's not the end of the world. We text and Facetime all the time. It's almost as good as the real thing."

"Almost." She laughed. "Except for the part that's missing."

"Yeah, that's a bummer," I said. "I don't want to gloat, but damn I'm happy. He makes me so, so happy."

"He's your soulmate," she teased.

"He is," I agreed. "He really is. I can't imagine not having him in my life. I love him. He loves me and I know he will love Lucy if he doesn't already."

"It's good to see you happy," she said on a serious note. "I know you've been going through the motions and you make people believe you are happy, but this is what real happiness looks like. You're glowing."

"I'm not glowing." I laughed.

"You are and it's not a bad thing. You're beautiful. You deserve this. You deserve to be happy and loved by a good man. He's going to make you very happy."

"I think so," I said. "I know so. I'm not going to fool myself into thinking it will all be easy, but I'm ready to tackle whatever comes our way."

"Yes, you are," she said. "You've been forged in fire."

"Isn't that the truth," I said.

"How's it going with the fundraiser?" she asked.

"Good. I've got to nail down a few last-minute details, but I think I have everything established."

"Is Case going to be there?" she asked.

"I didn't tell him," I said with a grimace.

"Why not?"

"I feel like I'm dragging him to all my stuff," I said. "I did one dinner with him and it didn't end well."

"I don't think he's keeping score," she said. "He'll want to do this with you."

"What if he feels obligated to donate?" I asked. "I don't want him to think I'm inviting him at the last minute because I want him to donate."

"Don't you think he'll be hurt if you don't tell him?"

She was right. "I'll call him and let him know it's happening, but he isn't obligated."

"You can tell him that, but I bet you a hundred bucks he's going to be flying his butt down here to attend with you," she said.

I couldn't help but smile. "You're probably right."

We finished our walk, picking up the pace and breaking a sweat. "I don't know if I have the right to ask him to move here," I said after we'd been walking.

"Have you thought about moving there?"

I grimaced. "I don't know if I want to live in the city with Lucy. He says he has a house, but I would have to figure out my business. Why did I have to fall in love with a man that lives so far away?"

"You act like you have cement shoes and can't move," she said. "You can go anywhere and do anything. Hire a manager for the factory. You can't let those things hold you back. You know you want to be with this man. People move all the time."

"Not me," I said. "I've established a home for Lucy. I don't want to uproot her."

"Again, families move all the time," she said. "Lucy is young. She'll recover. Besides, don't you think she would want to move if it meant having a solid life with him?"

"True," I said. "I don't know. I'm getting ahead of myself. We haven't talked about it. I guess we'll figure out the next move later."

We made our way back to the cars. "I'll see you at the fundraiser," she said. "Call Case."

"I will," I said as I got into my car.

I drove home and pulled out my laptop to work on the final details for the fundraiser before calling Case.

"Hello, gorgeous," he answered in that deep husky tone that sent chills down my spine.

"Hi, babe. What are you doing?"

"I'm sitting at my desk in my stuffy office while wearing a stuffy suit and dreaming about being naked with you," he answered.

"Well that is very specific." I laughed.

"What are you doing?"

"I just got home after a nice long morning walk with Jennifer," I answered.

"Did you get all sweaty?" he asked.

"Dirty, dirty man," I teased. "Your mind is in the gutter."

"My mind has been in the gutter since I left your bed," he said. "I hate being away from you."

"I hate it too," I said.

"Are you going into the factory?" he asked.

"Later," I said. "I'm working on finalizing details for a fundraiser I'm hosting."

"Fundraiser?" he asked.

"Yes, I do it every year. It's to raise money for cancer research."

"What kind of fundraiser?" he asked.

"It's not quite like what you are used to but imagine one of your events on a smaller scale," I said.

"And you're putting this on?"

"Yes," I said and there was a brief pause. "I wanted to invite you, but I don't want you to feel obligated to come."

"Babe, it's not an obligation," I said. "If you want me to be there, I would love to come. If you don't want me there, I'll stay away."

"No!" I gushed. "No, I don't want you to stay away. I would love for you to come but I just feel so guilty dragging you to all my stuff."

"When is it?" he asked.

"Friday night."

"What's the dress code?"

"Black tie," I answered.

"I'll be there," he said.

"Thank you." I smiled. "This means a lot to me. We dedicate it to Marie. I love being able to do something to honor her memory."

"I wouldn't miss it for the world," he said. "I'll be there. I look forward to being a part of something that is so special to you."

"I guess this is one way to get you back in town," I teased.

"All you have to do is say the word and I'll jump to get my ass there," he said.

"I miss you."

"I miss you," he replied. "You're always on my mind. I can't get through an hour without thinking about you. I don't dare tell anyone. My brothers would give me so much shit. Just so you know, you've got me wrapped around your little finger."

"That's pretty powerful," I said. "I think I might be wrapped around your little finger. I want to make you happy."

"You've made me happy," he said.

I heard a phone buzz. "That's you," I said. "I'll let you go. Call me later."

"I will," he said. "I love you."

"I love you."

I hung up the phone and took a moment to relish the sound of his voice. I got back to work on the final details. I checked the time. I had an hour before I needed to pick up Lucy, which was just enough time for me to go by the hotel and check with the event organizer.

I walked in and found her in the office. "Hi," I said. "Do you have a minute?"

"Sure, come in, Emma."

"I don't want to hound you, but I was just hoping to check out the ballroom and see how things are coming along," I said.

"Come with me." She smiled. "I'll show you what we've done so far. We had an anonymous donor offer to cover the cost of the ballroom."

"What? Really?"

She smiled and nodded. "Yep, it came in yesterday. I was going to call you today and let you know."

"That's amazing," I gushed. "Did you get the decorations I sent over?"

"We did," she said as we walked to the ballroom. "I've got a team coming in tomorrow to get everything ready."

She pushed open the door. The room was empty with tables folded and pushed against the wall. "We just had the carpets cleaned. I want everything to be perfect for the night."

"Thank you," I said. "I really appreciate you going through the extra trouble."

"It's no trouble," she said. "I'm so glad we can be a part of the fundraising. The boxes over there are the decorations that have come in so far. We've already got the twinkle lights ready to go."

"Can I check the boxes?" I asked.

I tended to be just a little nervous about the fundraiser. I wanted every detail to be perfect.

"Absolutely," she said. "I was going to have the team tomorrow check everything against the invoice."

I pulled open one of the boxes. Dark blue tablecloths and white napkins were in it. Another box held an assortment of silver stars in a variety of sizes. "It's perfect," I said. "I can't wait to see it all done up."

"It's going to be beautiful," she said. "The theme is fitting for the occasion."

"It was her daughter's idea," I said. "Lucy always asks if her mom is in the stars. I used to read her a book and it was something along those lines. I love that she thinks that. I want other families that have lost loved ones to believe it as well."

"We have the stars that have been purchased in my office," she said.

"Great, make sure they have a prominent place to be displayed. I want to make sure the people that bought the stars can see them."

"Absolutely," she said. "We were going to use that wall over there to display them. We'll have stars available at the door for them to purchase if they want."

"Good idea." I nodded.

"Make sure everyone is carded," I said. "With an open bar, I can't afford anyone underage getting into this thing."

"Of course. We have an experienced staff to handle all that stuff."

"I have a few vendors that want to setup early in the day. Is that going to be okay?"

"Just have them check in with me," she said.

"I will."

I looked around and felt a little anxious about the coming event. Right now, it was a little hard to see the big picture with the wide-open space. I knew it would come together. I planned on spending the day making sure everything was perfect.

"Thank you," I said. "I've got to go but call if anything comes up."

"Take care, Emma."

I left the hotel feeling better about things. It was coming together. It would all be just fine. I just needed to have a little faith.

33

CASE

I tried like hell to get to her earlier, but a minor emergency at the office had me pushing my flight back. I was still plenty early for the fundraiser, but I wanted to be in town earlier. I could hear the stress in Emma's voice. I wanted to be there for her.

"Thanks," I said and hopped out of the cab with my tux put over one arm and my suitcase in my other hand. I rushed into the hotel and followed the signs for the event.

Emma was talking to someone and gesturing wildly. I immediately went to her. She looked up and I saw her relief. "You're here."

"I'm here. What can I do?"

She blew out a breath. "One of the vendors that was supposed to be selling bath products is late. They're going to get here ten minutes before this thing is supposed to start. It's going to look disorganized. I hate disorganized."

"Hey, it will be fine," I said. "Where are they supposed to be set up?"

She gestured to a red X on the floor. "Right in the middle."

"We'll move them to the side entrance," I said. "They'll be out of the way. No one is going to pay them much attention."

"We're short four tablecloths," she said. "I have to use white."

I looked around the room and saw the obvious white cloths. I wasn't ever going to be an expert in the décor department, but even I saw the glaring white. "Is there a local place that can get you more blue ones?"

"I've tried," she said. "I ordered the blue from a company out of state. It probably doesn't matter, but it sticks out to me."

"How about those tables be used for drinks or those little gift bags?" I suggested.

She gnawed on her lower lip. "I guess we can cut back on actual tables and have more people sit together."

"Babe, I think you've done a great job in here," I told her. "It's gorgeous. No one is going to be paying attention to those little details. You're doing something great for a good cause. People are far more forgiving when it's charity."

She sighed. "I spend so much time trying to get this perfect, and inevitably, shit always goes wrong."

"A few white tablecloths and a late vendor are pretty minor in the grand scheme of things," I said.

"I need to get dressed," she mumbled. "I was supposed to already be dressed. I always feel like I'm running uphill while towing a car behind me when I do these things."

I pulled her into my arms and hugged her close. "You're good. You're going to be just fine. The night is going to be incredible."

"Thanks," she said. "We can get dressed in the bathroom."

I knew what went into a woman getting ready for a black-tie event. "Sit tight," I said. "I'll be right back."

I went to the front desk and paid for a suite at the hotel. When I went back to the ballroom, she was once again fretting over another detail. "Come on," I said and took her hand. "Where are your things?"

She pointed to a corner. I saw a garment bag draped over a chair with a small bag on the floor. I walked over and picked it up with my own things. "Let's go," I said.

"Where are we going?"

"Upstairs," I said. "We have a room to get dressed in."

"You rented a room for us to get dressed in?" she asked with surprise.

"Yes," I answered and stepped into the elevator.

"Thank you," she said. "I get a little neurotic."

"You're fine. Let's get dressed and take a minute."

We used the full thirty minutes to get changed. I could feel her relaxing. I dug into the mini-fridge and pulled out two small bottles of champagne. I poured us each a glass and handed her one. "I shouldn't drink," she said.

"It will settle your nerves," I said. "Tonight will be great. Take a deep breath and remember why you're doing this. No one expects perfect. Just enjoy the night."

"I'll try," she said. "I have to give a speech in front of the crowd, which is the worst part. I don't know why I do this to myself. I stumble and bumble my way through a speech. I'm terrible at public speaking."

"You're going to do fine. Find me in the crowd. Talk to me."

"I'm so glad you're here," she said. "I'm sorry I didn't tell you about it earlier."

"I'm here now," I said. "You look beautiful by the way. Absolutely stunning. You are going to do great."

She drank the last of her champagne and we headed back down to the ballroom. There were already guests milling about holding glasses of champagne as they chatted with one another. I stayed close to her as the room began to fill. More people filed into the room. The noise level grew. I felt her relaxing. She was getting into the groove.

"I have to give my speech in a few minutes," she said in a low voice. "I hope I don't embarrass myself."

"You won't," I said. "Just be you. People are here because they want to support you and the cause. I'll be near the front. If you panic, find me. Look at me if you need to. I'll be right here."

She gave me a quick kiss and moved away. I watched my woman decked out in a gorgeous silver dress that made her stand out in the crowd. She took her place at the microphone on the small, elevated stage. "Excuse me, everyone," she said in a soft voice.

No one heard her. The conversations continued. I willed her to speak up. "Everyone, can I have your attention, please?" she said much louder.

People turned to face her. I saw the flash of panic and made a subtle move to stand in front of the stage. She looked at me. I smiled and nodded. I watched as she took a deep breath.

"Thank you, everyone, for taking time out of your busy lives to come together to support a cause that is near and dear to my heart," she said. "I know so many of you have also been touched by cancer whether it's yourself or a loved one. We all know the damage cancer can do to lives. Tonight, we're here to do what we can to ease some of the pain cancer causes. Every dollar will go to a fund set up to provide help to those families that have been hit by a devastating cancer diagnosis. Miller's Chocolates donates money to cancer research all year, but tonight is about the people. Tonight is about helping the moms and dads that need childcare while they get treatments. Tonight is about covering transportation costs and covering rent when a working parent is dealing with cancer. I want to thank all of you for helping out this cause."

She paused and looked at me. I was rooting for her. I knew what came next in her speech. It was the part that would be the hardest. She was putting a face to her cause.

"As many of you know, I lost my sister to this nasty disease," she said with her voice wavering. "Her fight was made more difficult by financial demands. We used to talk about how to help others that were in her same fight. How could we help other little kids that were going to lose a parent way too soon? This fundraiser is Marie's idea. Even when she was fighting her own fight, she was thinking about others. Thank you again for coming, and please, don't be afraid to open those wallets!"

There was a round of applause and more than a few tears as she stepped down. I walked right up to her and pulled her into my arms. She was shaking as I held her. "You were very convincing," I whispered. "Good job. Amazing job."

"Thank you," she said. "I had a longer speech planned, but every time I mention Marie, things get dicey."

"It was the perfect length," I assured her. "You got your point across."

She groaned. "I need a drink."

I laughed and led her to the open bar. "I better schmooze," she said. "Are you okay on your own?"

"Baby, I was literally born to do this." I laughed. "My parents had children so we could schmooze."

I spent the next hour putting my upbringing to good use. I chatted up the people I could tell had money. I did a little namedropping and used one of my mom's best skills. She had mastered the art of guilting people into reaching deep into their bank accounts and donating.

"It's time to announce how much we raised," she said.

"Do you know?"

She shook her head. "Nope. I open the envelope in front of everyone."

"What do you do if it's a low number?"

"Cry." She laughed.

"I think it's going to be good," I said. "I spoke with a lot of people, and it sounded positive."

Once again, she took her place on the stage. I hoped like hell there was a big number written on that paper.

"Thank you, everyone, for coming and spending the evening with us while we remember those we lost and doing what we can to help others get through what will be their most difficult time," Emma started. "I'd like to announce what we have raised tonight, but don't think it stops here. You can still donate online or drop your commitments in the box at the door. Who's ready to hear how much we've raised?"

There was a round of applause. I was close enough to see her hands shaking as she opened the envelope. The smile on her face told me it was a good number. I actually felt relief. "You guys are amazing!" she shouted. "Tonight, because of your generosity, we have raised one point two million dollars!"

There were shouts and a lot of clapping from around the room. I was thoroughly impressed. Someone approached the stage and gestured for Emma. She looked confused and stepped to the side. The man handed her an envelope while talking to her. I saw the shock on her face. She looked at me and I felt like I was in trouble. I didn't know what the hell was in the envelope, but I got the feeling she was blaming me.

She stepped back up to the microphone. "Everyone, I've just been given a check," she said with her voice shaking. "We have received another very generous donation. This is a check for another one point two million dollars!"

There was a collective breath taken. It was a brief pause before the crowd erupted. She looked at me directly. "Excuse me!" she called out. "I need to give a huge thank you to the Manhattan family for this generous donation. This is incredible and I promise, you have all helped changed lives for the better. Thank you!"

She was looking at me and thanking me. I didn't do it. I had written a check for five grand. She couldn't possibly know that. When she stepped off the stage, she launched herself at me. "Thank you," she said. "Thank you, thank you, thank you."

I held her and was happy to accept her attention, but it wasn't me. There had to be a mistake. I dreaded bursting her bubble, but I needed to do it before this went too far.

"We need to talk," I said and gently pulled her away from the crowd.

34

EMMA

I was shaking. The first million had set a new record. The second million was astronomical. I couldn't believe what we had accomplished. We were going to be able to do so much good. I wanted to take him up to the room and show him just how thankful I was.

"What's wrong?" I asked with concern.

The look on his face told me something had happened. Something was wrong. My excitement evaporated. "Emma, it wasn't me."

"What wasn't you?"

"I didn't write that check," he said. "That wasn't me."

"What?" I asked with confusion.

He shook his head. "It wasn't me. I didn't write that check. I wrote a check, but not that one."

"The check I saw came from the Manhattan Family Trust," I said.

He looked even more confused than I was. "Only my dad could have touched that account," he said. "I'm on that account, but I don't have the authority to make that kind of donation."

"Your dad?" I asked.

"It had to be."

"How did he know you were going to be here?" I asked.

"I told him I was going to be out of town for a few days," he answered. "I told him about the fundraiser, but I honestly didn't think he was paying much attention."

I nervously laughed. "Apparently he was."

"Holy shit," he breathed. "Congratulations."

"I need to talk to your father," I told him. "I need to personally thank him. This is a huge deal. Is this because of what happened at dinner?"

"I don't think so," he answered. "He's not one to buy forgiveness. He's more about doing what he does, and you like it, or you don't. He doesn't spend a lot of time worrying about what other people think about him."

"Does he donate like this?"

Case slowly nodded. "Yes. Not usually as big, but my family is big on supporting various causes."

"Tax write off?" I teased.

He grinned. "Exactly."

"Still, I need to reach out. Do you think he would be awake still?"

"You want to call him now?" he asked.

"Yes. This is not the kind of thing I want to put off. I was told the check was left blank. The guy that handed it to me works at the bank the check was drawn from. Whoever did it instructed the man to match the total donation amount."

"No shit?" he exclaimed. "Damn. That is crazy. I had no idea he had it in him."

"So?" I said and held out my hand.

"So?"

"Can I call him? I'm sure you have your phone."

He grinned and reached into his pocket. He pulled up the number and handed it to me. "I'd like to talk to him when you're done," he said.

"Sure," I said and listened to the phone ring.

"Hello, son," a deep voice answered.

"Sorry, it's not Case," I said. "This is Emma, Emma Miller. We recently met at your house."

"Yes, Emma, I remember you," he said.

"I just got your very generous donation and I wanted to personally thank you," I said. "It was an incredible gift and I promise it will be put to good use. You have changed so many lives. Thank you."

"You're very welcome," he said. "Thank you for the personal phone call. I'm glad I have you on the phone. I wanted to apologize for what happened at dinner. I was out of line. I didn't understand the situation and I thought I knew better. I'm sure my son has told you that I can be a little overbearing. I tend to get an idea about what I want for my kids and forget they're not little boys anymore. I worry about them, and I didn't stop to think he might actually know his own mind."

"It's okay," I said.

"It's not okay," he said. "I was a jerk. For what it's worth, he never told me it was fake. I assumed he was working a deal. That was all on me. Please don't hold my sins against Case."

"I understand," I said. "We've worked through it."

"Good," he said. "I look forward to getting to know you. I understand you have a little girl. We'd like to meet her."

I was so emotional. Tears burned the backs of my eyes. "We'll have to see about that," I said. "Case wants to talk to you. Thank you again."

"It was my pleasure," he said. "Take care, Emma."

I handed the phone to Case. "Hi, dad," he said.

I tried not to eavesdrop, but it was kind of tough. He thanked his father and promised to call him the following day. He ended the call and put the phone away. "Thank you for doing that," he said.

"It wasn't me." I laughed. "It was him. It was a generous gift, and a simple notecard wasn't going to be enough."

"You made his night." He grinned.

"He made my night." I laughed. "I'm ready to celebrate. I don't have to do any more speeches. Let's get a drink."

"I'm game," he said and placed his hand on the small of my back.

"You told him about Lucy?" I asked.

"I did. Was that wrong?"

"No," I said. "I was just surprised. He said he wanted to meet her."

"He does. They do. They've been hounding me to bring you back for dinner. I told them I didn't think we were quite there yet. He didn't exactly make the best first impression."

"I think your father loves you and he thought he was protecting you," I said.

He snorted. "Yeah, right. His idea of protection involves him making every life decision for me. He still checks up on me at work. He acts like I'm a fresh-faced kid straight out of college. He seems to forget I've been doing it for years and doing my job very well."

"I'm sure he is very proud of you," I said and patted his arm.

"We better start thanking donors," he said after we got a fresh drink. "Looks like people are starting to filter out."

"You're right. I'm about ready to get out of these heels, and this dress is pinching in places I don't want to be pinched."

"Do you need to go home?" he asked quietly.

"Lucy is at a sleepover," I said.

"I have that suite," he said with suggestion in his voice.

"You do." I grinned.

"You could say your goodbyes and we can sneak away."

"And order room service?" I asked hopefully.

"Absolutely." He nodded.

I kissed his cheek and drifted into the crowd. I shook hands, offered a few hugs, and said thank you so many times I felt like I was coming across very wooden. I didn't want my donors to think I was just saying it and didn't mean it. Case found me and expertly pulled me from a very long-winded donor.

"Thank you," I whispered as he walked me out of the room.

"I ordered burgers and shakes from a local twenty-four-hour diner," he said. "It will be delivered in about ten minutes."

"You did?" I smiled.

"I did. You need to relax. Get off your feet and celebrate your victory."

We got to the room, and because I hadn't planned to stay the night, I only had my jeans and tee. I stripped to my panties and put on one of the fluffy robes. I sat down on the couch and took a minute to just breathe. Case joined me wearing the other robe. He sat down and lifted my legs onto his lap and massaged my aching feet.

"What a night," he said.

"It was," I said. "I feel like I'm still humming. Tomorrow I will start the process of filling out notecards. I need to talk with the head of the foundation."

"But tonight, you can just sit back and relax," he said.

I sipped the champagne he had poured for me. "Yes, I can."

There was a knock on the door. "Dinner is here," he said and jumped up to retrieve the late-night indulgence.

We moved to sit at the table. "So, I know you've got a lot going on, but I would like to invite you and Lucy to come to New York with me."

"When?"

"Tomorrow," he said. "Whenever. My parents have asked me to invite you back for dinner. We all promise there will be no drama. They'd love to meet Lucy as well. We can take a long weekend."

I grimaced. "She'd miss school."

"We could make it a short weekend." He shrugged. "I just want you to come back. I want you to see more of the city. We can take Lucy to the zoo and the children's museum. We can take her to the park. Wherever you want to go."

I thought about it and figured missing one day of kindergarten wasn't going to ruin her education. "Okay," I said. "I'd like that."

"Really?" He grinned.

"You know I'm a sucker," I said. "I know Lucy will love the big city. She's going to be so excited."

"I'll call my mom in the morning," he said. "She'll want to make a big dinner."

We ate our burgers and talked about our weeks. It was nice to just have moments like this with him. I didn't have to pretend I didn't eat burgers. I didn't have to be prim and proper. I could eat and talk and lounge in a robe. This was what it was like to be in a relationship. To have a partner in life who knew everything about you and still loved you.

"I need to send out an email to the staff," I murmured.

"For?"

"To let them know I'll be gone for a couple of days. Then I need to pack. I need to let the school know Lucy will be absent."

"Slow down," he said and took my hands in his. "Everything will get done. We'll take a later flight."

"No, no," I said. "I'm excited to go. It won't take me long."

I got up and grabbed my laptop. While I sent off one email after the other, he massaged my shoulders. I quietly groaned and moved my head. I hadn't realized how tense I was until he started rubbing it away. "I'm never letting you out of my sight if you keep up with this." I laughed.

"Good. I don't want to be out of your sight. I think I like being in your sight all the time."

I finished the last email and closed the laptop. I was ready to go to bed with my man. We turned off the lights and left the food cartons on the table. We crawled into the large bed and snuggled close together. "I hate sleeping alone now," I told him and sounded slightly accusatory.

"Me too. You've ruined me."

"That's what I was going to say." I laughed. "I've never slept with a man. And I mean sleep, not sex. I didn't think I would like it. I do. It's addicting."

"We're going to have to do something about that," he said and squeezed me close.

We still needed to have the talk. Tonight wasn't the time. I was spent from a long week. I didn't want to waste the time we had left together talking about how we were going to be together more. I simply wanted to be quiet and still and in the moment.

35

CASE

"Are you ready?" I asked Lucy.

Her eyes were wide as she nodded. "I got my coloring books and crayons. Mom said I could color on the plane."

I noticed she was calling Emma mom a lot more often. I liked hearing it and I knew it made Emma happy as well. "Yes, you can," I said. "It's a short flight."

Emma came downstairs with her hair piled on top of her head. "Okay," she said. "I think we're ready."

"Are you sure?" I asked.

"I am. No, wait. I'll be right back."

She jogged back upstairs. Lucy and I exchanged a look before I laughed. "She does this all the time," Lucy said.

"She has a lot to do," I said.

When she returned, she held up her hands. "Now we're good. Let's do this."

We were taking a cab to the airport. The guy had been waiting for ten minutes. I had handed him a hundred to wait. He probably would have waited another thirty minutes if needed. I put our bags in the trunk and took the front seat with Emma and Lucy in the back. Lucy chattered the whole way to the airport. When we told her we were going to my house for a few days, she had nearly blown a gasket with her excitement.

Emma looked stressed as we juggled our carry-on items with Lucy bouncing around. I thought it was the best thing ever. I felt like this was our first trip as a family. Despite the chaos and Lucy needing to go to the bathroom three minutes after we made it to the gate, it was exciting. She did amazing on the short flight and chatted with anyone that would listen.

I took them to my apartment to drop off our bags and to take a minute just to breathe. "Where to first?" I asked Emma.

"I'm thinking the Children's Museum of the Arts," she said. "I think that's where she will have the most fun. As much as I would like to do it all, I'm not sure she can hang for a full day. Are we still on for dinner tonight with your family?"

"Yes." I nodded. "I told mom to make it early. I'd like to take you guys out to my house. I think she'll enjoy herself a lot more at the house versus here in the apartment."

"I'm excited to see your house." She smiled.

"I'm excited for you to see it," I said.

We took a car to the museum. We were hoping to squeeze in a couple of museums today. Lucy held my hand as we walked in. I walked with her leading the way as we explored the first museum. "Can I make a picture?" she asked when we approached the craft area.

"You can." I nodded. "Go ahead."

Emma and I stepped away and let her do her thing while keeping a close eye on her. "She's having a blast," Emma said.

"Do you want to do another museum? We could take her to FAO Schwarz."

"Oh my gosh, she would love that," she said. "I'm not sure my credit card would."

"It's an experience," I said. "We'll get her all the culture she needs later. I think every little kid should get to run through the toy store at least once."

"I want to go." She laughed. "I've never been. It sounds fun. I think it might be wise to do the toy store and then take her back to your apartment for a nap before dinner. I don't want her to be cranky and act up in front of your family."

"My mom raised six boys," I reminded her. "Trust me, she's seen a temper tantrum or two."

"Just a short rest," she insisted. "And I want to put her in the dress."

I put my arm around her and hugged her. "Works for me. I wouldn't mind a little nap."

"Me too." She smiled.

After Lucy finished her picture, we headed for the toy store. The joy I saw on the little girl's face hit me hard. I loved the little thing. She was a good kid and I wanted to be a part of her life. I wanted to have more of these adventures with her. I loved watching the joy on her face as she saw new things. Watching Emma watch her was just as rewarding. I suddenly understood why my parents had so many damn kids. This kind of feeling was addicting.

"Is everything okay?" Emma asked.

"Yes, fine, why?"

"You have a look on your face," she said. "I don't know what it is. You look deep in thought."

"I was just thinking how much I like doing this," I said.

"The toy store?"

"All of it," I said. "I would be happy anywhere with the two of you. We could be walking through a landfill, and I would be cool with it. I love being with you guys. I love watching her see new things. Her innocence is so pure."

Emma turned to look at her niece. "She is a lot of fun. She is a bright light on a dark day. I love her so much. I cannot imagine my life without her. When we first decided I would be the one to raise her, I had been terrified. I tried to tell Marie she was crazy to give me her precious baby girl. The first months were so overwhelming. I look back on those days and I'm so glad we stuck it out."

"Me too," I said. "Do we dare tell her it's time to go?"

"Brace yourself," she joked.

"Bring it!"

There was some arguing, but eventually she caved and did as asked. Emma laid her down in the spare room while we lay down in bed. "Do you think things are going to be weird tonight?" she asked.

"No. I know you didn't get a great first impression of my family, but I swear, we're usually very normal," I told her. "We don't do high drama. We are normal people that sit around and eat meatloaf and potatoes while talking about our day."

She laughed. "Meatloaf? Really?"

"Okay, mom likes to dress it up a bit, but she has made it before," I conceded.

"You live a very different life than I do," she said. "We're nothing alike. Do you really think this can work between us?"

"I know it can," I said. "We're not that different. I can live any life you want. I was serious when I said I would give it all up. I will be a stay-at-home dad if you want me to. I'll be the guy that mows the lawn on Sunday and learns how to make meatloaf. I'll go grocery shopping and do all the things you want me to. I'm not defined by my name or my career. I'm flexible."

"We'll figure it out," she said.

"Yes, we will."

We drifted off to sleep and were awoken by Lucy wondering if it was time to go yet. We all changed and got ready for dinner with the family. I was certain things would go better, but there was always someone in a shitty mood.

"Lucy, you are going to be a good girl, right?" Emma asked as we walked up to the front door.

"Yes."

I rang the bell and waited. My mother answered the door. "Hello," she greeted with a warm smile. "Come in, please."

"Mom, you remember Emma," I said. "This is Lucy."

I didn't have to get into who Lucy was because I had already explained the situation. My mom bent forward to speak to Lucy on her level. "It's very nice to meet you, Lucy. I'm Nina."

"Hi, Nina," Lucy replied.

"How old are you, Lucy?" mom asked.

"Five," she announced proudly.

"Well, Lucy, my son has told me a little about you. He said you love to draw and paint. Is that true?"

Lucy slowly nodded. "I like to paint."

"Why don't you follow me?" mom said. "I got a few things I hope will keep you busy. I know hanging out with a bunch of adults can be very boring."

Emma looked at me, silently asking what my mother was up to. I didn't have the vaguest idea. Instead of going into the living room, mom led us to one of the lounge areas they rarely used. I stopped in the doorway and was shocked by the transformation. "Mom!" I gasped.

Emma put a hand over her mouth. "Mrs. Manhattan, you didn't have to do all this for her!"

"Nonsense and please call me Nina," mom said and walked into what could only be described as a child's version of heaven. There were shelves with children's books and toys. A thick rubber mat was in the center of the room with a variety of toys in a neat bucket. In front of the windows where houseplants used to live was now decked out in a small painting easel. Another shelf with paints and coloring supplies was close by.

"Mom, when did you do this?" I asked.

Emma was with Lucy as the little girl ran around the room discovering my mother's overabundance of toys. "When you mentioned you were serious about Emma, I figured it was time to get ready for the idea of grandkids. We've been pestering you boys to give us grandchildren. I wanted to be ready. I'll add more age-appropriate toys as the need comes. For now, I thought Lucy would feel more at home if she had something to do other than sit around listening to the adults talk."

"Has dad seen this?" I asked.

"Of course," she said. "He's on board."

Lucy was already making use of the easel. Emma came back to us and took my mother's hands in hers. "This is so thoughtful," she said. "Thank you. She is thrilled. You have made her day."

"Good," mom said. "I want her to feel welcome to visit anytime. I want you guys to be able to come over and hang out without worrying about her being bored."

"You've definitely ensured she won't be bored." Emma laughed.

"Alright, you two get yourself a drink," she said. "I need to get back to the kitchen."

Mom walked away.

"I can't believe she did all this," Emma whispered. "Is this normal? I hope she doesn't feel guilty about the way things went last time I was here. I'm over it. This is so over the top generous."

"She wanted to do it," I said. "My mom has been angling for grandkids for a while. Lucy just happened to be the first one in her life. I would expect her to be spoiled from this point forward."

"I don't even know what to say," she said as she looked around the room. "*Thank you* feels inadequate. After your father's donation and now this? You have a pretty awesome family."

I pulled her against me. "They might be showing off just a little." I laughed. "Do you want a drink? My brothers should be here soon. Things might get a little rowdy."

"Yes," she said and then looked back at Lucy.

"She's fine," I said. "We'll be across the hall."

She nodded and together we left. My brothers showed up ten minutes later. Edwin decided the playroom was more fun than hanging out with what he called the boring stiffs in the den. We could hear him and Lucy from across the hall.

"I'm not sure who's having more fun," I said.

"Edwin," Hans and Bram said at the same time.

"You know he's still a child," Hans said.

I sat back with my arm draped over Emma's shoulders. I listened to my brothers talking about clients and things they'd been up to over the week. Emma asked questions and joined in the conversation. They spoke with her like they had known her for years. I was on

Cloud Nine. This was going to be good. My life had taken a huge turn for the better. Having a ton of money was great and all but having this was what life was all about.

36

EMMA

"Are you ready?" Case asked as I sat in the kitchen talking with Nina.

"Yes, we should probably get going."

"Are you going out to the house?" his mother asked.

"Yes," Case answered.

She put her hand on mine. "It was so good of you to come back and give us another chance. I hope we can have more dinners together. I so enjoyed having a young child's laughter in the house again."

"You have Edwin," Case scoffed. "He was the one laughing."

His mother shooed him away. "Stop it."

We said our goodbyes with the promise to return again soon. Our bags were already loaded in the car that was taking us to his house. I was anxious to see where he called home. The apartment was nice, but it felt a little sterile, like a rental and not a home.

Lucy fell asleep fifteen minutes into the drive. "I think we wore her out," I said.

"She can sleep in tomorrow. We can hang out at the house and just have a lazy day."

"That sounds perfect," I agreed.

I leaned my head against his shoulder and watched as the city lights started to fade away. An hour later, the car paused at a gate before it slid open. Perfectly trimmed evergreen shrubs lined the driveway. As the car pulled around, the house came into view. My eyes nearly popped out of my head. I turned to look at him. "This is your house!"

He smiled and offered an impish shrug. "Yes."

Lucy woke up just then. We climbed out of the car and stood in the circular driveway as the car pulled away. I could only stare up at the massive white house that looked very much like a castle. The French Tudor home was huge but yet understated. There were trees all around that offered privacy while giving it a very parklike appearance. I just knew Lucy was going to have a field day tomorrow when the sun was out.

"Shall we go in?" he asked.

He opened the massive front door and gestured for us to go inside. Lucy had no shame. She rushed in like she did with everything she did in life. Lights came on with a touch of a keypad by the door. I stepped into the foyer that was lit with a massive chandelier overhead.

"Should I take off my shoes?" I asked. The gray tile gleamed under the lights. The place was spotless. A wide spiral staircase was to the left with a massive open room straight ahead. Hallways cut to the left and right. "I might need a map," I murmured.

"It's not so big," he said with a laugh. "Do you want a tour?" he asked Lucy, who had already run into the big room.

He led us from one room to the other. Huge picture windows faced the back of the property with a view of the lake. In the darkness, I couldn't see much, but I knew it was going to be spectacular. We meandered around the ground floor before taking the stairs up. "How many bedrooms?" I asked.

He almost looked embarrassed. "Ten," he answered.

"Ten! You have a ten-bedroom house!"

"I know it's a little big, but it was the property I fell in love with. I'm on eight acres that are one giant park. I can take a walk around the property, and no one is going to take my picture or ask me who I'm dating. The house was not the selling point. It was the land and the view."

"How big?" I asked. "How big is this place? I don't think we've covered half, and I already know three of my houses would fit in here."

Again, he looked a little embarrassed. "About ten-thousand square feet."

"Holy shit!"

"Mom!" Lucy called out.

"Sorry," I said and reminded myself to watch my language.

"Do you want to check out the backyard?" he asked.

"Yes, sure, please," I said.

The grounds were well lit. The massive swimming pool was currently covered behind the tall fence. "That's the dock down there," he said, pointing. "There's a gazebo to the right. I love to sit out there and watch the boats and birds. It's very peaceful."

We walked back inside and promised Lucy we would play in the gardens tomorrow. I put her to bed in one of the spare bedrooms closest to the master. I went back downstairs and tried to take it all in. The house was a little homier, but it still seemed to be lacking that lived-in feeling. It took me a few wrong turns before I found him in the smaller living room in front of the fireplace he had going on high. He was sitting on the couch with our usual glass of wine waiting for me.

"Well, you are full of surprises," I said and sat down.

"How so?"

"You said you had a house," I said. "I thought you meant a house. This is bordering on a castle. I don't think I fully understood just how wealthy you were. I don't mean that in a bad way. I'm just a little shocked. I don't know what to think about all this."

"I don't brag about money," he said. "I've learned to keep money out of the equation. Part of the reason my dad is so protective is because of the money. We've all been burned more than once. We think a person is a true friend or a good girlfriend only to find out it was the money they were interested in."

"I would never," I said, slightly defensive.

"I know you wouldn't, and I never thought that," he said. "Not ever. It's just not something I go around talking about. Most of my acquaintances don't know about the house. My family does and a few people at the company, but I prefer to keep things private."

"I guess I could understand that," I said.

"Now that you've seen the house, do you think you could ever see you and Lucy living here?" he asked quietly.

My initial, knee-jerk reaction was to laugh. Then I realized that if I wanted to be with him, I had to be okay with his wealth and what that afforded. It wasn't like it would be a chore to live in a place like this. I could imagine doing Lucy's room in her favorite princess pink and making a toy room like Nina had set up. The natural light that would come through the windows would be amazing.

"Is that something you would want?" I asked.

"Yes," he said without hesitation. "I would love for us to live here, but I will move to Pennsylvania if that's what you want. I know I want to be with you. I don't want to only see you on the weekends. I want to be with you all the time."

I had to laugh. "You giving this up to live in my house in Pennsylvania is nonsense," I said. "I bet they have some amazing schools here."

"The best," he said eagerly. "I don't want to pressure you. I wasn't kidding when I said I would go wherever you want me."

I mulled it over. "I've always thought about opening a satellite store in New York," I said.

He leaned forward and twisted to look at me. "Really?" he asked breathlessly.

"Yes." I nodded. "I would love to have a small storefront here. I would have my factory where it is, and I could hire a manager to run operations while I worked from here."

"You're serious?" he asked.

"I'm very serious," I said. "I want this. I want to be with you. I'm not sure when I'll have the time to clean this house, but we'll worry about that later."

He leaned forward and kissed me. "We'll hire a housekeeper. Technically, I already have a housekeeper, but we'll bring her in more days."

"Are we really going to do this?" I asked as reality hit me.

"Yes," he said. "The sooner the better."

"Lucy should finish out her year," I said as the wheels started to turn. There was so much to do. I had to pack and decide if I would keep my house or sell it. What about Jennifer? Would the company be okay without me?

"You're getting in your head," he said and got up. He pulled me up. "You don't have to nail down every detail right this very minute. We've got time. We'll plan and execute and make this a smooth transition. Everything is going to be okay. We have each other. We have Lucy."

"I'm freaking out a little here," I said and felt my heart beating faster. "It's a good freakout, but it's a freakout."

"I know a cure," he said and took my hand. We walked up the winding stairs and down the hall to the massive master bedroom.

He slowly undressed me, dropping kisses over my jaw and down my shoulders. Every kiss calmed me down just a little more. When it was my turn, I gave his body the same attention he'd shown me. I kissed over the back of his shoulders while sliding my hands down his bare skin. I slid my breasts against his back as I rounded his body and came to stand in front of him.

"I love you," he whispered. "We're going to make this a home. I want Lucy's toys strewn about. I want those cute little throw pillows you love on the couch. I want to see those cool pictures you have on your walls on these walls. I want to make more memories and frame them."

I smiled and traced my finger over his lips. "I want all of that too."

He reached down and lifted me. He carried me to the bed before gently laying me down. He stood over me and stared down. "You're so beautiful. This will be the first night together in our home. It will be our home."

"Yes," I sighed as his body came over mine.

My hands slid up his arms, relishing in his strength before grabbing his face in my hands to pull him in for a kiss. His tongue lashed against mine before he moved over me. I opened my legs to him. He slowly pushed inside. I didn't think I would ever grow tired of making love to this man. He was breathing hard as he pushed himself off me with his hips still pressed firmly against mine.

"Damn," he groaned. "You're so fucking wet. I can't hold back. I get inside you, and I just want to let go."

I smiled and reached up, stroking my hand down his chest. Then I sat up just a little. "Make love to me, Case. Show me how you feel."

His eyes darkened. With superior strength, he supported himself on one arm and pushed me back down to the bed before he started to move. His hips rocked and thrust. My hands reached out and grabbed the blankets. I attempted to hold on, but every thrust moved me up the bed inch by inch until my head was pushed against the headboard.

"That's it," he growled. "Give it to me."

I moaned and wrapped my legs around him. "More," I begged. "Please, more."

He let out a muffled grunt and dug in deep. I watched his abs flex and his jaw clench as he thrust into me over and over. A moment later, he hit the right spot and I was crying out with pleasure. He rocked and groaned until he was gasping for air with his body stiff as a board.

"That's it," I soothed. "That's my love."

He collapsed against me and showered me with kisses. "Oh my god," he gasped. "I'm not sure I'll survive living with you."

I laughed softly and patted his back. "I think we'll find a way."

37

CASE

I watched her sleep and found myself thinking about the future once again. Now that I had a clearer picture of it, I knew what I needed to do. I quietly got out of bed and dressed before checking on Lucy. She was sound asleep as well. The poor girls were tuckered out after the very busy day yesterday. I grabbed my cell phone and went into the office. I closed the French doors to keep the sound of my voice from carrying upstairs and waking them up.

"Why are you calling me so early?" Edwin complained.

"I need to talk to you," I said. "It's important. Wake up."

"What's wrong?" he asked. "Did you already fuck things up with Emma?"

"No, asshole. I need you to find me a storefront."

"What?" he asked on a yawn.

"I need you to find me a storefront for Emma's chocolate shop," I repeated.

"Right now?"

"Yes, now," I said. "This isn't something that can wait. I'm trusting your judgment. I can't get into the city. Find me something. Preferably midtown area."

"You want me to find you something right now?" he repeated.

"Dammit, Edwin. Get your ass up. I don't have a lot of time. I need this done like yesterday."

He yawned again. "You do know it's not quite that simple."

"Yes, it is," I replied. "I'm at my computer. Hurry up and send me the listings. I'll narrow it down and then you'll video chat me so I can see it in virtual person."

"I will?" he asked.

"You know you want to make a fat commission," I said. "Hurry up."

I ended the call and left the office. I was in the kitchen making breakfast when Lucy came downstairs first. It was a gloriously sunny day. The kitchen and dining room were flooded with natural light. She walked right to the windows and looked outside. "Wow," she exclaimed. "It's so pretty."

"Yes, it is," I agreed. "After breakfast we'll go for a walk. I'll show you the stuff you didn't get to see last night."

"Is Aunt Em—I mean mom still sleeping?"

"Yes, she is, so we need to be very quiet," I said. "I'm making French toast. Do you want to help?"

"I don't have my stool here," she pouted.

"Just this one time we'll have you stand on one of the chairs, okay?"

She smiled and ran to grab one of the dining-room chairs. She dragged it across the floor and climbed up. "Did you have fun yesterday?" I asked.

"I want to go to the toy store again," she said.

I laughed and handed her a fork to stir the egg mixture. "I bet you do. They had a lot of really cool stuff."

"I want a new Barbie house," she declared. "And one of those painting hangers like Nina had."

"We'll have to see about that," I said.

I was leaving it to Emma to tell her about their future moving plans. I had no idea if it was something Lucy would actually want. I didn't want to traumatize the girl.

"Good morning," Emma said as she walked into the kitchen. "You guys let me sleep in late."

"You needed it," I said. "Coffee is ready to go."

"Thanks." She gave Lucy a kiss on the cheek. "Are you making breakfast?" she asked.

"Yep, and then we get to go for a walk," she announced.

Emma took her coffee to look out the windows. "This view is incredible," she said. "It's so serene."

"I know," I said. "I told you the house was worth the view."

We put breakfast on the table and dug in. I heard my phone vibrating on the counter and assumed it was Edwin. "You ladies finish up. I need to check something."

I went back to the office and pulled up the email from Edwin. There were three links to potential properties. I quickly dismissed the first two, but the third looked perfect for my needs. I called him immediately.

"How soon until you can get down there and give me a tour?" I asked when he answered the call.

"It'll be an hour," he said. "I should charge you double."

"But you won't," I said. "I've got to go. Call me when you're there."

Emma and Lucy were clearing the table when I returned to the kitchen. "Sorry about that."

"No worries," she said. "Is everything okay?"

"Yes, fine, just a quick problem handled. I told Lucy we could check out the grounds this morning. Then I was thinking we could go into the city and do a little sightseeing. Do you think she'd like to see the Statue of Liberty?"

"Oh yes." She nodded. "That would be perfect."

We all showered and dressed for the day. While Emma was brushing Lucy's hair, Edwin called. I pretended to have to check something in the garage and quickly escaped.

"I'm here," he said. "What do you want to know?"

"Is it worth it?" I asked. "What kind of foot traffic does it get? How much renovations will be needed?"

We talked business, with him showing me around the space via video chat. It looked perfect. "Okay, I'll take it."

"You want to make an offer?" he asked.

"No, I want to buy it. Get with the seller. I want to do an all-cash offer with a three-day close."

"Do you know how hard that is to get done?" he asked.

"That's why I have the best realtor in New York," I said.

"Do you know what you're doing here?" he asked.

"I do," I said. "Emma is moving to New York. She wants to open a storefront to sell her chocolates. I want this to work. Anything I can do to speed along that process, I'll do. I need you to get some kind of paperwork with the deal made today. I need the keys as well."

"Man, you're getting way ahead of yourself," he warned. "It doesn't work like that."

"I'll get an insurance policy on it," I said. "I'll call Nico. He'll get me hooked up. The seller doesn't have to worry I'm going to trip and fall and sue him. Just get me the keys."

"You are very demanding," he said.

"I know. Thanks. I'll find a way to pay you back. I've got to call mom."

I hung up the phone while he was still talking. I called mom and filled her in on my plans and what I needed from her. Emma and Lucy were already in the backyard when I returned. "Ready?" I asked.

"Can we go in the pool?" Lucy asked.

"It's a little cold for that right now," I told her.

She pouted and stared longingly at the pool as we walked by on our way to the dock.

"Does she know?" I asked quietly.

"No, I was thinking we could tell her together."

We walked the length of the dock before going to sit in the gazebo. Emma looked at me, silently asking if now was the time. I nodded in reply.

"Lucy, do you like it here?" Emma asked.

"Yes," Lucy said. "I love it!"

"Do you think you would want to live here?" I asked.

Lucy's eyes grew big as saucers. She looked from me to Emma. "For real?" she squealed.

"For real," Emma said with a smile.

"I can have a bedroom here?"

"Any room you want," I said.

"Can I have a princess room?" she questioned.

"Yes." Emma nodded. "You'll be going to a new school. Are you okay with that?"

"Yes!" Lucy jumped up and down. "Can I have a swing set?"

"Absolutely," I answered.

She was shouting and running around on the grass. I turned to Emma. "I guess that means she's on board with it."

She laughed. "I don't think it was a hard sell to begin with."

"Then it's final," I said. "We'll worry about the details later. Let's load up and head into the city."

I drove one of my vehicles which was an SUV into town. The visit to the Statue of Liberty was as expected with lots of lines and everyone clamoring to get the right picture. "Excuse me," I said to a gentleman that had just taken a handful of pictures. "Do you mind taking a picture of me with my family?"

"Sure," he said. I handed him the phone and posed for a few pictures before thanking him.

"These are going on the wall," I told Emma. "We've got lots of wall space to fill. Every inch is going to be pictures of us on our grand adventures."

"Works for me," she said. "I'll start some photo albums as well."

We finished up at the Statue of Liberty, and because I knew it was something that would appeal to them both, I took them to Li-Lac Chocolates.

"What is this place?" Emma asked.

"Your future competition." I laughed. "I figured we should check it out before everyone knows who you are. You're undercover."

The moment we stepped inside, I heard her sharp intake of breath. "It smells divine."

"I thought you might like that."

"Oldest chocolate house, huh?" she asked as we meandered through the store and checked out what they had to offer.

"Everything is purple," Lucy declared.

"Yes, it is." I laughed. "That's how you know you're in the right place."

"This is pretty fancy," Emma whispered.

"Your place is better," I replied.

She laughed and moved to the counter. We ordered an assortment of chocolates and left the store. "Can we walk?" Emma asked. "I'd love to just take in the vibe."

"Sure," I answered. "Whatever you want to do."

We walked and sampled the chocolates before finding a place to eat some lunch. "What do you think about New York?" I asked Lucy.

"It's really cool," she said. "There's so many people."

"There is definitely a lot of people," I said.

My phone rang with Edwin calling once again. Being in the restaurant gave me a perfect excuse to get up and leave them for a few minutes. "What's up?" I asked. "Did they take it?"

"Of course, they took it," he said. "It's not like you made it possible for them to reject it."

"You got the keys?"

"I did," he answered.

"Did mom call you?"

He laughed. "Yes, she did. For the record, I think you're crazy."

"I'm sure you do," I said. "I've got to get back in there. Leave the keys with my doorman. Thanks for everything. I'll see you later."

Now, I had to think of an excuse to get them back to my apartment so I could leave them for an hour. I hoped she didn't think I was ditching her. "Hey, I need to meet a client with some tax emergency," I said when I sat back at the table. "My apartment isn't too far. You guys can hang out there while I meet him and then we'll get on with our day. Does that work for you?"

Emma was giving me a skeptical look. "Are you sure everything is okay?"

"Yes, fine. We'll go to the apartment and you guys can decide what you want to do next."

"Okay," she said. "We'll be fine."

I took them to my place and then headed down to the doorman to get the keys. "Thanks," I said and set out to put the rest of my plan in motion. I felt like I was running against the clock. This was what happened when you only saw the woman you loved a couple of days a month. It was hard to cram everything in.

38

EMMA

I stared out at the city below and wondered what Case was up to. He'd been acting off all day. I didn't think it had anything to do with him freaking out about us moving to New York. He seemed almost giddy. He definitely had something up his sleeve—I just didn't know what.

He kept sneaking off to take phone calls and now leaving us at his place while he went to deal with an emergency tax problem. That seemed just a little fishy. If I didn't know him and believe he was madly in love with me, I would be prone to think he had a side piece. I knew that wasn't the case, which meant he was up to something else. I just had no idea what it could be. With him, I couldn't even begin to guess. He tended to be a little eccentric.

"When are we going to live with Case?" Lucy asked.

"I'm not sure," I answered. "Maybe a couple of months. There is a lot we need to do before we move."

"I want to live here," she said. "I like it here."

"Me too," I agreed. "Do you like Nina and Britt?"

"Nina said I could call her grandma," she said thoughtfully. "Should I?"

I couldn't help but smile. "I think if you want to, you can. It's up to you."

"I'm going to call you mom now," she said. "Will I call Case dad?"

My heart felt like it was being squeezed. "I don't know," I said. "Maybe. We'll have to wait and see."

"We're making a family."

"Yes, we are." I smiled.

There was a knock on his door. I wasn't sure I should answer it. I knew there was a doorman, but what if the person had the wrong door? I got up and looked through the peephole. It was his mother. I pulled open the door. "Hi, Nina. He's not here right now, but he should be back soon if you'd like to wait."

"Actually, I'm not here for him." She smiled. "I came by to see if I could steal this little bundle of fun."

"Me?" Lucy asked with a bright smile.

"Yes, you, my darling," Nina replied.

Now I knew there was no way this was some random visit. "Did Case tell you we were here?"

Nina flashed me a knowing smile. "I think he was hoping to spend some time with you."

"Oh, Nina, I appreciate that, but you don't have to watch her. Case and I can spend time together later."

"Oh no." She shook her head. "You don't understand. I asked if I could have her for a bit. I was hoping she could help me make cupcakes."

Again, I knew there was more to the story. "Are you sure?" I asked quietly. "I'm sure you have other things to do."

"I have nothing to do that is more important than spending time with this little lady." She smiled. "Case would really like to take you out for a bit. I hope you don't mind us plotting."

"It's hard to mind when it's done with such kindness," I said.

"Can I go?" Lucy asked. I knew Lucy had an ulterior motive. She wanted to get her hands on that playroom.

"Yes, but you have to promise me you will listen to Nina. No running in the house."

"I will." She nodded.

Case returned at that moment. "Oh," he said. "I thought I would get here before you did, mom."

I gave him a look. "Plotting?"

"Sorry," he said. "Do you mind?"

"No." I smiled.

I helped Lucy put her coat on and gave her a kiss. "Be good," I said.

"We'll see you later," Nina said with a wave.

I watched her walk out the door and felt a little apprehensive to leave her in the care of someone I didn't really know. I trusted Nina, though. I couldn't be a helicopter mom.

"Well, well, well, mister," I said with my hands on my hips. "What are you up to?"

"I was hoping we could go by my office," he said. "I want to show you the family businesses."

"I'd like that," I said.

The office was closed, which meant we got it all to ourselves. "This is my office," he said and pushed open a door.

"Your family owns the building?" I asked.

"All three," he said. "We occupy a portion of each and rent out the other floors."

"Wow," I said with awe. "That is pretty amazing. So basically you all do work together."

"Yes." He laughed. "If I want to talk to a cousin, aunt, or uncle, I just have to take an elevator."

"That's pretty cool. I love how close you are with your family."

"Like I said, we don't always get along, but most of the time we do. When push comes to shove, we stick together."

We left the building and we walked around the city for a bit. We bought hot chocolates and ended up in Times Square once again. "Listen," I whispered as we walked past a busker on the corner.

The woman was playing a guitar and singing. "She's good," he said and pulled out his wallet. He dropped a ten in her guitar case before stepping back.

"I love how much culture is here," I said. "I know people say it's dangerous here, but I just feel like I'm in another world. I love that people are so different and coexist."

"I wouldn't recommend you come down here and roam about on your own," he joked. "You look like a tourist. These people will eat you alive."

"I guess I need my big, bad man at my side."

"Yes, you do," he said and led me down the sidewalk.

"Where are we going?" I asked when he took a turn into an alleyway.

"It's a surprise," he replied.

"Uh, are you planning to mug me?" I teased.

"Baby, I'll mug you tonight." He grinned.

He pulled out some keys and jangled them. He walked to a door, and because I was still so confused, I didn't notice the paper sign taped to the door. I watched him slide the key into the lock. "What are you doing?" I hissed.

"Breaking and entering," he shot back.

That was when I looked at the sign. I recognized his handwriting. "What is this?" I asked again.

He opened the door a couple of inches and slapped his hand against the sign. "Just what it says."

"Miller's Chocolates?" I asked with confusion.

"Miller's Chocolates." He nodded. "Would you like to see your new store?"

My jaw dropped. "My what? How? When?"

He laughed and pulled open the door. He turned on the lights and illuminated the backroom area. "Your store," he said.

"When did you do this?"

"This morning," he answered.

"This morning?" I repeated.

"Yes." He laughed. "I wish I could have done a bit more, but here it is."

"I don't understand."

"Last night you said you dreamed about a storefront in New York.

I hope you won't mind me finding one for you. If you don't like this location, we can look for another place."

"You did this all this morning?" I repeated.

I remembered how long it took me to find a factory location. How long it took to find a house. He made a phone call and found me a store in a few hours.

"My brother is a real estate guy, remember?" he said with a laugh.

"But how did you get the keys?"

"Money talks," he said and led me up front. "We can get a crew in here as soon as you know what you want. We'll get the remodel done in a hurry. You just tell me what you want, and I will make it happen."

"It could be nice dating a guy with money," I teased.

"Check it out," he said. "Let your imagination run wild. Tell me what you want."

I walked around the old counter that was full of dust and cobwebs and envisioned my name on the wall. I wanted it to resemble my shop at home. I would have glass cases and elegant displays all around. We would keep up with our usual free sample offerings. I let my imagination go wild.

I turned to look at him and found him on one knee. At first, I thought he might have tripped over some of the scattered debris on the floor. Then I noticed the little blue box in his hand.

"Case?" I breathed his name.

He grinned. "Hi."

"Case, what are you doing?"

"I would hope it would be self-explanatory, but let me break it all down for you," he said without getting up.

"I—"

"I love you," he said. "I think I knew I loved you almost from the beginning. That first day when I bulldozed you, I was enamored with you. Getting to know you these last few weeks has been the best time of my life. I know I'm moving faster than a speeding freight train, but I don't want to stop. I've been racing toward this moment my whole life. I know this is right. I feel it in every cell of my body. My entire being hums when I'm around you. My soul knows you're the one. I want to marry you. I want to make us a family. You and Lucy have made me feel so much more love than I ever knew was possible. I want to be her daddy. I want to be your husband. I promise you, if you say yes, I will bust my ass to be the man you deserve. I will bend over backward to make sure you feel how much I love you. I know this is fast and I'm probably freaking you out right now, but it doesn't have to be tomorrow. I want to ask you to marry me now because I need you to know where I'm going. I need you to know you are the one for me and nothing is ever going to change that. If you want to wait five years to actually get married, I'll wait. I'll wait for you forever."

"Case," I breathed his name again. I was completely speechless. He took my breath away. He was so perfect it didn't seem real. He didn't seem possible.

"Emma Miller, will you marry me? Please?"

I couldn't help it. I knew it wasn't how this was supposed to go, but I dropped to my knees in front of him. "Yes," I said through tears. "A million times yes."

He pulled me in for a kiss. I heard something hit the floor and remembered the ring. I didn't even look at the thing. He pulled back and grabbed the box, blowing off the dust before opening it. "I want you to wear this ring as a reminder I will marry you any day of the week. Whenever you are ready, you say so and I'll be there with bells on."

He pushed the ring on my finger. "It's so big and pretty," I said.

He grinned and helped me to my feet. "I don't want you to forget you're mine and I don't want any other man to think you're available."

"I think I could use this thing to land planes," I joked.

"Hey, go big or go home." He laughed.

"This has seriously been the best month of my life," I said. "When you bowled me over, I was ready to knock you out. I'm so glad you did. I would have suffered a hundred broken bones and a bruised butt if it led to this."

"I promise I will be more careful in the future."

I held out my hand and looked at the diamond flashing in the light. It was big, but it wasn't ostentatious. It was perfect. "I can't wait to tell Lucy. She's going to be so excited."

"We can take as long as you need," he said again. "I don't want you to go into panic planning mode."

He knew me well. "I will take my time, but not too much time. I want to lock you down before you can change your mind."

"Baby, I am never changing my mind. If I die and come back as another person, animal, or whatever, I'm going to search for your soul and make you mine again. This is forever for me. I hope you're okay with that."

"I'm definitely okay with that," I said. "Is this why your mom took Lucy?"

"Yes." He laughed.

"That was very sweet of her."

"Speaking of my mom, they're waiting for us at their house," he said.

"Did they actually think I might say no?" I laughed. "I mean, come on, I'm the luckiest girl in the world."

"I'm glad you feel that way," he said and kissed me again. "I know I'm the luckiest man in the world."

39

CASE

I felt like I was floating as we locked up the store. I had hoped she would say yes, but there was a little part of me that had been worried she would shoot me down. Even if she rejected me, I was ready to keep asking her until she said yes. I knew she was the only woman I would ever love. I felt lucky the first woman I fell in love with was as perfect as she was. I was lucky that she said yes.

I hailed a cab and we headed back to my parents' house. I was hoping my parents and brothers had come through on the second half of my surprise. When the cab pulled to a stop, I helped her out of the car.

"Before we go inside, I want to steal one more moment of privacy before things get crazy," I said with her face cradled in my hands.

"Crazy?" she asked. "Are your parents okay with you asking a commoner to be your wife?"

"Very funny," I said. "They love you. My mother is already crazy about Lucy. When you guys move here, just know we have a babysitter at the ready. She was already talking about transforming one of the spare bedrooms into a room for Lucy for sleepovers."

"Really?"

"Really," I said. "You're about to be a Manhattan. We take care of our own. You and Lucy are going to be part of a big, slightly crazy family."

Just then there was an uproar of laughter from inside the house. That told me they had managed to pull off the impossible. "What was that?" she asked.

"Let's just say the fact you said yes will save me from a very awkward moment." I laughed as I led her up the stairs. I didn't even get a chance to knock before my mother pulled open the door. Her eyes immediately went to Emma's left hand.

She let out a scream. "She said yes!" she shouted.

Like ants crawling out of the woodwork, my brothers all came into the foyer. Emma looked completely shellshocked as she was hugged and passed from one brother to the next. Lucy was standing to the side wearing the little pink apron my mother had bought for her.

"What happened?" Lucy asked.

I went to her and picked her up. Emma turned to us and smiled. She held up her hand with the ring on it. "Case wants to be a part of our family," she said. "We're going to get married."

Lucy turned to me. "You are going to be my daddy!"

I suddenly had dirt in my eyes. I could only nod before passing her to Emma. I tried to be cool when I wiped my eyes, but no one missed the emotion. Edwin put his hand on my shoulder and gave a hard squeeze before walking away. My dad did the same thing. "Congratulations, son. You got yourself a good one."

"Thanks, Dad."

"Come on, come on," my mom said. "Everyone's in the living room. I've got appetizers coming out soon. Britt, open the champagne."

Emma looked at me and laughed. "Now I understand why this could have been very awkward."

"Don't worry, sweetie, I had scotch and beer on hand just in case it went the other way," Mom said and walked to the kitchen.

"Jennifer!" Emma squealed when her friend popped her head around the corner.

"Surprise!" she yelled. "And congratulations!"

Emma hugged her before turning to me. "You did this?"

"I knew you would want your best friend here." I shrugged. "Again, this was my family. I put out the alert this morning and everyone jumped in to help out."

Emma teared up again. "Thank you all for making this such a special day. I don't know how to thank you all. You've all shown us so much kindness and generosity. I'm a little overwhelmed."

"That's why there's champagne," Hans said.

The bubbly was poured and handed out, with Lucy getting a champagne glass filled with apple juice. I stepped into the center of the room surrounded by my family and held up my glass to Emma. "You guys know how important this woman is to me," I said. "I never knew what life could be like until I met her. I strongly recommend you all find your own special lady. They'll never be quite as perfect as my Emma, but I dare you to try. Emma, baby, I love you. Thank you for being willing to marry me and to step into this family."

She smiled and clinked her glass against mine. "I couldn't think of a better family to step into."

There were more cheers before we all took a drink.

"Mama," Lucy said in a quiet voice.

We all stopped and turned to her. She was holding two cupcakes. One had an M and the other a D. "I made these for you guys," she said. "Grandma Nina said I could give them to you."

Mom was standing in the doorway with tears streaming down her face. When Bram tried to hug her, she shooed him away. "I'm fine. I've got to get the appetizers."

Mom didn't cry. She was of the firm belief a stiff upper lip was the only way to behave in polite society. Seeing her moved to tears meant a lot. "Thank you," I said to Lucy. "What's the D for?"

"Dad," she said as if it was obvious.

"And M is for Mom," Emma said.

Lucy nodded. "We made cookies and cupcakes for the party," she said. "But we can't eat them until we eat the good food."

I laughed at her sweet reciting of what I knew were my mother's words. "I think we can steal a bite," I said with a wink.

Lucy went off to play in the elaborate playroom while the adults settled in for some conversation. "So, what now?" Hans asked.

"Oh, did I forget to mention Case bought a store today?" Edwin said with a smirk.

"You did?" dad asked. "For what?"

"For me," Emma said. "I'm planning to open a storefront here."

"You'll be moving to New York?" Bram asked.

"Yes," she answered.

"When?" Hans asked.

"Soon I hope," she answered.

"Are you guys going to live in the city?" my dad asked.

"No," I answered before she could. "We want Lucy to have a quiet place to grow up. My house is more suited for an energetic little girl."

"Yes, it is," he agreed. "She needs room to run."

"When's the wedding?" Isac asked.

"Slow down," I said. "We've been engaged five minutes."

"And known each other for ten," Edwin teased.

"Hey, when you know, you know," I told him. "One of these days, you're going to know."

"Don't you dare put that curse on me," Hans said.

I rolled my eyes at the biggest player out of all of us. "It'll happen one day," I told him.

"None of us have to, now that you're going to get hitched," Edwin said. "You jumped ahead two spaces."

It was a reference to our usual competitions. "Mom will be satisfied with Lucy for a while, but don't think any of you are off the hook," I said. "She's going to want a lot more. You saw that room she put together. Lucy couldn't play with all those toys if she was here every day for the next year."

Mom breezed in carrying a large tray of little finger sandwiches. She put them on the table. "He's right," she said before walking out of the room again.

"Told you all." I laughed.

"So, Emma, does this mean we get free boozy chocolate now?" Filip asked.

She smiled. "I guess that depends on how much you help me get that store up and running."

She was going to fit in just fine. I was glad they liked her. It would have been tough if there had been some concerns about how fast we were moving this thing along. I wanted them all to be comfortable with my decision, but I wouldn't let any of them hold me back from what I wanted. She was going to be a part of my life regardless of what anyone thought.

"What do you think, Dad?" Edwin asked. "You've never had a daughter."

"I think it's just the addition this family needs," he said. "Your mom could use a few more allies."

I noticed Edwin get up and move to sit on the arm of the chair Jennifer was sitting in. I knew that move and I knew my little brother. He was putting the moves on her. Jennifer gave him a look before pushing him off the armrest. "You should know better," she teased.

My brothers laughed as Edwin sat on the floor and looked up at her with surprise. He wasn't used to being rejected quite so harshly. She was a model and was likely used to guys coming on pretty strong.

"I'm going to see if your mom needs any help," Emma said and got to her feet.

"I'll come with you." Jennifer followed her out.

I waited for it to be said. I knew it was coming. They were kind enough to wait at least thirty seconds for Emma to get out of earshot. Hans was sitting next to me and slugged me in the arm. "Shit, I never thought it would be you married with a kid first," he said.

"He's always been an overachiever," Bram added. "He doesn't understand you can just do something and be okay at it. He had to go all in and show us all up and maybe I'm not too far behind him."

"As usual," Filip chimed in.

"You're all just jealous," I said.

"Nope." Edwin shook his head. "Not a chance. What's up with the girl?"

"What girl?" I asked.

"The hot friend."

"She's out of your league," I told him.

He smirked. "No one is out of my league."

"She was making eyes at me," Hans said. "You're probably too young for her. She wants a man."

"I think she wants none of you," I said. "Don't any of you dare fuck this up for me. Emma and Jennifer are tight. You are not allowed to mess with the friend until Emma marries me. I don't need any of you pissing off what I assume will be the maid of honor."

Edwin laughed. "You don't even have a wedding date. How long am I supposed to wait?"

"As long as it takes," I told him. "I'm not pushing Emma into setting a date. She's moving here and she's going to be opening up a store. She's got enough on her plate. When she's ready, we'll set a date. I just wanted to get a ring on it and lock her down before she could change her mind."

"She's not going anywhere," my dad said. "If she was going to leave, she would have done it after she met me that first time."

"Good point," I said. "All of you better be nice or I swear I will cut your balls off."

Lucy walked into the room just then. "Case, I made you a picture," she said.

My brothers were all trying to hide their smiles. "You'll want to clean up that mouth of yours," my dad said before leaving the room.

"Thanks," I muttered and pulled Lucy into my lap. "What did you draw?"

"It's our cabin," she said.

I looked at the picture that looked a lot like the one I had colored earlier. "I love it," I said. "We'll have to start looking for our cabin very soon."

"Your cabin?" Edwin asked.

The guy had a nose for sniffing out a potential sale. "Yes," I said. "We want to buy a cabin upstate."

His big salesman grin nearly split his face in two. "I'll get right on it."

"With lots of trees," Lucy specified.

"Of course." Edwin nodded.

"And water," she added.

"A stream," I clarified. "And it better have running water. I don't think Emma is into roughing it."

"I'll get on it Monday morning," he said. "Should I send my findings to you or my niece?"

"Very funny," I said.

Lucy hopped off my lap. "I'm going to make another picture for him so he knows what to buy," she said and rushed out of the room.

"She's very specific," I warned. "Don't bring her anything less than perfect."

He let out a whistle. "She's going to be a tough client."

I listened to their teasing, but it was clear they were all happy for me. They accepted my girls as their own. I just knew we were going to have many more gatherings just like this.

EPILOGUE
EMMA

Six months later

I walked up front armed with Windex and a roll of paper towels. We opened last week, and the new Miller's Chocolate store was hopping. I had been on my feet for twelve hours and my feet were killing me. I had expected a bump in opening sales, but this was unprecedented. With the Manhattan family throwing their name behind the business, it had been the boost we needed to be officially on the map.

"Why don't you go home?" one of the girls said. "We can clean up."

"I just hate seeing the glass cases with fingerprints all over them," I said.

I squirted the blue liquid on the glass and wiped it down. There was something very satisfying about cleaning glass. I stepped back, examined it from another view, and attacked it again.

"Do you need me to come in early tomorrow?" she asked.

"You know, that might be a really good idea," I said. "I don't want to leave Jerica alone. If business is going to be as good as it was today, she's going to need the help."

"I'll be here," she said. "You need to take a day off. You are a crazy woman."

"I anticipated it would be like this the first couple of weeks after opening," I said. "I'm thrilled to do it. I love being here."

I finished cleaning the glass case and let out a sigh. "I'll be in the office," I said. "Then I'm heading home. You guys have my number if you need anything. Sophie is just down the road and can be here before I can if something major happens."

"We'll be fine," she said. "Go sit down. You look a little pale."

I felt a little pale. I had been burning the candle at both ends and was dead on my feet. I went into the small office in the back and called Lauren. She was my new manager running the Pennsylvania location. I had to hire a whole additional crew to keep the factory running two shifts instead of just the one.

"Hi," I said when she answered. "How's it going?"

"Good," she replied. "I was just getting ready to send you the reports for last week. Everyone has been working hard to stay on top of all the orders."

"I appreciate you guys all working so hard," I said. "I don't anticipate this pace to stay like this for long. It's just the newness of the place. Things will even out soon enough."

"Hey, no one minds the busyness." She laughed. "I was going to talk to you about hiring at least one more person to work up front. Ever since the New York location opened, we have a lot more foot traffic here."

"Do it," I said. "I trust your judgment."

"Thank you," she said.

"I'm taking the next two days off, but as usual, call me if you need anything."

"I will," she said. "Enjoy the time off."

I ended the call, packed up everything I needed to be out of the office for two full days, and left the store. Jennifer called on my drive home.

"How are you?" she asked with concern. "You didn't look so good today."

"I'm fine," I said. "I'm just a little tired."

"No kidding." She snorted. "You've been running at full steam for six months straight. I thought Case was going to lock you up."

"I'm taking the next two days off," I said. "We're going to hang out by the pool and do nothing."

"That's exactly what you need. Is Lucy loving her new room?"

"Yes, of course," I said with a smile. "Case had it totally redone. You have to come out to the house to see it."

"I will when I get back from my shoot next week," she said.

"How do you like your new agency?"

"I love it," she said. "I should have moved to New York sooner. I'm making so much more money and my assignments are very fun. I love New York!"

"Me too," I said. "Me too."

"I have to run, but I wanted to check in and make sure you were okay," she said. "You work too hard. Someone has to tell you when to slow down."

"I know, I know. I promise I'm going to relax all weekend. Case has pretty much insisted on it."

"Oh, before I forget, are we still on for the dress appointment the following week?"

"Yep. Are you going to be in town?"

"Yes, I've already made sure they know I can't work that day. This appointment has been pushed too many times. We need to get you a dress or you won't be getting married next spring."

"I know," I sighed. "There's just been so much to try and get done."

"The store is open. You have a great staff. It's time to take a step back like you promised."

"I will," I said as I drove past a drug store. Before I knew what I was doing, I flipped around and pulled into the parking lot. "I'll talk to you later," I said and ended the call.

I ran inside, made my purchase, and headed for home. I didn't think it was the case, but the exhaustion and general ickiness I had been feeling had me buying a pregnancy test. The sooner I knew, the better. I was supposed to be getting married in six months. I didn't want to buy a dress and end up not being able to fit in it. And I wasn't about to walk down the aisle big as a whale.

When I got home, Case was in town with Lucy. I ran upstairs to one of the guest bathrooms to take the test. I stared at the test window as I watched the color move across the screen.

"Oh my goodness," I breathed when it came up positive.

I could only stare at the test. It was a surprise, but it wasn't. During the craziness of the move to New York and all the stuff with opening the store and trying to wedding plan had left me more than a little frazzled. I had forgotten to take my birth control on more than one occasion.

"Best laid plans," I said to myself.

I couldn't begin to guess how pregnant I was. Probably two months. I couldn't remember my last period. Maybe I was three months. I turned to look at myself from a side angle. I rubbed my hand over my belly that appeared a little fuller but nothing noticeable.

A baby. I knew Case was going to be thrilled. I was happy as well. It wasn't planned, but as he had told me a hundred times, plans were not set in stone. I hid the test in the garbage and went downstairs to start dinner.

"We're home," Case called out.

"In here," I said loud enough for him to hear from the front door. One of the pitfalls of a massive house was trying to communicate across thousands of square feet. He carried a few bags of groceries into the kitchen and put them on the counter.

"It smells delicious in here," he said.

"I was working on a new recipe," I lied.

"I can't wait to try it."

"Later." I winked.

"Oh, one of those recipes."

"We went grocery shopping," Lucy declared.

"I see that," I said. "Did you help him out?"

She nodded. "I pushed the cart."

"You're getting pretty good at the grocery thing," I teased.

"Nothing to it." He laughed. "I'm almost ready to make a Costco run by myself."

"Woah, buddy, let's not get ahead of ourselves." I laughed.

"Okay, soon. Not yet, but soon."

"Dinner will be ready soon," I said. "Lucy, go wash up please."

She bounced out of the kitchen. Case moved behind me and hugged me from behind. "How was your day?" he asked.

"Busy," I said.

"But you're still taking the next two days off, right?" he asked.

"Yes. I promise I'm not going anywhere. We promised Lucy a pool day, barbecue, and s'mores in the fire pit. I'm not going to let her down."

"Good," he said. "I bought you some of your favorite bubble bath and some new candles. Tonight, you are my queen. You're going to soak in the tub while I rub your shoulders."

"Or you could soak in the tub with me," I suggested.

"Ah, I could." He laughed. "So, what's this new recipe you've been working on?"

"You'll see," I said. "It's a surprise."

"I like surprises," he said.

"I hope you do."

"Mom said she'll take Lucy next week so we can go to the printer and lock in our invitations," he said. "I was thinking we could stay in the city and have a nice dinner, just the two of us."

"That sounds like a perfect plan," I agreed.

"Really, I think she wants us to be busy so she has an excuse to keep Lucy overnight," he joked. "It's like she has a new toy and doesn't want to let go."

"I'm glad she has taken such a liking to Lucy," I said. "It really warms my heart how your family has welcomed us in. It's a very different life than I was brought up in. Lucy is one very lucky little lady to have so many uncles that dote on her."

"They love her," he said. "I'll wash up and set the table."

While we sat at the table and ate dinner together, I found myself smiling more than usual. I was happy. Truly happy. Case put Lucy to bed while I took my bath. He came into the bathroom after she was down and sat down on the edge of the tub.

"I got you something," I said.

"You did?"

I pointed to the white pastry box on the bathroom counter. "I did."

"Oh, is this my special chocolate?" he asked and grabbed the box. "What's in it? Tequila? Rum?"

"Open it," I said.

He opened the box and stared into it. He said nothing, which made me just a little worried. He picked up the little note I had put in the box with a non-alcohol chocolate.

"Is this real?" he whispered.

I smiled. "It is."

"You're pregnant?"

"I am."

"You're pregnant," he repeated. "Holy shit, you're pregnant. We're going to have a baby!"

He reached into the tub, still fully clothed, and hugged me without a care that he was getting wet. He kissed me and stepped back. "I take it you're okay with this?"

"Okay." He laughed. "Baby, I'm about to jump out of my skin with happiness. Wait, what about you? Are you okay with it?" he asked and dropped to his knees beside the tub.

"I'm very okay with it. I know we didn't exactly plan this little guy or girl, but I'm so happy to get started growing our family."

"Me too," he murmured. "Me too."

"We'll probably have to move the wedding up or postpone it," I told him. He was all about the wedding. I didn't want to disappoint him.

"I don't care," he said. "We're going to have a baby. Lucy is going to be a big sister. She's going to be so excited."

"Yes, she is," I said.

"I'm not sure who's going to be more excited, her or my mom." He laughed. "Oh god, my mom is going to lose her mind. How far along?"

"I have no idea." I laughed. "I've been so busy I haven't really paid attention."

"That's it," he said. "I'm putting my foot down. You're resting. You are officially my baby mama and I'm going to pamper you."

"Baby mama." I smiled. "I think I like the sound of that."

"We're going to be so happy," he said. "You finish your bath. I'm going to do some online shopping."

"Case, we have time," I called out to his back.

He was crazy and he was mine.

The End

ABOUT THE AUTHOR

 After ten years of helping his wife, Ali Parker and brother-in-law, Weston Parker develop love stories of their own, Jacob Parker has decided to take the plunge with a new twist on the romance story.

He's a romantic guy in real life and wanted to bring the world of the Manhattan Men to life with his wife, Ali.

He lives in Tennessee with his family, loves to golf, also writes as J Stark, and can be found working in his wood shop when he's not writing.

OTHER BOOKS BY JACOB PARKER

The Manhattan Men
Rich, Right, Real

Printed in Great Britain
by Amazon